SKIN LIKE SILVER

A selection of recent titles by Chris Nickson

The Richard Nottingham Mysteries

THE BROKEN TOKEN
COLD CRUEL WINTER *
THE CONSTANT LOVERS *
COME THE FEAR *
AT THE DYING OF THE YEAR *
FAIR AND TENDER LADIES *

The Inspector Tom Harper Mysteries

GODS OF GOLD *
TWO BRONZE PENNIES *
SKIN LIKE SILVER *

* *available from Severn House*

SKIN LIKE SILVER

An Inspector Tom Harper Novel

Chris Nickson

Severn House Large Print
London & New York

This first large print edition published 2016
in Great Britain and the USA by
SEVERN HOUSE PUBLISHERS LTD of
19 Cedar Road, Sutton, Surrey, England, SM2 5DA.
First world regular print edition published 2015 by
Severn House Publishers Ltd.

British Library Cataloguing in Publication Data
A CIP catalogue record for this title is available from the British Library.

ISBN-13: 9780727894649

Severn House Publishers support the Forest Stewardship Council™
[FSC™], the leading international forest certification organisation. All
our titles that are printed on FSC certified paper carry the FSC logo.

Typeset by Palimpsest Book Production Ltd.,
Falkirk, Stirlingshire, Scotland.
Printed and bound in Great Britain by
T J International, Padstow, Cornwall.

For my friend Candace Robb,
with thanks for the inspiration,
both then and now.

One

Tom Harper sat on the tram, willing it on to his stop and feeling foolish. As soon as it reached the bottom of Roundhay Road, he leapt off, scurried across the street hoping no one would spot him, then quickly disappeared through the door of the Victoria public house.

'You're looking dapper, Tom,' Dan called from behind the bar. He grinned. 'Better watch out, they'll have you for impersonating a toff.' As Harper opened his mouth to reply, Dan continued, 'Annabelle's out in the yard. Said could you go through as soon as you were home.'

He turned away to serve a customer. Why did his wife need him so urgently, Harper wondered testily. With a sigh, he slipped along the hallway and through the back door. Barrels and crates were stacked against the wall, by a brick shed that was secured with a rusty padlock. On the ground, flagstones jutted unevenly, a few ragged weeds showing between them.

She was waiting, hands on hips, smiling as she saw him.

'You took your time,' she said. Annabelle Harper was wearing a gown of burgundy crepe, trimmed with cream lace, that fell over a pair of black button boots. Her hair was swept up and

1

the sun glinted on her wedding ring. 'I expected you half an hour back.'

'It ran late,' he explained. 'What's so important, anyway? I want to change out of this get-up.'

'In a minute.' Her eyes twinkled with mischief. 'Just one thing first.'

She stood aside and he saw the photographer waiting patiently, his large camera resting on a tripod, the small developing cart behind him.

'No,' Harper said firmly.

'Come on, Tom,' Annabelle pleaded. 'You look so smart like that. It won't take any time at all.'

He was beaten, and he knew it. She'd have her way in the end; she always did. Instead, he popped the top hat on his head and stood up straight. At least this would be over quickly, more than he could say for the rest of the day.

It was the annual inspection of detectives, the time of year when they all had to turn up dressed like dogs' dinners to be reviewed by the chief constable. A frock coat, striped trousers, the sharp points of a wing collar pushing tight into his neck, boots shined and glowing to within an inch of their lives. And the top hat.

He couldn't avoid it. It was part of the calendar for Leeds Police, the one day that the uniforms could laugh at them. Standing at attention in the yard behind Millgarth station, the ranks of them all waiting, everyone looking uncomfortable. Detective Inspector Tom Harper hated it. The only consolation was that he was at the end of the line. His right ear, where the hearing kept deteriorating, was towards the wall.

He'd glanced over at Detective Constable Ash,

turning out for his first parade, clothes new and stiff, the pride of promotion showing across his face.

'That's fine, sir,' the photographer said after the flash had gone off with a puff of smoke, pulling him back to the warm evening. 'You can move now. I'll have the print in a little while, missus.'

Harper removed the top hat again, the black silk brushing against his fingers. Annabelle kissed him.

'You get can rid of your glad rags now, if you want, Tom.'

In the bedroom, he tossed them all over a chair and stretched, grateful for the freedom. He put on a comfortable shirt and old trousers, finally feeling like himself again, not some mannequin in a tailor's shop window. Every October it was the same, come rain or today's sunshine. A day wasted.

He filled the kettle, putting it to heat on the range, and settled into a chair, glad that it was all done for another year. Tomorrow it was back to real work. He had a woman to find.

It had begun the morning before, when Superintendent Kendall waved him into his office.

'Go to the Central Post Office,' he ordered. 'See the chief clerk.' His face was grave. 'I'll warn you, Tom, this one's bad.'

The building stood at the bottom of Park Row, two grand stone storeys looking across to the railway stations. All day long, people crowded

3

around the counters, waiting to send their letters and parcels. Upstairs, in the offices, things were more hushed.

The chief clerk was a fussy man, standing erect, too conscious of his position. But his gaze kept sliding away to the small cardboard box on a side table, brown paper and string folded back around it.

'I made the decision to open it,' he said. 'It was beginning to smell.'

'I see, sir,' Harper said.

'I've never seen anything like it,' the man continued. His hands began to fidget.

'What was inside, sir?'

'A baby,' he replied emptily. 'A tiny, dead baby.'

Harper peered into the box. There was just a scrap of threadbare blanket left. Nothing else. The box was tiny. Small, he thought. God, the baby must have been so small.

'You'd better tell me what happened.'

The parcel had been posted, but the delivery address didn't exist, so it had been returned and placed on a shelf until the stink of decomposition became obvious.

'How long had it been there, sir?'

'Two days. I ordered that it be opened yesterday afternoon, and we discovered the body.' He moved to the window and stared out, trying to hide the expression on his face.

The details came slowly. It had been posted three days earlier from this building. The clerk had asked all the assistants: no one remembered the parcel, but why would they? They handled thousands every day.

4

The body had been taken to the police pathologist. There was nothing more Harper could do here. He needed to go over to Hunslet.

They all called it King's Kingdom, the home of Dr King, the police surgeon whose mortuary lay in the cellar of Hunslet Lane police station. The smell of carbolic filled the air and rasped against his throat as he walked in. His footsteps echoed off the tiled walls.

'Here about the baby?' King asked. He had to be close to eighty, his hair pure white, a stained apron over a formal suit covered with the debris of this or that. But he was still deft in his work, his conclusions sharp and insightful.

'I am.'

The surgeon peeled back the sheet from a small object. A naked baby, a boy, a cowl of dark hair on his scalp.

'There you are, Inspector. That's him, the poor little devil. As sad a thing as I've seen in all my years here. God only knows what the mother was thinking.'

'Was he dead when she put him in the parcel?'

'Definitely,' King said with certainty. 'If he wasn't stillborn, he died minutes after.' He held up a finger to stop the next question. 'And no, she didn't kill him. It was natural.'

'Is there anything else you can tell me?'

The doctor sighed. 'The baby weighs two pounds ten ounces. I put him on a scale. Do you know anything about children?' He glanced as Harper shook his head. 'That's nothing at all. If I had to guess, the mother was malnourished, probably young. From what she did, she probably didn't want anyone to know about the child.'

He'd thought that, too. But she'd taken a devious route to hide it all. A servant, maybe, or someone who'd hidden the pregnancy in case she lost her position. He'd find out.

'Would she have showed much, do you think?'

'Hard to say,' King replied thoughtfully. 'Most women do. But with a very small foetus . . . if she was young and dressed carefully, perhaps not. Otherwise . . .' He shook his head. 'I wouldn't like to give an opinion, Inspector.'

It was a slow, sorrowful walk back across Crown Point Bridge into Leeds. All around, smoke rose from chimneys and the streets were noisy with the boom of manufacturing. He tried both the dispensary and the infirmary, but they'd had no women brought in with complications after childbirth. By the end of the day he had no idea how to find her.

Now the annual inspection was over and tomorrow he could begin the search again.

Just as the tea finished mashing, she came up the stairs, the bright click of her heels on the wood.

'Take a look,' she said, holding up the picture. 'He really caught you, Tom.'

It was true. The image captured him perfectly, the jut of his chin, the stance, one leg forward, his deep-set eyes and sly smile. But those clothes . . . it wasn't how he wanted anyone to remember him.

'It's good,' he agreed mildly.

'But?' Annabelle asked. 'You don't look too happy.'

6

'I don't know. I'm not used to seeing pictures of myself, I suppose.'

'Cheer up.' She gave him a peck on the cheek. 'You look handsome. You do to me, anyway.'

He set out cups, sugar and milk, moving a book from the trivet to make room for the pot. *The Condition of the Working Class in England*, he saw on the spine. Not a novelette, he thought wryly. But none of the volumes that filled the place these days were.

The change had begun in March. The new bakery in Burmantofts was doing so well that Annabelle had put Elizabeth, the manager, in charge of all three shops. They were thick as thieves, together two and three times a week for business that was also pleasure.

The pub more or less ran itself, and without the other businesses to look after, Annabelle had an empty space in her life. Idleness wasn't something that suited her. She'd started out as a servant in the pub before marrying the landlord, inheriting the place when he died, then opening her first bakery. She was wealthy now, but still never content unless she was busy at something, filling every waking hour to overflowing.

He'd come home from a long day in the early spring rain to see her reading a pamphlet. *Votes for Women*, it said on the cover.

'What?' she asked sharply when she saw him staring.

'I'm just surprised, that's all,' Harper told her. She'd never shown much interest in politics.

The tale poured out, her eyes blazing. The old coalman had retired, and the new one had come

7

that morning. When she complained about the quality of the coal, he rounded on her, telling her that maybe he'd do better dealing with her husband, then saying she needed someone who'd give her a good clout to keep her in line.

She'd seen him off with a spade from the yard. Still seething, she'd taken a walk, barely noticing where she was going. Down by the market a woman had stopped her with a gentle touch on her arm.

'Are you all right?'

'No, I'm not,' Annabelle said through clenched teeth. 'I'm bloody fuming.'

'Trouble with a man, luv?'

Annabelle laughed. 'Something like that.'

'They're useless, the lot of them.' The woman shook her head. 'Here, you look like you need this,' she said with a warm smile, handing Annabelle the pamphlet before vanishing back into the crowd.

'I don't know, Tom. It was just so odd. Almost like I'd imagined it. I came home and started reading it.' She held it up. 'You know, there's a lot of common sense in here.'

Within a fortnight she had books on all the tables, devouring each and every one. She began going to the suffragist meetings held in halls around Leeds, talking with other women, coming home glowing with excitement and possibilities for the future. But that was Annabelle, Harper thought. She never simply dipped her toe into something; she always had to immerse herself.

She didn't ignore the businesses. She still kept

a close eye on them, totting up the accounts every week and making sure the money rolled in.

'Are you sure you don't mind?' she asked one evening after she returned from another meeting.

'Mind what?' he asked, surprised.

'Me getting involved in all this.'

Harper was astonished. 'Don't be daft. Why would I?'

'I don't know,' she answered. 'Plenty of men would.'

'I'm proud of you,' he told her. He loved the way she could just fearlessly dive into something. And they still had their time together; she made sure of that.

The evening slid by, warm enough to leave the window open. 1891 had been a strange year for weather. So much snow and bitter cold to start, then a blazing summer that still hadn't withered as October began.

It had been an odd year all round. He'd missed Billy Reed at the parade, and regret flowed through the inspector's heart. They'd never resolved the resentment that seemed to hang between them at the start of 1891; they'd barely spoken in the last few months. Back from his injuries, the sergeant had quietly transferred to the fire brigade; it was part of the police force. The man had made his decision. He'd done what he believed he had to do. But it was a blow Harper had never expected. Billy had a sharp mind, and a clear, concise way of looking at things. More than that, Reed had been a friend, someone he'd always trusted completely. Harper knew it was his own fault.

9

His insistence on a lie. But he couldn't turn back time.

At least Ash had come on quickly. He'd become an excellent detective, not afraid of hard work, observant, with a brain that was quick to find connections. In his own way he was just as good as Reed. But it could never be the same.

The image of the dead baby slipped back into his mind again. Tomorrow, he thought. There was time for it then.

The grandfather clock gave its chime for half past nine and he stood. She was gazing at the photograph, propped against the mantelpiece.

'What are you thinking?' he asked, placing a hand on her shoulder.

She turned. 'That I'm lucky to have you.' There was love and tenderness in her eyes. 'And how I'm hoping you'll suggest it's time for bed.'

He put his fingers over hers. 'That sounds like a wonderful idea,' he said.

He'd been slowly stirring, still half-dozing, not wanting to move. Somewhere outside, beyond the open window, he could hear the first trills of the dawn chorus as the birds began to sing and chatter.

Then the explosion. Louder than thunder, deeper, a dull sound that rippled and boomed. And then it was gone, leaving a sudden, dead silence that seemed to hang in the air.

Harper sat up abruptly, looking at the clock. A little after half past four, still full darkness outside.

'What was that?' Annabelle's voice was a sleepy mumble.

'I don't know,' he said. He parted the curtains. Off in the distance, down towards the river, he saw the raw glow of a fire. For a moment a tongue of flame rose into the sky. 'I need to go.'

Two

It was too early for the trams or omnibuses. He dashed along the road, staring at the horizon. The fire must be close to the railway station. Off to the east, dawn was just a pale blue band at the bottom of the sky, but to the southwest the light was brighter and fiercer. Already he could taste the smoke in the air, acrid and hot.

Millgarth police station was almost empty, only the night sergeant behind the counter.

'Where is it?' Harper asked him urgently.

'Down at New Station, sir. We've got every fire engine in the city there. The insurance companies have even sent theirs. I've had to give them all our constables to keep order.' He pinched his lips together and shook his head. 'There's no one out on the beat.'

Harper ran out of the door, running through the market. The early traders were just setting up, gossiping and stopping work to glance nervously into the distance. Along Boar Lane the noise of the blaze grew. Even with the hearing in his right ear worsening month by month, it was still a fearsome roar. By the time he reached New

Station it had become overwhelming. All around, the heat was intense.

Men were running and yelling, light flaring up and fading with the flames, the smoke thick as fog. His eyes stung and his throat was raw. He coughed. Hot ashes floated in the air. It was like walking into a furnace.

Harper searched for anyone familiar in the confusion. Someone who knew what he was doing. But all he saw as he wandered were people unrecognizable under the soot and grime.

Finally he made out a face he knew. Dick Hill, bellowing orders to someone. He threaded his way through the press of people.

'What's happened?' He had to tap Hill on the shoulder and shout in his ear before the man turned. The two of them had started on the force together, but Hill had transferred over to the brigade early on. Now he held the rank of inspector.

'Started in the Arches.' His voice was hoarse. Harper leaned towards him, trying to make out the words. 'Can't tell anything more until it's out.' He turned away to direct a constable. 'We've got everything we own here and it's still getting worse. We'll be lucky if it doesn't destroy everything.'

'What can I do?' Harper shouted.

'Find one of the engines. Get pumping. Over there.' He gestured vaguely towards the river and Harper pushed his way between people until he found a fire engine.

The inspector stripped off his jacket, rolled up his sleeves and took over from a man whose face had turned almost as red as the fire.

12

After five minutes his arms and shoulders were sore. He was dripping with sweat, but the heat from the fire was so intense that the clothes simply dried on his back. Someone passed him a canteen and he drank thirstily, emptying some of the water over his head before handing it on. Blisters formed and broke on his palms, but he kept on pumping, finally taking a break after an hour, stumbling away and trying to find a few lungfuls of clean air.

He knew it had to be daylight, but all around it was impossible to tell; the smoke was too thick. It was like walking through hell. Harper kept coughing and spitting, but he couldn't get the taste out of his mouth. After ten minutes he returned, hands so sore he couldn't even close them, and started pumping again.

It was like being in a furnace. The fire at the station roared like a monster, one that couldn't be beaten.

Billy Reed pulled the hose, trying to change the angle. But it didn't matter what they tried, the inferno simply kept blazing. He felt as if the air was singeing his lungs and fell back a few feet, trying to catch his breath.

It was spreading, he could see that. He just prayed they'd be able to beat it back without any of his men losing their lives.

The bell had brought him instantly awake. For a moment Sergeant Reed thought he was back in the army, in Afghanistan. He groped for his rifle, surprised it wasn't there. Then he knew exactly where he was: the central fire station on Park Row, and the alarm was ringing.

He dragged on his jacket and boots and joined the others by the engine. One man was already fixing the horses in their traces, another checking the hoses on the reel. They had one of the brand-new steam engines. The best around for dousing a fire quickly, everyone said.

Reed glanced at the clerk's scribble on a piece of paper.

'New Station,' he told the others. 'You all know what to do. I don't want anyone taking stupid chances.' He paused, letting the words sink in, looking from one face to the next among the crew. 'If there are people in danger, save them. Forget about property. We're there to put the fire out.'

The man with the horses cried, 'Ready,' as the crew climbed on board and the doors opened. As soon as they were on the street they could see it, the curls of flame and the clouds of smoke.

'Just remember what you've been taught and you'll be fine,' he told Jem Hargreaves with a wink. The man had only finished his training the week before and kept his gaze fixed on the distance.

Reed had been leading the crew since his arrival in April. They'd been wary of him at first, new and untested, but he'd quickly proved himself. They'd tackled fires on almost every shift since he started and by now they trusted him. But this would be the biggest. It looked as if half of New Station was in flames.

He was already thinking ahead. Run the hose down to the river, bring up the pressure in the boiler. Plan, that's what he'd been taught. Be aware. Every fire could kill: they'd drummed it into him when he began. Always know your way out. Look after your men. And don't take chances.

He closed his eyes and thought about Elizabeth and the children, praying that he'd live until the end of the day to see them again. In his army days Reed had had no one. Living or dying had never worried him then. Now he possessed something valuable, something that mattered. These days he was more careful with his life.

'All back safe,' he said, and everyone on the engine echoed it. Their watchwords whenever they went in. They looked out for each other. They had to.

Elizabeth would already be working, starting her round of the bakeries. When he told her he couldn't be a detective any more, she sat and listened to his reasons, then held him and simply said, 'Just do what you think is right, luv.'

And in his heart he'd had no choice. He'd perjured himself so Tom Harper could have his conviction. He knew the inspector had covered for him in the past when he'd been drunk or violent. He'd done it gladly, too many times. But once he said the words in court, all those debts were paid. After that, he needed something fresh, something clean. Off the sick list, he'd passed the physical examination and put in his transfer.

'Are you sure?' Superintendent Kendall had asked. 'I don't want to lose you, Sergeant.'

'Positive, sir,' Reed had replied, waiting while the man signed the paper.

The driver reined in the horses. The men jumped down, pushing the engine into position.

15

'Right, lads,' Billy yelled. 'You know what to do. Everyone back safe.'

Eight hours later and they were still there. Bruised, battered, hair singed by the embers, skin smeared with soot, they had hardly enough strength left to guide the hoses on to the flames. Billy could make out their eyes. Everyone was drained, utterly exhausted. God help people if there were any other fires in Leeds, he thought; every engine in town was here. More from the surrounding areas, too, and they still hadn't put out the fire. He didn't care what had started the blaze. The only thought in his head was beating it back.

He wiped a dirty hand across his mouth, tasting nothing but smoke. The rails for the trains lay buckled and twisted into grotesque shapes, still glowing red hot.

A hand on his arm made him turn. It was Inspector Hill. The man brought his lips close to Reed's ear.

'Go home. The next shift's here.' His voice was cracked from all the hours of shouting orders. Billy nodded and began to gather his men, making sure they were all there. But they hadn't marched more than a hundred yards before the earth seemed to give a groan. Everyone stopped, and for a moment the world seemed to go quiet, as if drawing a breath.

Then came the crashing of stone and concrete. Half the platforms vanished into the space below, down among the broken arches and a dust storm rose. Billy turned towards it.

16

'Come on,' he told the others as he ran. 'Bloody come on.'

It was late afternoon by the time he arrived home. He stank of smoke; it was in his uniform, in his hair, on his skin. He'd been too tired even to wash off the soot and dirt. Inside, he closed the door and leaned against it, ready to drop.

'Billy,' Elizabeth said as she bustled out of the kitchen. She stopped, looking at him, then hugged him close. 'Thank God. I've been worried sick all day. Are you hurt at all?'

Reed shook his head. He felt as if he couldn't walk another step or say a single word.

She took down the tin bath and started to heat water, then washed his uniform, rinsing it three times before all the dirt disappeared.

At supper, the children were eager to hear about it. But what could he say, Billy wondered. It wasn't exciting; he'd been as terrified as everyone else. He'd never forget the sound as the platforms gave way. Or the looks on the men's faces when the word spread that a fireman had died. He glanced at Elizabeth, stuck for words.

'Just leave it,' she told them quietly. 'You can see he's dead on his feet.'

In bed, the last of the daylight outside, Reed closed his eyes. As soon as sleep came, he was back in the fire.

Harper stood in the superintendent's office the next morning. His palms were bandaged and tender but they'd mend in a few days. Annabelle has fussed around him, putting on a lotion that burned before it soothed. He ached all over.

'I need you to go down to have a look at that fire,' Kendall told him. 'Take Ash with you.'

'I thought they'd put it out.'

'They have. I want to make sure it wasn't anarchists who caused it.'

The man was as immaculately turned out as ever, suit pressed, moustache and side whiskers trimmed, the crease in his trousers as sharp as a blade. But his face was lined with worry.

'I thought they were all talk,' Harper said.

'They are,' the superintendent replied. 'But you know how it happens. All it needs is one hothead taking that "assault on the system" line of theirs to heart.' He shook his head. 'Stupid. Work with Dick Hill until he's established a cause. Just in case.'

'Yes, sir. I have that dead baby, too.'

'I know. What have you found?'

'Nothing.' He paused, thinking of the tiny corpse on the table. 'Honestly, I'm not sure if we ever will.'

'Keep trying, anyway. Your hands, Tom . . .'

'From the pumps yesterday.' He held them up. 'Blisters. They'll heal soon enough.'

'You'd think the criminals would have been running free, what with every officer down there,' Kendall said. He took his pipe from his waistcoat pocket and lit it with a match. 'But there was nothing reported.' He arched his eyebrows. 'Think about that. Not a single crime anywhere in Leeds.'

There was just enough of a breeze to bring a sense of freshness, the hint that autumn might

18

arrive soon. Harper walked side by side with Ash, the constable quiet as they passed the Corn Exchange. Carts clattered quickly along Duncan Street. Piles of horse dung were flattened on the road. Men ran, pushing barrows piled with goods to deliver. A tram rolled by with the grinding sound of wheels in the iron tracks. The air smelt burnt and dead as they neared the station.

'How did you like the inspection?' Harper asked.

'It was right enough, sir.' He gave a small grin. 'My missus thought I looked that smart all dressed up.'

'Mine made me have a photograph taken wearing it.'

'They must love the top hats, those women.' He shook his head and tapped his old bowler. 'Me, I'm more comfortable in this.' He paused. 'I heard one of the firemen died yesterday.'

The inspector nodded. 'When the platforms collapsed. Nothing anyone could do. They couldn't even get in to bring the body out.'

'Sad business, sir.'

They'd become used to working as a team since Reed had left. They functioned well together, although there'd been little to tax them too hard. All the crimes they'd investigated in the last few months had been straightforward. Profit or passion, and a simple matter to find the culprit.

Harper doubted there'd be much for them here, either. He didn't believe any anarchists were involved. The only problem would come if Hill said the fire was arson.

New Station was filled with rubble and

19

wreckage. Thick dust clung to piles of bricks, and charred wood still smoked lightly. But passengers were already crowding the three undamaged platforms, craning their necks to see all the ruin, and most of the trains were still running. Harper shook his head in amazement; after all the destruction, he wouldn't have believed it possible. Or safe.

They found Hill down among the arches that had once supported everything. All the surfaces were black with soot, the smell of fire and destruction heavy and cloying, and he started to cough. A yard or two below them, the River Aire rushed by.

'Hello, Dick,' Harper said. 'We've been sent down to help.'

Inspector Hill looked haunted. He was still wearing the uniform he'd had on when the blaze began. There were rents along the seams, the blue so covered with dirt that it seemed to have no colour at all. Dark rings lined his eyes.

'Tom,' he answered and let out a sigh. 'We just brought out that man who died. Schofield.'

'One of yours?'

Hill shook his head. 'He worked on one of the insurance company engines. The floor just gave way underneath him.' He stared up at the sky. 'Ten years and I've never seen anything like it. As best as we can guess, he must have crawled forty feet after he fell. Almost made it out, too, poor bugger. It's a miracle there was only one, really.'

Ash broke the silence that grew around them. 'Any idea where it started yet, sir?'

'Oh, we know that.' Hill pointed to an empty space, nothing left at all. 'You see that? It used to be Soapy Joe's warehouse. Packed full of tallow and resin. Tons of the bloody stuff. That's where it began. And that's why it burned so hard and long. Once that went up there wasn't a chance.'

'What caused it?' Harper asked.

Hill shrugged. 'A spark? An accident? Deliberate? There's not enough left to tell. I wouldn't even like to guess. The best I'm ever going to be able to say is that it happened. It's nothing to worry CID, anyway.'

'The superintendent wondered about anarchists.'

'I don't see it.' He shook his head wearily. 'Honestly, Tom, I don't. I'm going to dig around but I don't think I'll find any evidence of anything.'

'You should get some sleep, Dick.'

'Later.' Hill brushed the idea away. 'I need to take care of a few things first. We've never had anything as bad as this before in Leeds.' He waved a hand at the damage. 'Look at it. It's going to cost a fortune to rebuild. But the railway's already had engineers out this morning. Can you believe that?'

'They want to be making money again,' Harper said.

'Sir! Sir!' The shout echoed off the stone, making them all turn. A fireman was picking his way through the mounds of stone and brick. 'There's another body down here. It looks like a woman.'

21

Three

They ran, scraping their way over the debris. Dust rose around them as they scrambled.

'Over here,' the man called. He was standing by a pile of rubble. 'You can just see her foot over there.'

They gazed. Half a button boot, the leather torn clean away to show bloody flesh. The rest of her was buried under chunks of concrete.

'Must have collapsed right on top of her,' Hill said grimly, taking off his uniform jacket. 'Let's get this shifted.'

Ash glanced at Harper's bandaged hands.

'Will you be all right, sir?'

'I'll manage,' the inspector told him as he stared at the foot.

It took them a quarter of an hour to move everything, sweating and grunting. Blood seeped through Harper's bandages. He grimaced and worked on.

'Christ,' Hill said quietly.

Most of her clothes had burned away. Her hair was gone. She was part-flesh, burned and black. But it was the rest of her that made them draw in their breath. Patches of metal across her body that glinted in the light. Skin like silver: the thought came into his head.

'What?' At first he didn't even realize he'd spoken.

'Must have been the girders,' Hill said. He couldn't take his eyes off the body. 'They melted in the heat and the metal dripped down on her.' He wiped a hand across his mouth. 'I just hope to God she was already dead.'

Harper took a deep breath and squatted, moving this way and that around the corpse. Only the shape and size of the body and the torn button boot showed she'd once been female. Now . . . he could scarcely believe what he saw. Two dark, burned holes where her eyes had once been. The smell of her, like charred meat. The glittering metal. Dear God, it was grotesque. A statue of death. He shuddered as he stood again.

'What the hell was she doing down here?' he wondered.

'Looks like there's something for you, after all, Tom,' Hill said grimly. He slung his jacket over his shoulder and shook his head. 'I need to go, I've too much to do.' He took two steps and paused to stare at the woman again. 'Since it happened here I can let you have someone to help. How about Billy Reed?'

The inspector stiffened. 'He might not want to . . .'

But Hill was insistent. 'He's worked your side of the fence and he knows fires by now. I don't think there's anyone better suited.'

'Billy's good,' Harper agreed after a moment, keeping all the feeling out of his voice. 'If he's willing, I'll have him.' He couldn't pull his gaze from the corpse with its silver skin. 'We're going to need someone else.'

'Well, sir,' Ash said as the firemen walked away,

'going to be like old times, isn't it? I'll get this poor lass taken down to Hunslet.'

Dr King, smoking a cigar to cover the fumes of carbolic and formaldehyde, waved them to the side of the room.

Harper and Ash waited expectantly. Reed, dressed in plain clothes, stood beside them, sullen and quiet, as if he didn't want to be there.

'Well, gentlemen,' King began. He was standing by the slab where a sheet covered the body. 'I want to thank you. I can honestly say this is a first for me.' He seemed to relish the experience.

'Doctor,' the inspector said. 'We need to know what killed her.'

He hoped King wouldn't display the woman. It was something he never wanted to see again.

'Oh, I can tell you that, Mr Harper,' the man answered with pleasure. 'It wasn't the metal, although God knows that did enough damage to her. It wasn't those tons of concrete that fell on her either, even if they broke almost every bone in her body. It wasn't even the fire.' He gave a conjurer's smile. 'She was dead before any of that happened.'

'What?' Harper glanced at Ash. 'How? How can you tell?'

'Because she was stabbed in the back. Since she was lying on it, that escaped most of the damage. The blow went right through to her heart. Instant. A long, thin blade.'

Ash coughed. 'Pardon me asking, sir, but how do you know that's it? What was left of her

24

seemed to have plenty of cuts, if you don't mind me saying so.'

King eyed him sternly. 'Because I've been doing my job for a long time, Constable, and I'm very good at it. Believe me, that is what killed this woman.'

'What can you tell us about her?' Harper asked quickly, trying to smooth the waters.

King puffed on the cigar as he collected his thoughts, watching the smoke rise.

'I'd say she's probably in her early forties. There's a tiny bit of hair at the back of the scalp that didn't burn, and I found grey in that. What's left of her palms look smooth enough and well cared for. But,' he added with a flourish, 'if I had to guess, she's done work with them in the past. A small piece of her dress survived because it was stuck to her back. Good material, and that piece of boot you found is expensive leather. She had money.' He gestured towards a corner. 'Her things are in a bag over there. What little there is, anyway. Nothing to identify her.'

'Anything else, Doctor?' Harper asked.

'I can probably tell you more when I've opened her up. But that should be enough to get you started.'

They walked back quietly across Crown Point Bridge, sobered by what they'd seen and heard. On the river, barges moved along slowly, and vessels stood two and three deep at the wharves, swarms of men loading and removing goods, rolling barrels along flimsy gangplanks. Smoke rose from hundreds of factory chimneys, settling in a haze that blocked out the faint sunlight.

'It's good to have you back, Billy,' Harper said finally, but the sergeant just grunted and lit a cigarette.

'You heard what King said,' Reed told him. 'It's a job for the detectives now, not the fire brigade.'

'We'll still need an extra pair of hands, if Dick Hill can spare you.'

Reed stopped and pursed his lips. The inspector nodded for Ash to go ahead.

'Sir—' the sergeant began, but Harper cut him off.

'For God's sake, Billy,' he hissed, eyes flashing, 'it's Tom. How long did we work together? How long were we friends?' He paused, trying to let his temper settle. 'Look, I know I was wrong in pressing you to say something you didn't remember. I shouldn't have done that. But he was guilty. You know that just as well as I do.' When the sergeant didn't reply, he said, 'Well, don't you?'

'Yes,' Reed answered reluctantly, staring out over the water. Just a single, squeezed word.

'I'm sorry,' Harper continued. 'I put you on the spot. If there'd been another way, I wouldn't . . .'

'It's done.' The sergeant cut him off and tossed the rest of the cigarette down into the river, eyes following its descent.

'You're a good detective. I liked working with you. I wasn't sure when Dick offered your services, but this is going to need brains, and you have those.' He extended a bandaged hand. 'What do you say?'

Reed looked at the hand for a long time, then eventually gave a quick, small nod. 'All right.'

26

'Welcome back,' Harper. 'It's good to have you.'

'It's just for this case,' the sergeant told him. 'I'm still a fireman, remember that, sir.'

'For this case is fine.' It was a frosty beginning. But at least it was a start. He smiled. 'Come on, Ash'll be wondering if we've thrown each other off the bridge.'

'The first thing is to discover who she was,' Harper said, pulling the piece of dress from the bag. It was crumpled and burned at the edges and smeared in dirt, but inside the neck there was a dressmaker's label. Gently the inspector rubbed away the soot. 'Madeleine Harkness, dressmaker,' he read and looked at the others. 'Ring any bells?'

'Basinghall Street,' Ash answered without hesitation.

'Right.' The inspector handed him the cloth. 'Go over there and see what she can tell you.'

After the constable had gone, Reed asked, 'What do you want me to do?' A formal tone. None of the old friendliness.

'Go back to the Arches. Now we know she was killed before the fire it's worth a poke around. There might be something to find.' He paused for a moment. 'Maybe the murderer started the blaze to try to destroy her. What do you think?'

'No,' the sergeant said quickly. 'If he'd wanted to do that, he'd have dragged her closer to it.'

'You're the expert. See if there's anything.'

Harper was sitting at his desk, thinking, when the superintendent came out of his office.

27

'Like old times, having Reed back,' Kendall said.

'I hope it is,' he answered doubtfully.

An hour later Harper was sitting with a cup of tea when Ash returned.

'I've got a name for you, sir,' he said, easing himself on to a chair and taking out his notebook. 'Catherine Carr, that's what the dressmaker says. Bought the dress nearly two years ago.' He glanced up. '*Mrs* Carr.'

'Mrs?' the inspector said with surprise. 'I didn't see a wedding ring.'

'Nor did I, sir. I have an address, though. Out in Chapel Allerton.'

'That fits with money,' he said thoughtfully, tapping a thumbnail against his mouth. It was a village that had grown into a suburb after those with wealth moved away from Leeds for the fresher air.

The constable eyed Harper's cup. 'I don't suppose there's time for a brew first, sir?'

'When we get back.' He gathered up his hat and waited by the door. 'If the husband killed her, we'll have it all wrapped up today.'

Ash pursed his lips under his thick moustache and placed the bowler hat on his head.

'Never that simple, though, is it, sir?' he said with a weary sigh.

They alighted at the terminus, outside the Mexborough Arms, and asked directions, walking up a small hill. An imposing stone house stood at the end of a gravel driveway.

'Whoever Mr Carr is, he's not short of a bob or two,' Ash said.

'Doesn't mean a thing and you know it,' Harper told him. The woman hadn't been reported as missing; he'd checked before they left.

'I don't know, sir. They're usually the ones who have most to lose.'

'I'll talk to him. You have a word with the staff, see what they say.'

'Yes, sir.'

The maid who answered the door looked worried as the inspector announced himself, but led him through to a parlour at the back of the building, knocking on the door before entering.

'A policeman to see you, Mr Carr.'

The man was sitting in an armchair, staring out at the garden, a pair of walking sticks close by. He turned his head quickly.

'A policeman?' He had a deep bass voice that seemed to resonate around the room. Harper waited until the maid left, then said, 'Detective Inspector Harper, sir. You have a wife named Catherine Carr?'

'Has something happened to her?' There was urgency in his tone. Carr looked close to seventy, with a body that had shrunk and a wispy covering of white hair on his skull. But there was a quick, fiery intelligence in his eyes.

'Yes, sir, I'm afraid something has.' He paused for the briefest moment. 'I'm sorry to have to tell you she's dead.'

'I see.' The man lowered his gaze, silent for a few moments. 'How did it happen?'

A strange reaction, Harper thought. Not what

he'd expected. The man was sad but distant, as if the woman was a faint relative or acquaintance, not his wife.

'She was murdered, sir. In the Arches, under the railway station. My condolences.'

Carr closed his eyes and bowed his head.

'Perhaps you'd better sit down, Inspector,' he said finally.

Her maiden name was Catherine Sugden, Robert Carr explained, and she'd been in service in the house for many years. After his first wife died, they'd grown close. She was almost thirty years younger than him, a woman with a good head on her shoulders who deserved more than drudgery for the rest of her life. He wanted a companion. They married.

A little like Annabelle with her first husband, Harper recalled.

'We were perfectly happy for five years,' Carr said dolefully. 'She was a good wife, dutiful, all I could have wanted. I retired and let my son take over the factory. It was time to pass it on.'

A factory. That would explain the money.

'What do you make, sir?'

'Boots,' Carr replied. 'My father started it fifty years ago.'

Of course. Carr and Sons, down on Meanwood Road, the sign painted in bright red and white on the chimney.

'I gather something happened between you and your wife, sir?' the inspector asked tactfully.

The man sighed and reached for a crystal decanter of whisky on the small table next to his

30

chair. He poured a glass then held it up, offering one. Harper shook his head.

'She became a convert to all this suffragism and socialism.' Carr spat the words with distaste. 'I told her she didn't need that bloody nonsense. I could give her everything she wanted and more. But it became an obsession with her.' The inspector listened closely, hearing the bile and seeing the sorrow on the man's face. 'Then six months ago she told me she couldn't live here any more.' He looked around the room as if he couldn't understand how she'd abandoned the place. 'I pleaded with her. We argued. She left on the fifth of April, and that's the last I saw or heard of her.' He swallowed the whisky in a gulp and replaced the tumbler. 'I'd have had her back if she'd wanted. She knew that before she left.' Carr shook his head. 'Do you know who killed her?'

'Not yet, sir.'

'If she hadn't . . .' he began, then faltered. Carr raised his eyes. 'The suffragists and the socialists, Inspector. That's where you need to look. They turned her head. They poisoned her. It was always Miss Ford said this, Miss Ford said that. You need to start with her.'

Harper knew exactly who he meant. Isabella Ford. He'd heard Annabelle mention the name. A suffragist, a socialist. She lived out in Adel, a rich Quaker.

He wasn't sure how to puzzle out Carr's reaction, the curious mix of fury and sadness that seemed to make no sense. Perhaps the man had no idea how he really felt.

'I'm sorry, sir, but I have to ask,' the inspector said finally. 'Do you know where your wife went when she left? What she was doing?'

'No,' Carr told him bluntly. 'I looked. I even employed someone to search for her but he couldn't find anything. She just vanished. And now you come and tell me someone's murdered her.' He raised clouded eyes. 'What's wrong with this world, Inspector? All these strange ideas. People killing people.'

But it was nothing new, Harper thought. Things had always been that way. He gave Carr a few details, holding back far more. He didn't need to know that his wife's corpse had been burned by molten iron and crushed under tons of concrete.

'What about her body?' Carr asked.

'Sir?' He stiffened, wondering if he'd given away too much.

'I'd like to bury her. She was still my wife, even if she didn't want anything to do with me any more.'

'Of course. I'll make sure they write to you once they can release her.' At the door he turned back and said again, 'My condolences, sir.'

Ash was already waiting at the end of the drive. As they strolled back to the Harrogate Road, Harper told the constable what he'd learned.

'I'm not sure what to make of him. I don't know which was more real, the sorrow or the anger.'

'Maybe both, sir.'

The inspector turned to look at him. Maybe he was right.

'The servants didn't want to say too much,' the constable reported. 'You can't blame them, I

32

suppose, he's their employer. But there was one lass who looked like she was bursting to tell me something. I got her on her own. Turns out she'd been Mrs Carr's maid.'

'And?'

Ash pursed his lips under the thick moustache. 'Your Mr Carr isn't all he'd have you believe, sir. He liked a drink or two. After that he'd take to insulting his wife, then beating her. That's what the maid claims, any road.'

'I see.' It fitted. The burst of anger followed by regret. He'd seen it often enough. Perhaps it was no surprise she'd left in the end, or that he blamed someone else. 'Often?'

'Often enough, every month or so. Sometimes more. A lot of raised voices after she started getting all political, the maid said. He told her she had to give it up. Either that or get out.' He glanced at the house.

'And she chose to go.'

'Looks that way, sir. But they're all agreed it's six months since she left. They all remember that. Not a word since then.'

'That's what Carr said, too. April.'

'Do you think he could have done it?'

'I don't know.' Not himself, Harper thought. Not if he walked with sticks. But he had wealth, and that could buy a great deal. Death wasn't an expensive commodity. Carr was certainly a possibility. He sighed. 'Come on, let's get back and see if Billy found anything at the Arches.'

Four

But it had been a waste of time.

'With all that debris around, there's no chance of finding anything.' Reed didn't try to hide his frustration. 'I wouldn't even like to guess if she was killed there.' He brushed some of the dust off his suit. 'It's a bloody mess. You know they've already started plans for rebuilding?'

How? Harper wondered. He'd seen the destruction. How would they even clear it all away, let alone put it up again? He hadn't held out hope of the sergeant finding much, but they had to try.

'Right,' he said, 'we know she left in April. Where's she been since then? She needed a job to support herself.' He thought for a moment. 'Dr King said her hands were still smooth, so it wasn't domestic work. Any ideas?'

'Shopgirl,' Reed said quickly and the inspector nodded.

'Hundreds of shops in Leeds, though,' Ash pointed out. 'We don't even know where to start. She might not even have been using her real name.'

'We're going to need to talk to Miss Ford,' Harper said. 'Maybe she can tell us more about Catherine Carr.'

'Who's she?' Billy asked.

'Isabella Ford,' Harper explained. 'She's a suffragist. You know, votes for women. A socialist,

34

too. Organizes a lot of meetings, things like that.' He stood and glanced at Ash. 'You start on the shops. I know it's thankless,' he said as the man groaned a little, 'but it has to be done. Begin in town. You come with me, Billy.'

They set off through the market. Two o'clock and the traders in the square were gratefully packing up for the day; they'd been there since before dawn. Noise came from the hall, a burble of voices as business continued. They crossed Kirkgate and entered the small union office. Paint was peeling on the window frames and door, and the glass needed a good polish. Inside, there were piles of papers and books on the desks and shelves, scrawled notes scattered around. And a red-headed young man in an old checked suit sitting in one of the chairs, thinking.

'Well, Inspector,' he said with a grin that took five years off his age, 'I haven't had the pleasure of your company in a while. And an associate, too. Am I so dangerous it takes two of you to visit me now?'

Tom Maguire had grown up in a poor Irish family in Leeds, no more than a few streets from Annabelle. He was still only in his middle twenties, but he'd earned every bit of his reputation as a fiery speaker and leader. He'd organized the labourers and the gas workers and guided them to victory when they went on strike.

'I'm looking for some help,' Harper told him. 'This is Sergeant Reed. He's with the fire brigade.'

'A grand and dangerous job you do, too, Sergeant,' Maguire told him with an approving nod. 'My hat's off to you men. I was very saddened to learn about your colleague.' He turned to look at the inspector. 'What kind of information would I have for the police?'

'The fire at New Station . . .' the inspector began.

Maguire raised an eyebrow. 'Arson?'

'No. We don't think so. There were two bodies there.'

'The fireman.' He nodded grimly.

'There was also a woman,' Harper continued. 'That one *is* police business.'

'And what does it have to do with me, Inspector?' Maguire asked calmly.

'Her name was Catherine Carr. She was a suffragist. Someone killed her.'

'I see,' he replied slowly. 'So you think I might know her?'

'It's worth a shot,' Harper admitted.

Maguire gave a quick smile. 'Much as it may surprise you, I don't know everyone with political sympathies in Leeds, Inspector. If she was a suffragist, you need to talk to Miss Ford. Murdered?' He pursed his lips. 'Terrible business. But have a word with Isabella. If anyone knows, she will. She lives in Adel.' He gave a sly smile. 'Or you could start closer to home.'

'What did he mean?' Reed asked testily as they walked back along the street. There was enough of a breeze to cut the heat, and off to the west, the hint of clouds on the horizon.

'Annabelle. She's become a suffragist.'

'That's right. Elizabeth said something about it. I'd forgotten.'

'He has a point, though. And it's closer than

Adel.' They started out along Regent Street. 'Let's see what she knows.'

Annabelle was leaning against the bar, chattering away with two men from the chemical works up the road when they walked into the Victoria. She said something, then came around, taking Reed's hands in hers.

'I've not seen you in far too long, Billy,' she told him, beaming. 'We've missed you, luv.'

'Thank you.' He blushed a little.

'The way your Elizabeth goes on about all the things you've been doing with the brigade, I'm surprised your head still fits through that door.' She winked at him. 'I mean it. It really is lovely to see you again. I hope this one's treating you well.'

'I'm going to work him to the bone while I have him,' Harper told her with a smile. 'We need to have a talk.'

'With me?' She looked at him, confused. 'Dan's just down in the cellar, I'll give him a shout. Go on up, I'll be there in a minute.'

'What's happened?' she asked. 'Is someone hurt?'

The sergeant looked at Harper.

'That fire at New Station.'

'What about it?' Annabelle said, her gaze moving from one man to the other. 'I don't understand.'

'There were two people who died, a man and a woman.'

'I know about the fireman.' Annabelle stared at Reed.

37

'The other was a woman,' Harper continued. 'She'd been murdered. I think you might have known her.'

Her mouth dropped open in astonishment. 'Murdered? Me? Why?'

'She was a suffragist. A lady called Catherine Carr.'

'Catherine?' She frowned, searching her memory. Then her gaze cleared. 'Katie? Katie Carr? Oh God. But . . .' Her voice trailed away, and she scrabbled in the sleeve of her dress for a handkerchief, dabbing at her eyes as he put his arms around her and drew her close.

'It's always different when you know someone,' Harper told her gently.

'It can't be. I only saw her last week. She was murdered?'

'Did you know her?'

'Not well,' Annabelle answered after a few moments. 'We chatted a few times, that's all. But she was lovely, always ready to help. You know, do things.'

'Did she ever talk about herself?' he asked.

'No. She worked in a shop on Briggate, I remember that.' Harper looked at Reed and gave a small nod of acknowledgement. 'Mostly it was this and that. Talking about who was going to speak. Things like that. She always seemed to be at the meetings.'

'Did she say exactly where she worked?'

'No.' She frowned and shook her head. 'I don't think so. I remember her clothes looked very smart for a shopgirl, though. Why?'

He told her what they knew: about Catherine

38

Carr's marriage, the way she'd changed. But nothing about the way her body looked when they found her, the skin with its metal shine.

'What we really need is to find out about where she's been in the last few months,' the inspector finished. 'Where she lived.'

'She never told me any of that,' Annabelle said flatly. 'It's strange, though.'

'What?'

'Well, think about it, Tom. She was a servant, married the man she worked for.'

'Yes.' The similarities in the two lives, Annabelle's and Catherine's.

'If I'd known . . .'

'You didn't, though,' he said gently. 'I'd better go and see Miss Ford.' He turned to Reed. 'Find Ash. Go through the shops on Briggate. I'm off to Adel. We'll compare notes in the morning.'

'There must be dozens of shops along there. Why don't we wait until we have more information?' The sergeant stared. 'It'll stop us wasting our time.'

'Just make a start. We might get lucky.' They locked eyes for a moment.

'Billy,' Annabelle called as the sergeant walked away, 'I mean it. It really is lovely to see you again. You'd better not be a stranger here.'

He seemed about to speak then gave a quick, embarrassed nod before leaving.

'He doesn't look happy to be back,' she said.

'We'll rub along. He's good at his job.'

'Are you going to see Miss Ford now?

'I'd like to come out there with you, Tom.' When he hesitated, she continued, 'It might help.

She knows me a little. I go to the meetings, I've talked to her. And I liked Katie.'

He'd considered it on the way to the Victoria. Did he want Annabelle involved? Miss Ford might be more willing to talk with a woman around, a sympathetic face she knew.

'All right,' he agreed. 'We'll need a hackney.'

'Just give me five minutes to change. Charlie Waterhouse is down in the bar, he'll be able to whistle one up for us.'

Five minutes became ten before she emerged from the bedroom in a lemon-yellow gown, the silk rustling as she moved across the floor, a bonnet tied under her chin with primrose coloured cotton.

'I'm ready.'

Annabelle was quiet and grim-faced in the cab, lost in her thoughts. They'd been out to Adel the year before, just after their wedding, a summer's afternoon promenading and scrambling over the crags, finishing with a bite to eat at Verity's Tea Rooms. He remembered the laughter and the joy: very different from today's journey.

The houses became scattered, giving way to fields and farms, although they were no more than a few miles outside Leeds. The sky was clear blue, the air smelt clean and clear. Fresh.

'What about this husband of hers?' Annabelle asked finally as the carriage wound along a lane. 'Maybe he killed her.'

'It's possible,' Harper said. 'But I need to know a lot more first.'

She looked ready to say something, then gave

a tight shake of her head and remained silent for the rest of the journey. The house was as grand as anything he'd ever seen, the sun shining brilliantly on the stained glass by the entry. He knocked on the door. When the maid answered, he announced himself.

'I'm Detective Inspector Harper, Leeds Police. I'd like to talk to Miss Isabella Ford, if I may.' When the woman's eyes glanced at Annabelle, he added, 'This is my wife. Miss Ford knows her.'

She escorted them to a shaded parlour that overlooked a long back garden. A moment later Isabella Ford appeared. She radiated energy, her long hair gathered in a loose braid. Good clothes, but plain. An earnest woman, he thought. What he'd expect from someone who effectively ran the Leeds Women's Suffrage Society.

She beamed at Annabelle. 'Mrs Harper. Well, this is a lovely surprise.' As she caught their expressions, her smile turned to a frown. 'What's wrong?'

'I believe you know Catherine Carr?' Harper asked.

'Of course I do . . . Inspector, is that right?' There was confusion in her eyes. 'I'm sure your wife told you that.'

'I'm very sorry,' he began, 'but I have to tell you that she's dead.'

'What?' She stared at him in disbelief. 'But . . .?' Miss Ford took a breath and gathered herself. 'How?'

'The night of the fire at New Station. We found her under the platform, in the Arches.' He

41

hesitated. 'She'd been murdered.' He felt Annabelle's hand reach out for his and hold it lightly.

'I . . .' Miss Ford began to pace around the room, hand fidgeting. 'But . . . Katie . . .' She gathered herself. 'Do you know who did it?'

'No,' Harper replied. 'That's why I'm here. I need to find out more about her. I'm hoping you can help me.'

'Yes, yes. Of course. If I can, I will.' She tugged on a bell pull by the empty grate and waited until the servant arrived. 'Hettie, do you think you could make us some tea, please? I think we all need some.'

'Of course,' the woman answered. 'Are you all right, Miss Ford? You've gone all pale.'

'Bad news, I'm afraid. Thank you.'

By the time she was passing around the cups, Isabella Ford seemed in control of herself again. 'Can you tell me how she died, Mr Harper?' Her voice was even and she looked him in the eye as she spoke. When he didn't reply, she said, 'You'd tell a man, wouldn't you? I'm an adult, my sensibilities aren't any more delicate than a man's. Katie was a friend. I'd like the truth, please.'

'She was stabbed,' the inspector replied.

'I see.' She stirred her tea, gazing into the liquid for a moment. 'Since you know her name, I assume you've already found out a few things about her.'

'Only a few. We know about her marriage, that she became a suffragist and left. That's all I have. I need details.'

She was silent for a moment, then, 'Let me ask

42

you something. Do you think her husband murdered her?'

'I don't know yet. As I told my wife, I need to know a lot more about Mrs Carr first.'

'Do you know he humiliated and beat her?' Miss Ford stared at him. He felt Annabelle's grip tighten briefly on his hand.

'Yes. Her maid told us.'

'At first he was loving, then after they married he became more demanding. That's what Katie told me.' Her voice was so low that he had to strain to make out the words. 'He'd call her all the names under the sun and beat her when he'd had a few drinks.'

It confirmed what they'd been told. No woman was safe with the wrong man.

'When she started coming to meetings, she was very shy. Very nervous,' Isabella Ford continued. 'I talked to her and tried to put her at ease.'

'She became a believer?'

'An ardent one, Mr Harper. Katie was a convert, and I was glad to have her. She told me she needed to leave her husband. She was scared things would grow worse. I promised that I'd help her find a job and somewhere to live.' Miss Ford held up a finger. 'I know, you need that information. I'll give it to you.'

'Thank you.'

'Tell me, Mr Harper, do you have the vote?' she asked. The question seemed to come from nowhere.

'Of course not.' But she'd know that already.

'Do you believe women should be able to cast a ballot?'

43

He could feel Annabelle watching him.

'Yes,' he answered. 'You, me, all of us.'

Miss Ford smiled. 'Your wife said you were sympathetic. And I've heard your name from Tom Maguire.'

'Then why ask?' He felt as if he was being tested, and he didn't understand why.

'Because I wanted to be sure.'

'He might be a copper,' Annabelle said, 'but don't let that fool you.'

'Oh, I won't.' She turned to him. 'And believe me, Inspector, I'll do all I can to assist you.'

'I need to know everything you can tell me about Mrs Carr.'

'Of course.' Isabella Ford took a sip of the tea and began the tale. Katie Carr had attended meetings regularly, even when she was with her husband. It seemed as if the suffragist cause had helped her find the strength to leave. And when she'd finally done it, Miss Ford had done as she promised: she'd found the woman a position with Miss Worthy, a milliner with a shop on Briggate. There was also a room in a boarding house in Sheepscar, on Tramway Street, run by another Quaker, Mrs Timothy. On her own, Catherine Carr had seemed to divide her life between work and the movement, attending every meeting she could and volunteering for all manner of jobs.

'Are there ever problems at the meetings?' he asked. 'Any violence?'

'We're women wanting change, Mr Harper,' Miss Ford replied coolly. 'What do you think? Mr Maguire always makes sure there are a couple of union men available to stop any trouble.'

'Have any of you ever been assaulted?' From the corner of his eye he caught Annabelle's face, tight and guarded.

Isabella Ford gave a thin smile. 'I've been insulted to my face, I've had pieces of fruit thrown at me outside meetings. Men gather there and wait for us. We run the gauntlet. Stared at mostly, with hatred and fear. Pushed a bit as we walk along the pavement sometimes. Your wife knows. We've all experienced it.'

He looked at Annabelle. Her face gave nothing away. Someone could have followed Catherine Carr and killed her. He thought for a moment.

'What about the police? Where were they?'

Isabella Ford raised an eyebrow. 'Conspicuous by their absence, Inspector. Or if a constable does come by, he stands back and simply watches.'

'I see.' He felt ashamed. That wasn't the police force he believed in. He could apologize, but that wouldn't help. 'Tell me, did Catherine have someone? A man?'

'A lover, you mean?' Miss Ford replied. 'She never mentioned one to me.'

'She didn't have that glow,' Annabelle added. 'You know, when you're happy like that.'

He nodded. 'What about friends? She must have had some.'

'When she was married, the wives looked down on her because she'd been a servant, and the servants resented her because she was their mistress.' Miss Ford shrugged. 'I suspect Katie had felt isolated for a long time. She'd learned to keep herself to herself, Inspector. She didn't trust easily.'

45

They talked longer, but for now there was little more to learn. But he had places to begin. That was something.

On the way out, Annabelle stopped to admire a painting in the hallway.

'My sister,' Isabella Ford said proudly. 'She's an artist, a very good one, too. She's in London at the moment.'

The casual way she said it, and all the trappings around them, elegant things, good furniture, reminded him that she was a wealthy woman with no need to work for a living. But she was the one who'd organized the mill girls when they went on strike. She believed in things. She was strong.

Her carriage took them back to town. In the distance, he could see the pall of smoke hanging over Leeds. The place would be sticky, stinking, uninviting after the calm breeze and clean air here. But it was home.

'You never told me about the problems at meetings,' he said as the coach sped through Adel.

'I didn't want to worry you.' She set her mouth firmly. 'And I can look after myself. You know me, I'm not going to take any guff.'

'I know, but . . .'

'No buts,' Annabelle told him. 'Honestly, I've thrown worse than them out of the pub. If they think they can scare me, they've another think coming. They're the ones who are scared, Tom. They're petrified of women.'

'One of them could have killed Catherine Carr. Remember that.'

They were silent until the coach was jouncing down the Harrogate Road.

'I've been thinking,' Annabelle began.

'Go on.'

She took a breath. 'I know this is your case, but I could ask around at meetings and see who knew Katie. You know, what they have to say about her. Would that help? Only they're used to me, Tom, they'd be more likely to talk.'

It made perfect sense. He was the police. The force had done nothing to protect these women. Why should any of them trust him?

'I think it's an excellent idea,' he answered, and she smiled widely. 'I'd be very grateful.'

'That rooming house where she was living, it's only a stone's throw from us. I didn't even know. She could have come over, had supper with us one night.' Annabelle shook her head. 'All she had to do was say.'

He drew out his pocket watch as the carriage approached the Victoria. It had gone six, the evening stretching ahead. He was tempted to let the day go. But there was work waiting. Once Annabelle was inside the public house, he told the driver to go on to Millgarth.

There were notes piled on his desk. He'd put out the word to all the divisions about the dead baby at the Post Office, for the beat bobbies to ask for any word about pregnant women who'd vanished, and to check with doctors about anyone who'd come looking for treatment after giving birth.

He tossed most of them aside. A few needed investigation. There was one close by, just on Quarry Hill. It was no more than two minutes away.

The house was in a ragged court hidden away from St Peter's Square. The type of place where the sun never penetrated and hope never grew. A midden over by a crumbling brick wall, flies buzzing noisily around it. No gas lamps, no cobbles, just packed earth that would be mud as soon as it rained.

Harper knocked on the door. No answer. He stood back, glancing around. But round here doors were closed against the police. He'd get little help.

'Who are you looking for?'

The voice startled him. He hadn't heard anyone approach. His bloody hearing had let him down again.

'Barbara Waite,' he replied.

'I haven't seen her in a few days.'

The speaker was a gaunt man, wearing a cheap dark suit, with fair hair and heavy mutton chop whiskers. His voice was friendly, but he seemed tense, holding himself with unnatural stiffness

'Do you know where she might be? I'm Detective Inspector Harper with Leeds Police.'

'Flitted, probably. She's a sinful girl.'

Harper cocked his head. 'Sinful?' It was a curious turn of phrase.

'Unmarried and carrying a child. And she refuses the word of God.'

He was one of those. A Holy Joe.

'And can I ask who you are?'

'Patrick Martin.' He extended a hand. 'With Leeds Town Mission. I'm the superintendent for this area.'

Harper had come across them. Full of religion

48

and brimstone, passing out their tracts and Bibles, trying to bring the poor to God. A few of them were good people, helping where they could. Most seemed happy to condemn anyone who didn't think like them.

'You know Mrs Waite?'

'Miss,' Martin corrected him with a sniff.

'Why do you think she's gone?'

'It's the way, Inspector. Surely you know that. I've seen too many like her around here.'

'Like her?' Harper asked, feeling his hackles rise a little.

'A girl who liked to drink and made a living on her back. Someone who turned away from the true word.'

'Had she given birth?'

'I don't know.'

It didn't matter; he could find out.

'How old is she?'

'Twenty, perhaps. Probably less.' Martin shrugged. 'But her sins are as old as the devil.'

'Thank you.' He'd had enough. He didn't care for church at the best of times, and he didn't need anyone setting up his pulpit on the street.

'Harper,' the man said thoughtfully as the inspector turned away. 'Is your wife's name Annabelle by any chance?'

'Yes,' he answered in surprise. 'Why?'

'I heard that she'd married again, someone said it was to a policeman.' The stern mask seemed to fall away from Martin's face, showing a younger man for a moment. 'I knew her when we were children. She and my little sister were friends.'

49

'I'll give her your best wishes.'

The man blushed. 'I'm sure she won't remember me.'

'She might, Mr Martin. Annabelle has a good memory. If you hear anything about Miss Waite, I'd like to know. I'm just over at Millgarth.'

The man nodded, gave a small wave and vanished around the corner. Well, well, Harper thought, so the Holy Joe had once been sweet on Annabelle.

'Pat Martin?' she asked with a small laugh. 'My God, I haven't thought about him in years.'

'He must have thought about you. He knew we were married.'

'He always was an odd one.' She chuckled at the memories. 'His sister Cara, me, and Mary Loughlin – we were close as that when we were young. Started work at the mill together. Don't even know what happened to them now. He works with the Town Mission?'

'Yes.'

'That sounds about right from what I remember.'

'I think he was in love with you.'

'Me?' Her eyes widened. 'Don't be daft. I was just his little sister's friend.' She shook her head. 'I'll make us a cup of tea,' she said, and vanished.

'Oh,' she shouted from the scullery a few moments later, 'I saw Bob Hodges today. From the council.'

Harper steered clear of councillors whenever he could; he'd made too many enemies there.

'What did he want?'

'We were talking about the new tram.'

The electric tram. For the last three months the work had been making travel up and down Roundhay Road a misery as they erected the poles and strung the wires. It was going to start in Sheepscar, right by the Victoria, and run out to Roundhay Park. He knew she wanted to be on the first run later that month. But there chances were slim; everyone wanted to be there.

'Any luck?'

'I told him I'd put on a slap-up feast for them all if they'd squeeze us in.'

'That's very generous,' Harper said.

'You know what they're like. Hate to put their hands in their pockets.'

'It'll be like a flock of gannets descending on the place.'

Annabelle laughed. 'Worth it if it happens, though.' She poured boiling water into the teapot. 'Pat Martin turning up again, eh? Who'd have thought it?'

'Did you talk to him?' Elizabeth asked. They'd eaten, and the two youngest were already in bed. Emily was practising her writing with a chalk and slate, and John was out somewhere with his friends.

'I did.' Reed balanced the cup of tea on his lap, sitting on the hard chair. He'd spent the last few minutes lost in thought, turning the case over in his mind.

'Well,' she said, 'go on. You can't leave it at that. What did he say?'

'He apologized.'

'What else?' She waited patiently, darning one of his socks, fingers moving deftly.

51

'He admitted he was wrong.'

She rolled her eyes in exasperation. 'Honestly, Billy Reed, getting anything from you is like drawing blood from a stone. Go on. Have the pair of you made up?'

'I don't know,' he said. It could never be the way it had once been, he knew that. The comradeship he'd shared with Tom Harper had evaporated. And he wasn't sure he wanted to be on this Carr case. Damn Dick Hill. He'd thought he'd left all that behind. 'How do you do it?' he asked.

'Do what, luv?' Elizabeth asked.

'You and Mrs Harper. How can you be so friendly when your men are on the outs?'

She shook her head. 'Because we're women, you daft ha'porth. We know better. I bet Annabelle was glad to know you're working together.'

'I saw her today. We went by the Victoria. She said was happy to see me.'

'Billy Reed, I love you,' Elizabeth said. 'Even if you're like every other man and still no more than a little lad inside.' She bit off the end of the thread, picked the next sock off the pile and pushed the darning egg inside.

'I'm happy. Here, with you and the children. I just want a quiet life.'

'Good.' She stared at him. 'I'll tell you though, sometimes I think men don't grow up. You just go backwards instead.'

Harper was in the office, writing his reports on the previous day, when Reed and Ash arrived.

'If I talked to one shop owner yesterday, I talked to fifty of them,' Billy said with a sigh.

52

'I can make it easier for you today, then. I found out where she worked. Miss Worthy, the milliner.'

'That's up near the Headrow,' Ash said dolefully. 'We started at the bottom of Briggate. We hadn't got that far.'

'Find out everything you can,' Harper told them. 'She had a room in Sheepscar; I'll talk to the landlady.'

Superintendent Kendall was still in his office, reading through a sheaf of documents, when Harper tapped on the door.

'I swear there's someone whose only job is to come up with more regulations.' Kendall picked up his pipe and struck a match, filling the air with smoke. 'What have you managed to find so far?'

The inspector gave him a summary.

'We need to know where she went on the night she died,' Kendall said. 'Right now we have too many possibilities and no certainties. There's the husband, but I want to know more about those men outside the meetings. Our constables weren't doing anything? Is that right?'

'That's what I'm told,' the inspector replied.

'I'll soon put a stop to that. Anything more on that dead baby?'

'One girl so far, but she seems to have disappeared. There are some others to check.'

'Keep at it. How's Reed?'

'We haven't had a ding-dong yet,' the inspector said.

'Let's hope it stays that way. I don't know why there was bad blood between you two. And I'm not going to ask,' he said pointedly. 'How are the hands?'

He lifted them to show the bandages.

'Getting better.'

Five

Harper stopped in the small shop at the end of Tramway Street and asked where Mrs Timothy lived.

'Four houses down,' the girl told him. 'But you're wasting your time. She don't take no men, no matter how respectable you are.'

The woman had looked after her house. All the dirt was scrubbed from the step, windows clean, brick washed as high as she could reach; not too far, from the look of it.

And Mrs Timothy was certainly a small woman, barely reaching to his shoulder, with a head full of tight grey curls peeking from a mob cap, her face lined by age. Plain and straightforward.

'No gentlemen here,' she said as soon as she saw him. 'It's a lodging house for women only.'

'I know that, Mrs Timothy,' he answered with a smile. 'I'm Detective Inspector Harper with Leeds Police. I'm here about one of your tenants.'

She folded her arms. 'Why? Has one of them done something wrong? I'll have her out before tonight.'

'No,' he assured her quietly, 'it's nothing like that. Could I come inside to talk about it?' She wouldn't want her private business shouted all over the street.

'Go on,' she agreed grudgingly and stepped aside. 'Through the first door there.'

When they were both seated, she stared at him. 'Who is it?' she asked bluntly.

'Mrs Carr.'

The woman stared at him for a long time before she spoke.

'I thought maybe she'd gone back to that husband of hers. But it has to be bad if the police are here, doesn't it?'

'She's dead,' he told her. 'I'm sorry.'

Mrs Timothy closed her eyes.

'My God, poor Catherine,' she said after a few seconds, then took a bunch of keys from the pocket of her plain cotton dress. 'You'll want a look at her room, then.'

'Yes, I do. And I need to talk to you about her.'

'Miss Ford recommended her, and that was good enough for me. We talked a few times when she first moved here.'

'How long ago was that?'

'Six months?' she asked herself. 'Close enough. She'd left her husband and she had employment.'

The inspector rubbed his chin. 'What else did she tell you?'

'I don't know that she said much at all. I'd see her in the hall sometimes and we'd pass the time of day. Always pleasant, but that was it. A very private lady. Very quiet. She was hardly ever here, what with work and her meetings.'

'The suffragist meetings?'

'That's right. She was always busy.'

'What about a man? Was she sweet on anyone?'

'Her? No. No one ever called for her. The only man she talked about was her husband, and that was only once or twice, back at the beginning.'

'What did she say about him?' He sat forward on the chair, listening, head tilted to be sure he caught everything in his good ear.

'That he wasn't good to her. He beat her, that's what she told me.'

Nothing he didn't already know. Maybe there'd be more in her belongings.

'Can I see her room now?'

It was cold and bare. A neatly made bed, four dresses hanging on hooks behind the door. More clothes than a shopgirl would have, he noticed, and better quality. A cheap, flimsy desk and chair stood under the single window, a pen and a diary sitting open. A pile of books with long titles – suffragism, socialism. Two more volumes by the bed. Thick, political works. A bundle of pamphlets, tied with string, sat next to them. Everything sparse and ordered.

Harper closed the diary and slid it into the pocket of his suit coat.

'I'll need to take this,' he told the landlady. 'Did Mrs Carr have any friends among the other lodgers?'

'No. She didn't even take her supper here.'

Maybe she'd put more of her life on the page. God knew she seemed to hide herself everywhere else.

'Thank you.'

56

'What about her belongings?' Mrs Timothy asked.

'Box them up for now,' the inspector said. 'And if you find anything when you clean, please let me know.'

'Rum business, this,' Ash remarked as they walked up Briggate. The pavements bustled with people moving to and fro with quick purpose, men in suits, still wearing summer straw boaters, women in dresses and uniforms, each with an intent face. The smoke from the chimneys was starting to push down, a haze keeping the sun away and the heat pressed to the ground.

'Aren't they all?'

'Maybe so,' the constable agreed easily. 'How do you like the fire brigade, sir?'

'It's hard work,' Reed admitted. 'But at least you know what you're fighting.'

'I don't know. It always looked dangerous to me.'

'It is,' the sergeant agreed with a shrug. 'Plenty of injuries. But that's the risk. We're all well trained. What about you? Enjoying being a detective?'

Ash grinned under his bushy moustache. 'I am. I never thought it would be for me, but it suits me very well.'

'Get along with Mr Harper?'

'I've learned a lot from him.'

'How's his hearing these days?'

'Getting worse,' Ash said with a grin. 'You know what he's like – tries to keep it hidden, but I doubt there's anyone at Millgarth who doesn't know. We make allowances for him.'

The shop stood at the top of the street, close to the Headrow. Nothing too big or fancy. A bell tinkled lightly as they entered. Hats stood displayed on tables and shelves. Small ones shaped liked delicate flowers, and larger, sweeping bonnets in pastel colours, decorated with feathers and waxed fruit.

They waited, feeling awkward and clumsy among the smells of perfume and powder, until a girl appeared from the back. She was young and fresh-faced, hair gathered in a tight bun, wearing a grey blouse buttoned to the neck and a long, bustled skirt.

'Gentlemen.' She smiled widely. 'Can I help you?'

'I'm looking for Miss Worthy. I'm Sergeant Reed with Leeds Police.'

The girl stared at them, her eyes starting to moisten. 'You must be here about Catherine.'

'We are, luv,' Ash told her gently. She nodded, lips pulled tightly together. 'Is Miss Worthy here?'

'In the back.' She disappeared in a rush, returning in a few seconds, an older woman with a thin face behind her.

'I'm Miss Worthy.' It was an announcement; she raised her chin as she spoke. 'Come through, please.'

Girls worked, stitching hats from designs, their backs bent. The sergeant followed Miss Worthy, giving Ash a nod to stay and talk to the women. Beyond a door, Miss Worthy settled behind a cramped desk, papers in neat piles around her.

'Miss Ford sent me a note,' she explained, taking a deep breath. 'Poor, poor Catherine.'

'My condolences,' Reed said. 'How long had she worked for you?'

'Six months, Sergeant. She was a sweet woman, and a very diligent employee.'

'You liked her?'

'I took her on as a favour to Isabella,' she answered carefully. 'But yes, I came to respect her.'

'Reliable?'

'Utterly.'

Reed stood on Briggate, smoking a cigarette, letting the smoke cover the scent that seemed to cling to him.

He'd learned that Catherine Carr was a model worker, never late, never missing a day, always one of the last to leave when the shop closed for the evening.

Miss Worthy supported suffragism. She went to some of the meetings and gave the group money. It made sense, she insisted: she was a householder, she ran a successful shop, she believed she had just as much right to vote as any man.

But she kept that separate from work. The women who worked for her were free to believe what they chose; her only rule was that politics and religion should never be discussed at work.

And she kept a distance from her employees. It never paid to be too friendly, she insisted; people only took advantage. Whatever else Miss Worthy might be, she was made of steel when it came to business.

59

All he could hope was that Katie hadn't obeyed all the rules, that someone had managed to make a friend of her. But when Ash appeared, shaking his head, he knew it was just wishful thinking.

'Kept herself to herself. Polite and friendly enough, and they're all upset. But none of them were close to her.'

'So we're back where we started.' He grimaced.

'Piece by piece, that's how it goes, doesn't it, sir?'

The sergeant strolled along the Headrow and down by the Town Hall. It was the first time in months he'd had the chance simply to walk around, to look at places and faces. His world had become smaller: home, the fire station on Park Row, the dash to a fire and the tired journey back.

The fire brigade was like the army; you trusted the men around you because your life depended on them. The bond was familiar, reassuring. And there was the same roar of danger in the blood on the way to a fire. That sense of never quite knowing what lay ahead.

But he had to admit he'd missed this, the thinking and working it all out in his head. Picking up on a word someone let slip and following it to the end.

He let his feet carry him around town for half an hour before heading back to Millgarth.

Six

The inspector sat with a cup of tea, Katie Carr's diary on the desk in front of him. He'd spent the last five minutes staring at it like a man in a trance. Finally he opened the book and leafed through. The bandages on his hands made it awkward, but at least they were healing. A few more days and he'd be right as rain.

Katie Carr's writing was rounded and girlish, the spelling slapdash, half-educated. She'd begun the volume at the start of the year – the first item was dated January 1st. He read slowly, feeling like an intruder into her thoughts. But this was his job, to take all the shards and try to put them back together.

For the first month the entries were quite long, almost half a page each day. How she felt stifled by her life and her husband. How he dismissed the idea of women wanting to vote.

He calls it stupidity and frivolite. He says we are not ready and that we may never be ready. He says a woman can niver have the reason of a man and no matter how I talk and persuad him, he will not be moved.

In public, he treated her well, polite and attentive. But once they were alone, it would begin: the

61

hurtful remarks, his satisfaction at leaving her in tears. Sometimes the blows. As Harper read on, the entries became sparse. A line or two, then days with nothing.

If I dont leave, I might die.

After that she'd written nothing for a fortnight. When she began again, she was in her new life. A little about her job, the room with Mrs Timothy. Everything matter-of-fact. From there, it was mostly notes about meetings and work, a speaker who'd inspired her. But some lines jumped out at him.

I feel like I can breathe again.
I feel as if I can stand tall for the first time in years.

He read on. There was no mention of a life beyond her job and the work she did for her cause. A small, compacted life. But that was the sense that came through the whole diary. A mouse of a woman. Alone, no friends. Maybe she'd always been that way. His sense was of a woman who'd vanished into herself.

At least she seemed more content after leaving. Her life might be small, but it was her own. He turned the pages, then suddenly stopped.

I thought I saw him tonight, walking along the street outside my window. Then he was gone again.

It was dated two weeks earlier. Just that, nothing more. A few days later she wrote:

> I am not certin, but I believe I saw him standing by the gas lamp on the street tonight. Then I blinked and he had gone. Perhaps I imagined it. I pray to God I did.

He looked at it again. He? Carr? Harper flipped through it all urgently. There was just one more entry, from the night before Catherine Carr was murdered.

> It is him out there. He stepped back and I saw his face. But I will not be afraid.

He stared at the words for a long time then examined the rest of the book. No more words hidden away, no pieces of paper tucked between the pages.

> It is him out there. He stepped back and I saw his face. But I will not be afraid.

Who?

Harper sat for a long time, gazing at nothing. Images came into his head. Catherine Carr, lying under the debris of the railway station with her skin turned to silver. The tiny baby on Dr King's table. Nightmares just waiting for darkness to visit again.

'Anything much in there?'

The inspector jerked his head up. Dammit. He'd never heard Reed come in.

'Someone was watching her.'

'Who?' The sergeant sat at the other desk. He looked older, Harper thought, but happier somehow. The restlessness that tormented him for so long had gone. He seemed comfortable in his skin.

'I don't know. She only says *he*.'

'The husband?'

It was a few seconds before he answered. 'I can't see it.' With his walking sticks he seemed too frail. But he'd need to find out. He sighed. 'What did Miss Worthy have to say?'

'Hardly worth the time. The job was a favour for Miss Ford. Mrs Carr was an excellent employee.'

'But?'

'But Miss Worthy never gets close to her employees.' He shrugged.

'What about the other girls in the shop?'

'She kept herself to herself.'

'Didn't even talk politics?' the inspector asked.

Reed shook his head.

'Not allowed. It's as if she hardly had a life, isn't it?'

'Yes,' Harper agreed thoughtfully as he looked at the diary. 'Come on, Billy, I'm in the mood for a cup of cocoa.'

The Golden Cup stood halfway down Lower Briggate, its name painted on the roof in gilt letters. The place was already busy, most of the tables filled with women gossiping or men conducting business.

The inspector ordered two cups and sat back, studying Reed's face until they were served. 'Why are we here?' the sergeant asked.

'Because I need to say a few things. Better here than at the station.'

'What?' His chin jutted forward.

'If we're going to work together properly, we need to clear the air.'

'I thought we had,' Reed said sharply.

'Come on, Billy. You're not a fool. I can use your help on this, but I don't want to feel like you're begrudging me your time every day.'

'There are plenty of good detectives on the force.'

'Yes. But none of them are you.' The sergeant opened his mouth to speak but Harper cut him off. 'That's not flannel. I was wrong before. I know that. I'm sorry. But I'd do it again. I can have Dick Hill transfer you back, if that's what you really want. I'd like you to stay, though. This is going to be hard, I can feel it. I just can't have you acting like you're doing me a favour every time I give you an order. Understood?'

Reed glared, taking a cigarette from the packet and making a production of lighting it.

'Understood,' he agreed finally. Harper extended his hand. This time the sergeant shook it.

'Good.' The inspector sipped his cocoa. 'You're right, it's like Katie Carr was barely there. You know what I learned reading her diary?'

'What?'

'Nothing. Not a damned thing. I still don't have any sense who she really was. What made her laugh or cry. She just seemed to exist.'

'Maybe she was scared to have anyone close after her marriage.'

'Possibly,' Harper agreed. 'Read it for yourself.

65

She talks about her husband and how he treated her. Social engagements. That's it. It's as if she was walking through her life.'

'People do, you know. What now?'

'I want you to dig into her. Find out where she's from, what she did before she worked for the Carrs. Her family. And find out about Mr Carr, too. He'd been married before. What did his wife die of? He said his son runs the business now. How well is it doing? Are there other children? But keep it quiet. I want ammunition, but I don't want him to know I'm gathering it.' He saw the sergeant quietly smiling. 'What is it?'

'It's only been a few months, Tom. I haven't forgotten how to do the job. It's probably Carr who murdered her. Nine times out of ten it's the husband.'

'But it's the tenth that's the problem? And I don't know . . .' He drained the cup and wiped his mouth. 'I just have the feeling that there's more to this than we're seeing.'

'And sometimes the obvious answer is the right one,' Reed told him. 'Remember? You taught me that when I started.'

'Maybe I'm making a molehill into a mountain. But there's something about this that feels wrong. How the hell did she end up in the Arches? It's not somewhere she'd be likely to go with anyone.' He ran his hands down his face. 'I just want something that feels like an answer and not another bloody question.'

'Then we'd better get to work. I still think we can close this quickly.'

'Tell the super. He'll be happy to hear it.'

* * *

66

The information from Catherine Carr's death certificate had been added to the papers in the folder. God only knew where they'd found everything – her husband, Reed supposed. She was listed as a shop assistant, murdered. The date she left the world, and the date she came into it.

Catherine Jane Sugden had been born in Leeds on July 9, 1847. Forty-four years old when she was killed.

He had two facts. Now he could find more.

The recorder's office was in a musty corner of the Town Hall, tucked away down a corridor, far from the marble stairs. There was light from the window, but the three clerks inside still had the gas mantles burning as they worked. The only sound in the room was the rapid scratch of nib on paper.

'I need to see her birth certificate,' the sergeant said as he showed his identification. The man vanished into a back room, returning with a heavy ledger. He checked the date, going through the pages to find the entry, then nodded to himself. Delving into a deep cabinet, he finally brought out a piece of paper, blinking through thick spectacles to be sure it was correct. Then he laid it on the counter.

'This is it, sir. No one ever asks to see these things.'

Her mother had been called Margaret Emma, her father James William. Married, living in Leeds. He was listed on the paper as a painter and decorator. A catch-all, a label for a man who'd turn his hand to anything.

'I'd like to know if the parents are still alive,

67

whether there were any other children, and if they're living.'

The man pursed thin, bloodless lips.

'I suppose I can find that,' he agreed after a little thought. 'I'll need some time.'

'An hour?'

'I'll do my best,' the clerk promised.

He walked down the steps, between the lions in front of the building, and into Victoria Square. The Indian summer was going to break; there was the sharp scent of rain in the air and clouds building off to the west, and around him he heard people with bronchitic coughs. A girl ran down the street, her legs bowed with rickets.

An hour. Time to walk back to Millgarth. Or to go over to New Station and look at the killing ground again.

Teams of men were clearing rubble and loading it on to carts. Already the place looked completely different, daylight streaming through the space where the platforms had been, paths cleared through the debris below. For a moment he could only stare in wonder at the work. Another day or two and all this would be empty space.

The trains were still running on the three remaining platforms, steam gushing, the passengers queueing warily. Business had to go on. There were schedules to keep and money to be made.

The Arches were nothing more than a blackened ruin. Wooden gangplanks crossed the river. Workers with kerchiefs around their mouths pushed wheelbarrows filled with rubble. There was dust everywhere, men coughing and spitting as they worked.

A hand tapped him on the shoulder. 'What are you doing here?'

'I'm sorry. Sergeant Reed, Leeds Police. Fire Brigade, most of the time. You know about the woman murdered the other night?'

The man nodded. He was young, cheeks still shiny from that morning's shave, with curly, pale hair and a small, fair moustache.

'Eric Shaw,' he said and stuck out a hand. 'I'm an engineer with the railway. We don't want people coming in and staring. It's still dangerous enough as it is.'

He seemed impossibly young for such a job. 'Are those other platforms really safe?' the sergeant asked. 'I was here fighting the fire.'

Shaw nodded eagerly. 'I inspected them myself. Not a worry in the world.' He looked around the gangs of labourers. 'This is all a mess, though. It's going to cost a fortune to rebuild.' He smiled. 'I'll leave you to look at what you need, Sergeant. Just be careful. If you want anything, come and find me.' He strode away quickly.

Reed wandered along, looking at the ground and dodging men as they bustled quickly around. He hadn't found anything when he searched before. Now he could barely guess where the body had been. There was no sense of the madness from the fire, only the determination all around to sweep everything away and start again.

'What have you managed to find?' he asked the clerk in the records office.

'Here you go, sir.' The man gave a satisfied smile as he handed over several brown, curling pieces of paper.

'Thank you.' The sergeant laid them out along the counter. Death certificates for James and Margaret Sugden. His from 1857, the cause listed as injuries from a fall. Catherine would have been just ten, probably already in service somewhere. Margaret Sugden had lasted another two decades before consumption took her when she was fifty.

The clerk had been thorough. There was a marriage certificate for the Sugdens from 1846, with an address in Hunslet, and birth and death certificates for three children, none of them living past the age of three. But no more heartbreak than many families endured.

He came to the final sheet. Stanley Arnold Sugden. Born August 20, 1856. His father would have been dead before the boy ever knew him.

'He must still be alive,' the clerk explained. 'I can't find anything else on him.'

'You've done a good job.'

'Thank you, sir.' The man beamed. 'If the police are looking for someone in their records division . . .'

'I'll be sure to tell them.'

So Catherine Carr had a brother, he thought as he walked back to Millgarth.

Sergeant Tollman stood behind the desk. He'd been in the same place on Reed's first day as a copper. Now the man looked older, greyer, his belly larger as it bulged against the wood. But he was the one they turned to, the one with remarkable recall. Give him a name and he knew the offence they'd committed. All too often the sentence they'd been given, too.

'Stanley Sugden,' Reed said. 'Does it mean anything?'

'It might, sir,' Tollman answered after a long while. 'We've had someone like that. It's a fairly common name, though.'

'What did he do?'

The sergeant stroked his bushy side whiskers as he thought. 'Robbery with violence, as I recall. The judge gave him ten years, I remember that.'

'How long ago was this?'

'Must have been in '84 or '85,' he replied after a moment.

'Did he go to Armley?'

'I believe so.'

'Can you telephone to the governor there? I'd like to know if he's still inside.'

Harper sat in the office, reading through Catherine Carr's diary once more. It was a sad document. Lonely. He wondered how much joy the woman had ever known in her life. There was certainly none of it on the page. Even once she was on her own, every day seemed to be duty; no thought of pleasure.

Tonight he was meeting one of the union men who guarded the suffragist meetings. He'd arranged it through Tom Maguire. Maybe he'd learn something, a description, a name, anything useful.

Ash had gone back to Chapel Allerton and talked to the servants again. Mr Carr rarely went out at night. Sometimes he'd go and dine with his son, but that was all. He'd been at home the night his wife was murdered, and for several before that, suffering from gout.

Now Ash had gone to talk to the residents on Tramway Street. Half an hour earlier he'd talked to the constable who walked the night beat there.

'The sergeant said you wanted to see me, sir.' He looked young and nervous. A thin growth of moustache sprouted over his upper lip, trying to make him appear older. The uniform hung baggily where he hadn't grown into it yet. His eyes darted around the room.

'Sit down, Constable?'

'Smith, sir. Have I done something wrong?'

'Nothing like that,' Harper said kindly. 'Tramway Street is your beat, isn't it?'

'Yes, sir. Started there eleven months ago.'

Inside, the inspector smiled at the lad's exactness.

'Do you know Mrs Timothy's rooming house?'

'Course I do, sir.' He grinned. 'She's not the easiest to get along with. Like a hedgehog, if you know what I mean. But she has a good heart.'

'How often do you go by?'

'About every hour and a half. Never much trouble round there.'

'Have you spotted anyone loitering?' the inspector asked. 'Had to move anyone on?'

'Not really, sir.' He stopped himself. 'There was one thing, though, the night before the big fire.'

Harper leaned forward, elbows on the desk. 'Go on.'

'I turned the corner and I saw someone running off.'

72

'A man or a woman?'

'Man, sir, definitely. He was wearing a bowler hat, I saw it when he passed under a gas lamp.'

'What else?'

Smith shook his head. 'That's it, sir. I didn't get much of a glimpse, he was running away from me. Should I have gone after him? There didn't look to be anything out of order around there.'

'No,' Harper assured him. 'You didn't have a reason.'

'As soon as I saw everything was fine, I put it in my notebook and carried on.'

'Did you know Mrs Carr?' the inspector asked. 'One of Mrs Timothy's tenants.'

'Can't say as I did, sir. I read about it in the papers, of course. Do you think this might be connected?'

'I'm not sure. Thank you.'

But he did know. The feeling, the clench in his stomach like a fist. Catherine Carr hadn't imagined someone watching her. The man had been very real.

'She has a brother,' Reed announced as he came in. 'Stanley Sugden. Sent to Armley a few years ago.'

'Still inside?' the inspector asked.

'Tollman's checking.' He read from the notes he'd made during the morning. 'That's all I have so far.'

'Good work, Billy. I'll take everything you can find.'

'You still want information on the husband?'

'Yes,' he said after a little thought. Carr might not have wielded the knife, but he wasn't ready to eliminate him as a suspect just yet. 'The whole bloody family. Right now we have three possibilities. It could be this man she saw on her street at night. It could be her politics—'

'Those could be related,' Reed pointed out, lighting a cigarette.

'Maybe,' he agreed. 'Or it could be family. We need to follow up on them all.'

There was a tap on the door and Tollman entered.

'At the jail they said that they moved Sugden to the asylum out at Menston last year, sir. He's a lunatic. A violent one. I took the liberty of asking about the next of kin. It's a Mrs Carr.'

Seven

'Mr Hardaker? Thank you for meeting me.' Harper shook the man's hand and they took a table in the Pack Horse. Hidden away in an old court off Briggate, the sounds of the town were muted, just the soft rumble of trams passing on their metal tracks. 'Mr Maguire said you keep a watch at the suffragist meetings.'

'Aye, that's right.' Will Hardaker took a swig of his beer. He had a young man's face, no lines, eyes clear and playful. Big, too, easily six feet one and broad-shouldered. He wore an old, dusty jacket over a shirt and waistcoat, a pair of dirty trousers and heavy boots, with a cap jammed down on wild brown curls. Dirt was ingrained in his fingers. A labourer, a union man. 'Someone has to.'

'You know why I'm asking?'

'Mrs Carr.' He nodded his head. 'Can't say I knew her, but I must have seen her. You think one of that lot outside the hall did it?'

'I don't know,' the inspector told him. 'That's why I wanted to talk to you.'

'Might never be a problem if your coppers did their job,' Hardaker said, staring at him.

'I hadn't known about that. It's been taken care of now. I don't know if Mr Maguire told you, but my wife's one of those suffragists.'

'Tom mentioned it, aye.' With a long swallow he finished his beer and Harper signalled for more.

'Tell me about the men.'

'Hopeless, most of them,' Hardaker answered after a little thought. 'They just watch as the women go in and come out.'

'Young? Old?'

He shrugged. 'A mix. Middle-aged, mostly. You can see the anger on their faces, but they're too scared to do anything about it.'

Too scared in public, the inspector thought. That might not stop them committing murder if they had the chance.

'What about the others? The ones who cause trouble?'

'You have to keep your eye on them.' He brought a packet of Woodbines from his pocket and lit one, blowing out the smoke in a long draught. 'There's not many, but they shout a lot and throw things. Rotten fruit, stones sometimes.'

'Has anyone been hurt?' Harper asked sharply.

'No. We take care of that. There's me and a few other lads. We keep our eyes peeled and sort it all out.' He gave a smile. 'Teach 'em right from wrong.'

'How many of them?'

'Never more than five or six. And not often. They've always had a few drinks first, you know, for courage. You can tell.'

He understood. A group of drunks, pushing each other on.

'Has there been any real violence?'

Hardaker shook his head. 'Come close a few times. We make the ladies stand back, then me and the others form a line.' He curled his hand into a first. 'We're all big lads.' He smiled. 'Of course, it'd be easier if your coppers were there.'

'They will be in future,' Harper promised. 'Is it usually the same men outside?'

'Generally. I feel sorry for them. Nothing better to do than that.'

'You've seen them. Do you think any of them could attack someone if they had the opportunity?'

Hardaker took a long time to answer. 'I don't know. I suppose so.'

'Anyone in particular?' He was fishing, but it was worth a try. A face, a name might come up.

The man just shook his head. It was a useful conversation, but it wasn't going to put him on anyone's trail. He'd need to see for himself.

'When's the next meeting?'

'The day after tomorrow. Are you going to be there?'

'Yes,' Harper said, and sat back, curious. 'What makes you do this?'

Hardaker took a breath. His thoughts seemed to turn inward.

'My sister was married to a bloke who beat her. Finally he did it so bad that she began bleeding inside, and she died. The coroner called it death by misadventure.' He snorted and raised sad eyes. 'I reckon if women could vote then things like that might not happen.'

They would, Harper thought. There were some men you could never change. But he gave a nod of understanding.

Time to go home, he decided. It had been a long day. He'd spent the afternoon following more leads on the dead baby in the post. Barbara Waite still seemed like a good bet, but no one knew where she'd gone. He'd visited three more houses. In the first, everything was fine. Another, the child had been stillborn, already in a pauper's grave at Beckett Street Cemetery. And in the last, the father had shown him the baby, so small, barely clinging to life, the mother dead after bringing her son into the world.

Not much bloody joy.

The West Riding Pauper Lunatic Asylum stood away from the village. They alighted from the train, watching it steam away up Wharfedale. The air smelt clear and clean, so different from Leeds. Harper took a deep breath.

'Good, isn't it?'

Ash chuckled. 'Not sure it's right without all the soot, sir. Too healthy.'

It was easy to spot the place, the only large building along the road, with the tall clock tower standing out like a beacon. A high wall surrounded it, heavy iron gates at the end of the long driveway. The inspector showed his identification and their boots crunched along the gravel.

'Quite a place, isn't it, sir?' Ash said, then gave a small cough. 'Why are we out here, if you don't mind me asking? If he's a patient, he couldn't have killed her.'

'I'm hoping Sugden can tell us something about his sister. I've seen that diary, it's like trying to get hold of a ghost. I need to find out who she was.'

Men and women were working quietly in the garden, moving haltingly as they dug and hoed. From somewhere inside the building he could just pick out cries and shouts. Harper glanced at Ash. The constable raised an eyebrow.

'It's an asylum, after all, sir.'

At the entrance to the main building they were met by a short, wide woman in a heavily starched nurse's uniform. Under the cap, she had a formidable face, the same jowly stare as Queen Victoria, eyeing them coldly as they approached.

'Can I help you, gentlemen?' Her voice had authority. The matron, he decided. Someone used to being obeyed. He smiled and produced his identification again.

'Detective Inspector Harper, Leeds Police. I need to speak to one of your inmates.'

'Who might that be?' She stood at the top of the steps, looking down at him.

'Stanley Sugden.'

'What do you want with him, Inspector?' she asked. 'He's been here for over a year now. He's never tried to escape.'

'His sister's dead. I need to ask him about her.'

She turned on her heel and strode away down a long corridor. All they could do was follow, their footsteps echoing off the walls. The floor was laid with a mosaic, the white rose of Yorkshire and a trail of black daisies. The woman stopped at a heavy metal door, selected a key from a large ring, and turned it in the lock.

Suddenly there was noise. Yelling, soft moaning, the babble of nonsense. Inside, the matron began talking quietly to a nurse who pointed to a man standing alone by the window. He was stooped, a soft, defeated air about him, a book balanced in his hands. The hair on his head was thin and pale brown, but a full chestnut beard grew long on to his chest.

'You want to talk to Stanley?' the nurse asked in surprise. She was as tall as Harper, with a forthright, intelligent gaze.

'I do. I need to tell him that his sister's dead.'

'Dead?' She eyed him coolly. 'What's that to do with the police?'

The inspector hesitated a moment.

'It's not easy to say, miss. She was murdered.'

The nurse remained silent for a second, glancing worriedly over her shoulder at Sugden.

'You need to understand a few things about Stanley,' she began. 'He was sent here because of his rages. They couldn't control him at Armley. Most of the time he's very quiet, but anything can set him off.' She paused. 'The slightest thing.'

Harper looked across at the man. He was still staring out of the window, one hand fretting with his long beard.

'All right,' he said. 'What do you suggest?'

'Let me tell him,' she said. 'He knows me by now. He doesn't do well with strangers, sir.'

'Of course. Tell me, did his sister ever visit him here?'

'No.' She shook her head. 'Never a letter either, more the pity. He loves to read. Newspapers, magazines, books when he can. Anything he can get hold of.' She looked around the room. 'He's like most of them in here, locked inside his own head. We don't know why.'

'How many of these men are dangerous, miss?' Ash asked.

'Not so many.' She smiled shyly at him. 'We give them bromide and sleeping draughts. It keeps them quiet.'

'Mr Sugden,' the inspector said, and the nurse was attentive again. 'I'd like to know about his sister. About her past.'

'I can ask him,' she told him, 'but I doubt he'll say much. Not right away, anyway. He might suddenly come out with something tomorrow or the day after.' She pursed her lips. 'Wait a moment, please.' She walked away with a swish of starched cotton.

Harper watched as she spoke to Sugden. He didn't even turn to look at her, didn't acknowledge her. There was something eerie about the ward, he thought, the chafing mix of pained noise and silence. So this was what madness was like.

The nurse returned, shaking her head.

'I'm sorry. His mind's off somewhere else,' she explained. 'It often is. He can stand like that for hours.'

'Thank you, anyway.'

One more avenue closed. Before he left he took another look at the man, still as a statue, close to the window. In the grand corridor, he heard the key turn in the lock behind them.

'Quite an education, sir,' Ash said once they were out of doors and in the fresh, free air.

'Yes,' he agreed with a sigh, glancing back at the clock tower. 'Isn't it?'

Constable Richards, the bobby who walked the Arches every night, had been covering the area for the best part of twenty years.

'You know what it's like, sir,' he said wearily. 'Every which way you look, it's prostitutes down there. Dark as the grave, too, unless somebody strikes a match.'

'The same faces?' Harper asked.

'Some, them as I can see, any road. Mostly it's mill girls just needing a little extra to survive.'

'And always men around?'

'Oh aye. They vanish quick enough when they see me,' Richards answered with a grin. 'But as soon as I've gone, they're back again. Like bloody flies, if you'll forgive the language.'

The night of the fire had been like every other, he said. Before the blaze he'd seen nothing unusual, and he couldn't have picked out Catherine

Carr, if she'd been there. Just one of too many.

'How quickly did the fire take hold?' the inspector asked.

'Went up fast, sir. I didn't have to move them on. First lick of flame and they were out of there, screaming and yelling. There was nothing anyone could have done, not with all that stuff in Soapy Joe's warehouse.'

'And you didn't see anyone left there?'

The constable sighed. 'I don't think so, but I can't say for certain, sir. It was bedlam, and too many dark corners.'

He was sitting in the chair, eyes shut and close to sleep, when he heard the footsteps on the stairs. Not just Annabelle; someone was with her.

Harper took out his watch. Almost seven o'clock. He stood and stretched, wondering who she'd brought home. He'd walked back from Millgarth along Regent Street. Time to think, to try to sort out the fragments he'd learned, and see if he could piece them together. By the time he reached the Victoria they still made no sense.

She'd been gone when he arrived home, a note to say she'd gone to visit old Mrs Morgan.

She entered, followed by another woman, smaller, older, with a pinched face and iron hair gathered into a bun.

'Good, I'm glad you're home,' Annabelle said, kissing him on the cheek. 'I was out and I ran into Tilly. I thought you might want to talk to her. She knew Katie from the meetings.' She looked at the woman. 'I'll go downstairs and bring us a couple of stouts.'

'I'm Detective Inspector Harper,' he introduced himself.

'I'm Tilly Freeman,' the woman said as she looked admiringly around the room. The piano, heavy furniture, the fire in the grate. 'I never expected Annabelle would have anywhere as grand as this.'

'It wasn't always like this. She started out as a servant. Just like Catherine.'

'Yes.' Her face fell. In the soft light from the gas mantle he could see that her clothes were shabby, cheap cotton that had been washed too much, and her knuckles were gnarled and swollen. 'Poor bloody Katie.' Her voice had a hoarse rasp.

They didn't say anything more until Annabelle returned and setting a glass on the table, the beer inside almost black.

'Drink it up. It'll put hairs on your chest,' she said with a wink. 'There's more if you want it. Perk of the job.'

'Better than where I work,' Tilly told her. 'No perks in a mill.'

'Drink up while it's free, then,' Annabelle told her, watching as the woman took a long, satisfied sip.

'How well did you know Catherine?' Harper asked.

'As well as anyone, I suppose,' she said. 'She only lived two streets from me. We often used to walk home together from meetings.' Tilly stared at him. 'I expect you think I should be crying for her.'

'I wasn't thinking that at all.'

'I shed all my tears when Miss Ford told us

83

what had happened.' But there was no hardness in her eyes, and her mouth gave away her sorrow. 'I've lost a husband and five children in my time and Katie's the first one I've cried for since them.'

'Did my wife tell you I'm investigating her murder?'

'She did, luv.' Tilly nodded as she took another drink. 'And I'll tell you what I know, if it helps you catch him. Work and meetings, and she was happy enough with that. Do you know about her husband, Mr Harper?'

'That he beat her? Yes.'

'And all the ways he made her feel small. After that, slaving in that bloody milliner's shop seemed like freedom to her. She could be a funny lass that way.'

'Did she ever talk about her past?'

'Not really. She was just looking for something better when she accepted his proposal, I suppose.' Tilly paused for a moment. 'The same as the rest of us, searching for a pot of gold. Or happiness. Thought she'd found it, too, until he showed his true colours.'

And there'd been no one she could turn to. Who'd believe her word against a respectable businessman? She'd been lucky enough to marry up. No one would want to listen, not even the police.

'Did she ever say where she'd worked before?'

The woman shook her head. 'I never asked. It was her business.'

'What else did you talk about?'

'This and that. Getting the vote. Work. She was in that shop, I'm down at Marshall's mill.' She shrugged.

He paused, framing the next question carefully.

'Did she seem scared at all?'

'Scared?' Tilly considered the word. 'No. Maybe she looked over her shoulder a bit more in the last few weeks, but that's nothing unusual. If you're a woman out at night, you learn to do that.'

'And she didn't seem at all different recently?'

'No. She was never the outgoing type. Half the time it was like pulling teeth to get her to talk.'

'Quiet?' he asked.

'She could natter on, if the mood took her. She was passionate about votes, she could talk about that. She'd read a lot, she knew it all.'

'Did she say anything about a man following her in the last few weeks?'

'Katie?' she asked in surprise. 'No. Why, was there?'

'Possibly,' he answered.

'She never said.' Tilly sat and thought for a little while then shook her head again. 'No, there was nowt. Katie wasn't acting strange. She was just her.' The woman finished her drink. 'Thank you for that, luv. Hit the spot after all that talking.' Tilly turned to Harper. 'I'm sorry I can't help you more. I really am.'

'You already have,' he assured her.

'Tom'll make sure you get home, won't you?' Annabelle said.

'Of course.'

It wasn't far, just up Chapeltown Road, no more than two minutes from Tramway Street.

85

'Did she ever talk about her family?' the inspector asked as they walked.

'No. I reckoned she was like me, they were all gone.'

'And you never visited her in her lodgings?'

'Never invited me,' Tilly said. 'I don't think she wanted anyone to see it. She was a very private person, Mr Harper. It was like she had a wall, and no one could get past that.'

'No one?'

'Not as I ever saw.'

He took his time walking home in the darkness, thinking about what he'd been told. It was a piece or two more, but he still didn't have a picture of Catherine Carr. There were too many blank spaces. Maybe all the things she kept hidden were going to remain that way.

Harper climbed the stairs and opened the door, surprised to see Annabelle talking to a uniformed constable. The man looked awkward, embarrassed to be talking to the wife of a superior officer, while she chattered away nineteen to the dozen.

'Tom,' she said, 'this young man needs to see you.'

Stone, he remembered. That was the lad's name, not too long on the force. If they sent someone out at night, it was never good news.

'What can I do for you, Constable Stone?'

'The sergeant said to come and tell you, sir.' He glanced nervously at Annabelle before he spoke. 'There's been something else at the Arches.'

'What?' he asked. 'A body?'

'No, sir. It's a woman, that's all I know. They want you there.'

'Tell them I'll be there as soon as I can.'

Eight

'I need to go,' he told her.

'Did Tilly tell you anything more?'

'I'm not even sure there *is* anything more.'

She laid her head on his shoulder, close to his good ear.

'A woman,' she said emptily. 'Poor thing. You look after yourself down there.'

Even with half the platforms gone, the Arches were dark and frightening. Trains rumbled somewhere above, the river rushed below. No wonder the prostitutes liked it, he thought; you could hardly see your hand in front of your face down here. A constable was waiting with an oil lamp to guide him through the rubble. The water roared close, booming off the bricks, bringing a chill like December.

The girl was sitting on the ground, an old blanket around her. Someone had brought a mug of tea and she held it in both hands while Constable Richards gazed down on her like a father. Another girl squatted close by, staring at the cobbles.

'Her name's Nellie Rider, sir,' Richards said quietly, and drew the inspector away.

'What happened?'

'She and another lass came down. They're mill girls, not earned a penny this week, thought they might make a little bit down here, if you know what I mean.'

He nodded. Selling their bodies for the change in a man's pocket.

'Go on,' he said.

'To cut a long story short, sir, she made an arrangement with a chap and he took her back there.' He pointed to one of the deep recesses that pocked the place. 'When he was done, he refused to pay and brought out a knife. Threatened to kill her.'

'What did she do?' He glanced over at the girls.

'Started screaming the place down. He cut her face, then he ran off. But she had a decent look at him when he lit a match to see her. With what happened before, I thought . . .'

'You did right,' Harper assured him. 'Who's the other one?'

'The lass she came down with. Maud Wilson.' Shaw patted his notebook. 'I've got their addresses and the like.'

'I'll need statements from other girls who were down here, too.'

'Yes, sir. I wouldn't expect too much, though. That's just how it is here.'

He approached them carefully and knelt, smiling. He could see the wound slicing down the girl's cheek. The blood had dried, but she'd carry the scar for the rest of her life. The other one, Maud, was biting her lip. She was a slip of a thing, all bones and angles.

'I'm Detective Inspector Harper,' he told them

softly and held out his hands. 'Come on, let's get out of here, shall we?'

Nellie was a tall girl in a thin cotton dress and worn clogs, a shawl covering her head. She put a hand over her cheek as they walked. Harper didn't try to say anything more for now. They came out into the night by the railway station.

After such deep darkness, the gas lamps seemed too bright, the sound of voices and the clamour of engines too loud. He took off his mackintosh and draped it around Nellie's shoulders, Maud on his other side.

He could see them properly now. Maud, so small, with her long dark hair, a face too pinched to ever be called pretty. Tracks on her cheeks where she'd been crying. Nellie hunched into herself, desperate to forget everything.

The Scarborough Taps was still open, lights brilliant in the windows. He guided them across, sat at a table and ordered brandy for them both.

'Drink that down,' he said. It would help with the shock. Maud looked at him doubtfully then swallowed it in one gulp that left her coughing. Nellie patted her on the back and looked at him suspiciously, then sipped hers slowly. He waited until the colour started to come into their cheeks before turning to Maud.

'Tell me what you remember,' he said gently.

'Me and Nellie, we work at the mill in Armley.' The words spilled out in a raw voice. 'But there's no work this week, and we didn't have no money.' He nodded. 'We walked in by the canal. We'd done it before. Thought there might not be too many girls around, what with that murder an' all.'

'Were there?'

She nodded. 'Men, too. How much for this and that, things you wouldn't do for a guinea. We weren't doing owt 'cept stand there, just trying to earn a few pennies. Then this fellow came up to Nellie.'

He looked at the other girl. 'Tell me about him.'

At first she couldn't speak, opening her mouth but no words coming out. For a moment he thought it was his hearing, then Maud put her arm around Nellie's shoulders.

'It's all right now, pet. He's a copper. Just go on and tell him.'

The tale came one small piece at a time. The man had looked pleasant enough, smiling. A lad of maybe twenty. Fair hair, dirty face. Thin side whiskers.

'He spoke funny,' she said suddenly.

'How?'

'Like he couldn't say an s proper. Came out sounding sort of *th*.'

A lisp. Good. That would help to find him.

They'd fixed a price and he'd followed her into one of the alcoves. But once they were alone he put his hand on her throat.

'He just seemed like he wanted to hurt me,' Nellie said softly and a blush rose from her throat. 'Really hurt me.'

She hadn't asked him for the money beforehand; the jingle in his pocket has been temptation enough. When he finished, she told him how much and he refused to pay.

90

'He brought out a knife,' she continued.

'Did you see it?' Harper asked.

Nellie shook her head. 'He put it agin my cheek. I could feel it.' Without thinking, her fingertips moved to the cut. 'He said he could kill me and they'd never find him. I started to scream. I thought I was going to die.'

The inspector ordered another brandy for her. She was no more than a girl, so shaken it would take a long time for her to recover. If she ever did. And she'd always carry his mark. Was he the same man who'd murdered Catherine Carr?

He had more questions, but she had no answers to give. She'd only seen his face for a moment. He was taller than her, but that was all. Finally he told them, 'I'll have a constable walk you home.'

'What am I going to tell my mam?' Nellie asked.

'Don't worry about that for now,' Harper told her. 'You're safe, that's what counts.'

By four he'd written up his report and was waiting when the café at the market opened. Bacon, eggs, tea; it helped. He felt weary. Another lost night.

Constable Richards had talked to all the other girls from the Arches that he could find. One man was much the same as another to them, as long as he had money. They never looked at faces or listened to voices. One thought she remembered a lisp, but she couldn't be sure.

A murder and a rape in the Arches at night. There could be a connection. But the description could fit so many men. The only distinctive thing was the lisp.

'Incident in the Arches last night,' he told Reed when the sergeant arrived.

'What?' He paused, overcoat half off. 'Another murder?'

'Rape. But he cut her when she screamed and threatened to kill her.'

'Do we know what he looks like?'

'Not really,' Harper said in frustration. 'She got a glimpse, that's all. He had a lisp.' He ran a hand through his hair. 'What did you find out about Carr?'

Reed settled at his desk. 'Took over the boot factory from his father forty years ago. He's expanded the business and brought in some big contracts. They supply half the boots to the army now.'

'Impressive,' Harper said. It explained why Carr could afford his big house in Chapel Allerton.

'Employs four hundred. Quite a ruthless character, from what people say.'

'How do you mean?'

'A bit of *baksheesh* here and there to make sure he gets people to sign on the dotted line. Palms greased. A lot of his business is in the Empire. India, Africa.'

'What about his workers?' the inspector asked.

'No better or worse than anyone else. I looked at the death of his first wife. No talk of foul play or anything suspicious.' He glanced at his notebook. 'Married Catherine Carr seven years back. Friends thought he was mad to marry a servant. Probably half of them were jealous.'

Ash arrived as he was speaking.

'Who runs the factory now?' Harper asked.

'Neville. He's the oldest son. Been in charge for three years now and raking in the money. There are two other children. The daughter's married to someone in London and the other son's in the army.'

'At least he won't want for boots,' Ash added drily.

'See what else you can find on Catherine Carr's brother, too.'

'I thought he was in the asylum,' Reed said. 'He couldn't have done it, could he?'

'No.' Harper thought about Stanley Sugden, wondering how he'd reacted to the news of his sister's death. If he'd even taken it in yet. 'But it might shed some light on things.'

'All right.'

'Tramway Street?' Harper asked Ash. 'Anything useful?'

The constable grimaced. 'Half of them were at work. A few remembered hearing some fast footsteps, but that's all. Nothing to help us. I'll go back when more of them are home, sir. Might have better luck then.'

'Let's hope so. I'm going to need you both this evening. There's a suffragist meeting at the Mechanics' Institute. I want to see the men who gather outside.'

'What are we looking for?' Reed asked.

Harper sighed. It was a good question. Before he could answer it, Superintendent Kendall marched through the office, summoning the inspector with a wave of his hand. Harper raised his eyebrows to the others and followed.

'Yes, sir.'

'What the hell's going on, Tom? We had one murder in the Arches. Now there's a rape there, too. Almost another killing, from what I heard.'

'I don't know if they're related yet.'

'What do you think?' he asked.

All Harper could do was shake his head. 'It's too soon to tell. Possible, that's as far as I'd go.'

'What are you doing?'

He explained, watching the superintendent nod.

'So we're no further along?'

'Not a jot. We're not going to be until we have more information. And getting it is going to be the problem.'

'I hear you've had Reed looking into Carr.'

'Yes, sir. We know he beat her when they were married. Like I said, I'm looking into everything.'

'Just tread carefully. That's my advice. He has the ear of the chief constable.' Kendall brought an old briar pipe from the pocket of his jacket. As he lit it, the raw smell of shag tobacco filled the room. 'And don't go dragging him in here. Not unless you have something very solid. Do you understand me?'

'Perfectly sir.' How often had they had discussions like this over the years? But this time he'd do what he was told. He didn't have anything on Carr, anyway.

Harper sat at his desk, reading through one of the folders that had arrived. Sugden's records from the asylum. He'd handed the other to Reed, everything the police had on the man.

The governor at Armley jail had sent Sugden

out to Menston because of his sudden, ungovernable rages. He seemed to have calmed; there were only two reports of them in the last year. Still, if they were giving him regular doses of bromide and sleeping draughts, that wasn't a surprise.

He talked little, either to the staff or other patients and spent most of his waking hours reading or staring out of the window, exactly the way Harper had seen him. What was in his head? What had happened to him?

He glanced up at the shadow over the desk. Reed, the folder open in his hands.

'I've been saying your name for the last minute,' he said.

'Sorry. I was caught up in this,' he lied. 'What is it?'

'Sugden. The last job he had was at Carr's factory. He got into a fight with a foreman and they sacked him. Spotted him outside three times after that.'

Did it mean anything, he wondered? He didn't see how it could relate to the murder.

'There's more than that,' the sergeant continued, 'Sugden was in the army. Joined as soon as he was old enough. Served in Afghanistan during the war.'

'What happened to him?'

'I don't know, but he was back on the street by '82. Looks like he never settled properly, couldn't hold a job. He had a temper.'

His voice trailed away. Harper knew what Billy was thinking: there but for the grace of God. Reed had spent ten years with the West Yorkshires, he'd fought over there. He'd lived on the razor

95

edge of violence for years. It had blunted since he'd met Elizabeth and stopped drinking so much. Sugden was the man he could quite easily have become if the dice had rolled differently.

'Take a look at Catherine, too,' he said. 'Maybe there's something to find in her past.' It might be worth a visit to the boot works to discover what had happened out there with Sugden. And it would be a chance to meet old Mr Carr's son.

But first he needed to give some time to the dead baby who'd been put in the post.

A visit to Mabgate, another to Cross Green. In both cases the reports were wrong, mothers and babies both fine. Barbara Waite still seemed the likely candidate. He made his way back to Quarry Hill and knocked on the door where no one had answered before.

Nothing.

He glanced through a cobwebbed window. There was a battered table inside, but not much else. No clothes, no sign that anyone lived there. He tried the knob, feeling it turn, and entered.

'Miss Waite,' he called. 'Are you there?'

It was empty. A rusted iron bedstead in an alcove, stripped bare. No clothes. All he could find in a corner was a bloody rag, some string, and a piece of brown paper, the type anyone would use to wrap a parcel. He picked them up.

Back at Millgarth, he waited as Tollman finished talking to a man complaining about a hackney driver. As the man left, the desk sergeant rolled his eyes.

'I don't know what he expects me to do,' he muttered. 'What is it you need, sir?'

'I'd like to talk to the beat man for Quarry Hill.'

Tollman glanced at the clock. 'I can have him here in a quarter of an hour, sir.'

'Thank you.'

Constable Robb looked as if he'd walked the beat for the last forty years. He had a broad, kindly face under a moustache heavily peppered with grey.

'This'll be about Barbara Waite, sir?' he asked.

'Yes. It looks like she's flitted.'

'I'm not too surprised, sir. Haven't seen her for a few days now.'

'Tell me what you know about her.'

There wasn't much. She'd only lived there for three months. A prostitute, everyone knew that, already well along with the bairn by the time she moved into the place. She was a small girl who looked younger than her years, and the baby didn't show too much. Men came and went regularly, but there was no trouble, no complaints from the neighbours.

'Any family?' the inspector asked.

'Not a clue, sir,' Robb answered. 'I heard she came from Burmantofts, but I don't rightly know.'

'I see.' Not much help, but it was a start. As an afterthought, he asked, 'Do you know Mr Martin?'

'From the Town Mission? I run into him most days when I'm on my rounds.'

'What's he like?'

The constable shrugged. 'They've had worse in the area. He's very earnest, but he really does try to help people when they need it. He'll put

97

his hand in his pocket if he has to, and that's more than you can say for most of them religious types. Why, sir?'

'I met him, that's all. He seemed to be . . .' Harper tried to think of the right word. 'Very ready to judge.'

Robb grinned. 'Like I say, he's not as bad as some. I know he looks stern, but there's a decent heart beats under it.'

Burmantofts, he thought. He knew someone there . . .

'Hello, Elizabeth.'

She was standing at the back of the bakery, watching as the girls served customers. Harper wasn't sure if she'd be here; she ran all three of Annabelle's bakeries, dividing her day between them. She turned at the sound of his voice, then her face broke into a smile.

'Hello, Tom.' Then he saw the flicker of fear. 'Has something happened to Billy?'

'Nothing like that,' he assured her. 'I just want to pick your brains, that's all.'

'Come through. We can talk in the back.'

It was a small room. In the mornings he knew it was full of loaves and cakes. Even now, half-empty, it still had the heady, welcoming scent of fresh bread.

She perched on a high stool. 'I haven't seen you in too long.'

'I know. It's good to be working with Billy again.'

'I think he likes being back,' she told him with a smile. 'But he'd never admit it.'

98

Harper had his doubts but said nothing.

'He's a good fireman. That's what Dick Hill said.'

'Every time he leaves for work I just pray he'll be home later.'

He nodded. It was the most dangerous job on the force. 'Sooner him than me. But I need to ask you a question. Some local knowledge.'

'Go on.'

'Do you know a family named Waite? They're supposed to live up this way.'

Elizabeth pursed her lips and thought. After a little while she shook her head.

'It doesn't ring a bell.' Then she cocked her head. 'No, there's a fellow who comes in sometimes. Someone called him Waite. Let me think.' After a few seconds she was able to place him. 'He's at the brick works. What's he done?'

'Nothing. He might be able to help me, that's all.'

'He's the only one I can think of.'

'It's a start. I'll let you get back to work.'

The brick works were filled with dust. It clung to his skin and tickled the back of his throat, making him cough. He'd barely gone ten yards into the place before he was covered in the stuff, wiping his lips to clean them.

'I'm looking for a man called Waite,' he told the clerk in the office. The man looked up, impressed by a policeman here.

'Not here,' he replied dully. 'He left last week.'

The inspector felt a tingle. 'Another job?'

The man shrugged. 'Just said he was leaving and wanted to be paid what he was owed.'

'Do you have his address?'

The clerk muttered a complaint, took a ledger from the shelf and leafed through it.

'Fifteen, Industrial Street.'

'Thank you.'

Harper stayed in the yard for a few more minutes, trying to talk to some of the workers. They eyed him suspiciously, none of them willing to say anything. Protecting Waite or loathing coppers? It didn't matter; either way the result was a threatening, sullen silence.

Industrial Street was what he expected, back-to-back houses that had stood neglected for too long. Even as he knocked on the door of number fifteen, he knew no one was there. There was something about the sound, hollow inside. He looked through the window and saw a bare room.

'They've done a flit, luv,' a voice said. He turned to see the woman next door, standing with her arms folded. 'Left last week.'

'Do you know where they went?'

'Didn't tell anyone they were off. Piled it all in a cart one night. I watched them go.'

'Was there someone in the family called Barbara?'

The woman cackled. 'Her and her sisters. Little trollop. He kept kicking her out and her mother kept taking her back. Quieter round here since they've gone.'

'And you've no idea where?'

'Don't bloody care, neither.'

Barbara Waite. He rolled the name around.

More and more it sounded as if she was the one who'd put her dead baby in a parcel. What the hell was she thinking? She'd gone, her parents had gone.

He'd have the local beat constable ask questions. There might be bits of information he could pick up. The picture of the child, lying there in Dr King's mortuary, came into his head. And after it he saw Catherine Carr, the metal covering her like a second skin.

With a shake of his head, Harper walked on. He had work to do. Last night's rape. It might be connected to Carr's murder. All they had was Nellie's description. Even with the lisp to go on, he couldn't see how they'd ever find the man. He didn't have any idea where to begin.

'You look different in plain clothes,' Inspector Hill said with a grin.

'Feels different, too, sir,' Reed said. There'd been a message waiting at Millgarth; report to the fire station on Park Row.

'How's the investigation coming along?'

'Slowly. It's nothing to do with the fire, though.'

Hill lit a cigarette. The sergeant could see the man's eyes studying him.

'Do you want me to pull you off it, Billy? It'd be easy enough.'

He took a long time to reply. It was tempting. Back to the routine he'd come to know, the roar of excitement in his head as the engine sped along the street. Home to Elizabeth at the end of a shift. Dead on his feet, maybe, but there.

'No. I'd like to see this one through, sir, if

that's all right.' He wasn't sure why he said it. Maybe it was the way to clear things properly with Tom Harper.

And the thinking, asking questions, trying to look two or three steps ahead, it had all slithered back under his skin. The uncertainties that came with being a detective.

'That's fine. I can spare you.' He chewed the skin at the edge of a broken fingernail. 'I've been watching you since you joined the brigade, Billy. You've done well.'

'Thank you, sir.'

'You picked things up quickly and the men respect you. When you come back I'd like to train you as a fire investigator.'

'Sir?' The suggestion took him by surprise.

'You know about fires now. You know how to think, how to ask things. You'd be ideal for the job if you're interested.'

'I am, sir. Yes.'

'Good.' Hill smiled. 'That's settled. Tell Tom Harper to get this one solved fast. I want you back here.'

The evening had grown chilly. He stood in the shadows, watching women filing into the Mechanics' Institute for the suffragist meeting. Hardaker, the union man, stood on the steps, nodding his greeting, two other big lads close by.

Harper saw Annabelle, deep in conversation with a woman he didn't recognize, his eyes following her until she vanished through the doors of the building. Reed and Ash were close, in an alley next to the Coliseum, just up Cookridge Street.

A group of men stood on the pavement, staring at the women. He could see the anger in their eyes. Why, he wondered. What scared them so much about women wanting the vote? There were perhaps ten of them, one or two young, most middle-aged. Some looked like labourers, one of two wore suits like clerks.

Voices came from inside the building and Hardaker wandered over, pulling a pipe from his pocket and lighting it.

'Those are the usual ones,' he said. 'Sometimes more. This lot don't cause any real trouble.' A policeman passed on the other side of the street, head down, rain cape covering his shoulders. 'First one of your lot I've seen on the beat round here in months.'

'He won't be the last,' the inspector assured him. He kept his eyes on the men. 'What about the ones who do cause trouble?'

'If they come, they'll be along later,' Hardaker told them. 'Some Dutch courage first so they can taunt women.' He spat. 'Wait around and they might appear.'

He'd stay until it was over, then go home with Annabelle. But the men standing there now worried him more than the ones who might arrive later. Silent, or muttering quietly amongst themselves, they had a bitterness burning deep inside. If they could get away with it, who knew what they might do.

Someone came down the street, boot heels echoing on the pavement. Harper glanced up, recognizing the face as the man moved under a gas lamp. Patrick Martin. He seemed about to stop, then noticed the constable starting back up the hill and moved on briskly.

'That one who's just gone by,' the inspector said to Hardaker. 'Does he ever stand here?'

Hardaker nodded. 'Always looks like he's praying.' He chuckled. 'Your lad must have scared him off. Good bloody riddance, too.'

Interesting, Harper thought. What would Patrick Martin be doing outside a suffragist meeting? And why hadn't he stayed tonight?

Time passed slowly enough for him to feel all his aches and pains, shifting from one foot to the other. Then he heard the scraping of chairs and the women began to emerge. He waved Reed and Ash across and they stood together, close to the union men.

'What do you think?'

'Ugly bunch,' the sergeant said.

'Make sure they don't follow any of the women. If they try, take them in and question them.'

'I know one of them,' Ash said. 'Him at the end. He lives two streets from me. Arthur Jones. Quiet sort.'

'Does he live alone?'

'Married. His wife's a timid little thing.'

'If nothing else happens, walk home with him. Have a quiet word,' Harper ordered. 'Hardaker said the real troublemakers sometimes turn up now.'

But tonight was quiet. The women passed under the glare of the bystanders and went on their way. Finally Annabelle emerged with Miss Ford, the

104

two of them finishing their talk at the top of the steps before parting.

He waved and she approached with a smile.

'Three coppers waiting for me?' she laughed. 'I didn't know I was that dangerous.' She gave Harper a kiss on the cheek. 'Hello, Billy, hello, Mr Ash. So what are you lot doing here?'

He explained it later as they walked up the Headrow.

'You think it might be one of them who killed Katie?' she asked, and shuddered.

'I don't know,' he answered truthfully. 'But just keep your eyes open.'

'I asked around again tonight, if anyone knew her. She was always there; I thought she must have talked to someone.'

'Any luck?'

She shook her head. 'It's so sad, Tom.' She put her arm through his. 'We all thought someone knew her and none of us did. If I'd just sat down with her.' Annabelle sighed. 'Come on, let's have a drink before we go home. We had to give one of the girls at the new bakery the sack this afternoon. I need some laughter.'

'Inspector Hill said that?' Elizabeth asked. 'Wants you to be an investigator?'

Reed nodded. 'He said I'd start training with him when this case is done.'

'Do you want to do it?'

'Yes.' He smiled. He'd walked all the way home, along York Road and Beckett Street, and barely noticed the distance. It would be the perfect job.

105

'That's wonderful news.' He folded her in his arms and he heard her slow sigh of contentment. She'd come in after him, barely had time to take off her coat before he was bubbling over with the news. 'Where are the children?'

'John's not back yet. The others are playing. I gave them supper.'

'You're a good man.' She pulled away to fill the kettle and slide it on to the hob. 'We had a problem this afternoon.'

'What sort?'

'One of the girls was thieving at the Burmantofts shop. I thought the takings didn't look right, so I asked Annabelle. She came over when she was collecting all the bakery money. It was Lorraine; do you remember her?'

'No.' The faces all blurred into one.

'She'd only been there two months. Took over a fiver in that time.'

'What did you do?'

'We had her in the back. She denied it at first.'

'They always do,' Reed said.

'She's on her own with three little ones.'

'You have four and you never stole.'

'I know, but . . .'

'You pay a fair wage,' Reed said. 'You told me that.'

Elizabeth gave a sad nod. 'I was the one who had to let her go. She walked out in tears.'

'She's lucky you didn't call the police.'

'That's what Annabelle told her. Gave her a right dressing down. I know we did the right thing. It just felt so hard, that's all.'

He held her close and let her cry. She had too

good a heart. She'd seen something in him and hadn't let him run away.

'She's the one who chose to steal,' he reminded her. 'She brought it on herself.'

'I know. I could understand, though. Maybe that's why I feel so bad about it.' She wiped the tears from her eyes. 'Anyway, tell me about this new job. What will you be doing? Will you still be fighting fires, too?'

They were late home, but for once he didn't care, sitting in the hackney with his hand on her knee. People had been singing along to the piano in the Horse and Trumpet and Annabelle had joined in, letting herself go and roaring with laughter when it was done.

'That was good,' Harper said. He leaned back, closing his eyes. His head felt clearer, refreshed.

'I enjoyed it.' Annabelle turned her head lazily. 'Just make sure you're not too tired when we get home, Tom Harper. Not when I've put my good gown on.'

Nine

Harper looked through the notes waiting on his desk. Dr King had released Catherine Carr's body. The beat man in Burmantofts hadn't found more on the Waites, but he thought they had relatives in Cross Green; he'd try to find out more.

There was nothing more he could do on the dead baby case for now. Good, he thought. He had enough on his plate without that. He'd find Barbara Waite eventually.

'What did that chap who lives near you have to say?' he asked Ash when the constable arrived. 'Why does he stand outside the suffragist meetings?'

'He doesn't feel women should have the vote, sir.'

'How does standing and watching help?'

'I'm not rightly sure.' He exhaled slowly. 'He tried to tell me, but it didn't make much sense. He thinks if enough of them stand there, the women will know men don't want it.'

'What does he think they'll do?'

Ash shrugged. 'No idea, sir. Like I said, it didn't make a lot of sense. But I don't think he'd hurt anyone. He was shocked when I told him about Mrs Carr.'

'Some people can play-act very well.'

'He seemed genuine to me.'

'What about you, Billy?' Harper asked as Reed entered. 'Anyone following women last night?'

'No. All quiet.' He took off his overcoat and stretched.

Outside, it was still dark. Soon enough it would seem like there were only a few hours of daylight. Already it seemed as if half of Leeds had winter coughs. It would only grow worse, Harper thought.

'Right,' he started, 'this is what—'

The door banged open and Tollman marched in.

'I thought you'd better know, sir. I just had a telegram from the asylum in Menston. That Stanley Sugden escaped last night.' He paused. 'More than that, a farmer out there told them this morning that his shotgun is missing.'

This changed everything. Why had he gone, Harper wondered. Why now? What did he want? Sugden was a lunatic, he was violent, and he was probably armed.

'Billy, find out all you can about him,' he ordered quickly. 'You said he was sacked from Carr's?'

'That's right,' Reed replied.

'I'll go out there and warn them.' He turned to Tollman. 'I want an officer keeping watch at the factory on Meanwood Road. Ash, you come with me.'

He had too bloody much to do. And after last night he wanted a word with Patrick Martin. Another relentless day, and he still had no idea how to begin looking for the rapist in the Arches.

Soldiers were marching on the parade ground at Carlton Barracks. Reed stood for a moment, watching. The rhythm of tramping boots was too familiar. The barked commands, the rushed obedience of the company. But the recruiting office was quiet. No one joining up today. Only the corporal in his dress uniform, sliding the newspaper out of sight as he smartly stood to attention.

'Can I help you, sir?'

'Detective Sergeant Reed with Leeds Police.

I'm looking for the records of someone who served with the regiment.'

'Of course.' The man smiled. 'You look like you were in yourself.'

The comment didn't surprise him. One soldier could always recognize another.

'A while ago.'

'Afghanistan?'

Reed nodded.

'You had it bad out there, sir.'

'Yes,' he answered shortly. 'We did. Where would I find the records?'

'Administration building, the next one along from here.' The corporal saluted. 'An honour to meet you, sir.'

They found what he needed. He sifted through the papers, copying details into his notebook. Sugden had grown up in Hunslet, joined the army as soon as he was old enough. In Afghanistan from '78 to '80. Mentioned twice in despatches and put up for a medal. That was impressive; he must have seen some heavy fighting. Stayed in for another two years after he came home, but his disciplinary record had grown worse. Finally he'd been discharged in '82. Reading between the lines, it was probably only his gallantry abroad that had stopped them court-martialling him. The regiment didn't do that to a hero. He skimmed back, looking at the training Sugden had undergone. He'd been a sniper and a scout.

Christ, thought Reed.

The smell of leather hit them before they reached the gates, mixing with the putrid stink of the tannery down the road. The regular thumping of machinery came from inside the factory, and smoke poured from the chimney.

Harper was pleased to see a bobby already on duty there, eyeing everyone who arrived. He gave the man Sugden's description and moved across the cobbled yards. Two boys were struggling to load boxes on to a cart. A foreman strode purposefully from one building to another. The noise grew louder as they walked.

'I'll see Neville Carr,' Harper said to Ash. 'You talk to the people in the office. Find out why Sugden was dismissed, and who else was involved.'

'Right you are, sir.'

The office was as luxurious as he expected. Heavy leather armchairs, a thick rug, a large desk stacked with papers. Neville Carr was a younger version of his father, face already jowly, hair receding, a dyspeptic expression under his thin moustache.

'What is it?' he asked testily, removing a pair of spectacles and putting down his pen.

'I'm sorry to disturb you,' Harper said. 'But I wanted you to be aware that a former employee of yours named Stanley Sugden has escaped from a lunatic asylum.'

'Well?' Carr stared at him. 'What's that to do with me?'

'He was dismissed from here. He has a shotgun and he's violent. I have a constable guarding the entrance.'

'Then it's taken care of, isn't it?' He dismissed the matter.

111

'There's one more thing, sir. He's the brother of your father's wife.'

Carr gave an exasperated sigh. 'Bloody woman. Bad enough when she was alive, now she's gone and she still can't leave us alone.'

'You didn't care for her, sir?'

The man rubbed his chin. 'No,' he answered bluntly. 'I don't know what my father was doing, marrying a damned servant. It wasn't as if anyone was going to accept her.'

'He said they were happy.'

'He just wanted someone around. A companion. Then she started getting all those strange ideas. The best thing she ever did was leave.'

'And now she's dead,' Harper said.

'Brought it on herself. Associating with people like that. The world would be a better place without them.' He replaced the glasses on his nose. 'Is there anything else, Inspector? I have work to do.'

'No, sir. That's all.'

As the inspector went back down the stairs, he believed he could learn to loathe Neville Carr.

He met up with Ash at the omnibus stop. The constable nodded and folded his newspaper away as Harper approached.

'What did you learn?'

'Sugden was dismissed for getting into a fight with his foreman, sir. He'd been told that he needed to keep his beard covered or shave it off. He wasn't too happy at the order.' The constable gave a grim smile. 'Seems they had a bit of a ruckus. Took two other men to pull Sugden off. He was in a rage.'

112

'Did you talk to any of them?'

'The foreman. He said Sugden seemed completely mad. He's going to be very careful for a while, I think. What about Mr Carr?'

'Nothing.'

As they settled on a seat inside the 'bus, Ash brought the newspaper out again.

'You might want a look at this, sir.' He pointed at a notice with a thick finger.

Harper read quickly. A notice announcing the burial of Mrs Catherine Carr, to take place at St Matthew's Church in Chapel Allerton. In the end, leaving had been for nothing at all; in death, her husband had reclaimed her.

'Is this today's paper?'

'Yesterday's, sir. It might explain a lot.'

If Sugden had seen this in the asylum, it could be the reason he escaped. He read it once more. The funeral was tomorrow.

'I think we'd better make sure we attend.'

'Yes, sir.' Ash gave a grim smile. 'How are your hands?'

'Pardon?' He'd seen the man's lips move, but he hadn't caught the words.

'Your hands, sir.'

'Oh. Getting better.' Annabelle had changed the bandages that morning. The skin was still raw and pale. Another day or two and he'd be back to normal. More than he could say for his hearing.

'Sugden grew up in Hunslet,' Reed said. 'I've told the station over there.'

'Good.' The inspector nodded his approval.

Kendall stood close, listening carefully.

'I've sent out a general alert,' the superintendent said. 'And I'll make sure there are uniforms close to the funeral tomorrow.'

'One more thing, sir,' the sergeant told him. 'He's trained as a sniper and a scout. He's going to be hard to find.'

With his rheumy eyes and heavy jowls, Barnabas Tooms looked like an old bloodhound who'd lost the scent. But appearances were deceptive; he was sharp, perhaps the keenest political operative in Leeds. In a fawn suit and loud, checked waistcoat, he held court every day in the snug at the Griffin Hotel on Boar Lane.

More than any councillor, he knew how the system of government worked in Leeds, and how to turn it one way or another. He collected information and dispensed it. He gave and demanded favours, and he cast a very long shadow. Some said he was worth thousands. Some said he had nothing. Probably no one knew the truth.

He wasn't a source the inspector wanted to use. It put him in Tooms's debt and that was a bad place to be; he had a habit of wanting payment in awkward ways. But Harper needed to know more about Neville Carr. The man had rubbed him the wrong way. It was nothing more than a gut feeling, but over the years he'd learned to trust them. If there was gossip and muck, Tooms would know it all. He'd tell, then exact his price in the future.

'Inspector,' he nodded. 'Have a seat.'

He pushed an empty plate aside, cutlery and

crockery clattering. He was a tidy man with bushy white whiskers that grew down to his chin, the top of his skull almost bald.

'Busy, Mr Tooms?' The man liked a sense of respect.

'This and that.' He gave a brief, insincere smile. 'What can I do for you?'

'Carr. The boot man.'

Tooms pursed his lips and shook his head. 'That's business, not government.'

'You hear things.'

'Father or son?' Tooms asked briskly.

'Both,' he replied after a moment. If he was selling his soul to Tooms, he might as well get full value.

'You're looking into the wife's murder, then.'

'Yes.'

Tooms pulled a toothpick from the pocket of his waistcoat, cleaned it with a thumbnail and stuck it in his mouth, eyeing the inspector.

'The old man's a nasty piece of work. Always has been. Isn't that why she left him? He'd sell his mother for a big order. The army investigated him twice for overcharging on goods delivered. The way I heard it, some money changed hands and they stopped asking questions. Civil enough to your face, but he always had the knife ready to go into your back.'

'Nasty enough to kill?'

Tooms considered the question.

'Not himself,' he said finally. 'He's too frail nowadays. But he knows plenty who'd do it for a fee. I wouldn't put it past him, if that's what you mean.'

115

'I don't mean anything,' Harper told him blandly. 'I'm just here to listen and learn.'

The man snorted. 'You're groping, Mr Harper. You'd never come and talk to me otherwise.'

He looked like a carrion bird waiting for a feast.

'The son,' the inspector prompted.

'Neville's more than a bootmaker.' Tooms dangled the phrase and grinned at Harper's interest. 'He has his eyes on a council seat, maybe even a member of Parliament in time. He's ambitious.'

'Is he like his father?'

'You know about Neville's marriage?'

'I don't know anything about him.'

'He got a girl in the family way and they had to get married. She's from a decent family, so it was all hushed up. He keeps a girl on the side, of course, but most do, don't they?' He didn't wait for a response. 'Very discreet, hides her away in Headingley and pretends that no one knows.'

'What's her name?'

'I can find out if you need it.' He made the offer sound like a threat. 'But if you want my advice, you'll keep clear of him. Neville's spent the last two years cultivating the right people and putting money in their pockets. He'll stand at the next election and he'll win. A term on the council and then parliament, that's our plan. And it'll happen.'

The inspector ignored this. 'He has a child?'

'Four of them. The oldest one, Gordon, he can be trouble. He has his moments. I just make sure no one hears about them.' He rubbed his thumb

116

against his fingers. Money. 'Nothing that can affect Neville Carr's chances when people go to vote.'

'What's Gordon done lately?' Harper was curious.

'You're the copper,' Tooms told him, 'you find out. Anything else?'

'Is that all the dirt?'

'It's all I'm giving you. Unless your pockets are deep enough to pay for more.'

'You know the answer to that, Mr Tooms.'

'Then I'll wish you good day.'

Whenever he talked to Barnabas Tooms, he always felt the need to wash after, as if there was slime clinging to his skin. He dealt with snouts and grasses every day, good people and evil; no one else had that effect on him.

Patrick Martin was busy on Sykes Place. Harper spotted him talking to a woman at the door of a house and slid back around the corner to wait. The man arrived soon enough, his face grim, one hand clutching a Bible, tracts stuffed into a pocket of his coat.

'Hello, Mr Martin,' the inspector said brightly.

'Mr Harper.' He stopped suddenly. 'Sorry, you took me by surprise.'

'A bad day?'

Martin shook his head. 'People come around eventually. Sometimes it takes a while to pry open the door to their hearts.'

He'd heard wisps of the conversation on the doorstep, blown to him on the wind. Martin had spent half his time berating the woman, telling her she'd go to hell if she didn't repent.

'I saw you on Cookridge Street last night,' the inspector said. 'By the Mechanics' Institute.'

'I was on my way home from a meeting with my superior. It happens every week.' He gave a smile, more relaxed now.

'I'm told you often stand outside suffragist meetings.'

'I do.' Martin stiffened his back. 'Someone has to pray for their souls.'

'Pray for their souls?' He didn't understand.

'*Wives, submit yourselves to your own husbands as you do to the Lord. For the husband is the head of the wife as Christ is the head of the church, his body, of which he is the Saviour. Now as the church submits to Christ, so also wives should submit to their husbands in everything.*' It's in the Scriptures. Do you know it?'

'No.'

'It's from Ephesians. These suffragists wanting the vote goes against the word of God. They should do what their husbands desire. That's why I pray for them – so they see sense.'

'Do you know one of those suffragists was murdered?'

'I heard. It's terrible.'

'Isn't there a commandment about that?'

'Of course,' Martin answered seriously.

'Have you ever talked to the women after the meetings?'

'I've tried to hand out tracts. None of them wanted to know.'

Harper could hardly blame them. The man was a symbol of all the opposition they faced.

'Have you ever followed any of them?'

'No.' Martin's voice was reasonable enough, but the inspector could see the worry on his face. Somewhere in the distance came the sound of a barrel organ, joyful in the grimy dusk.

'You keep a journal, don't you?' He'd heard somewhere that each superintendent had to account in detail for each day.

'It's part of my job.'

'Could you bring it to Millgarth? I'd like to take a look at it.'

'Am I under suspicion, Inspector?' There was anger in his eyes. And more. Fear.

It's was Harper's turn to smile.

'No, sir. Just following through and checking. Nothing more than that.'

There was one more thing to do today. He walked over to Briggate, the taste of soot on his tongue, seeing the dark clouds on the horizon. Henry Reeve was in the bar of the Central Hotel, scribbling in a notebook with a glass of beer by his side.

'Still working on that book?' Harper asked.

The man shrugged. He had thin shoulders and long, graceful hands. A careless appearance, with a shock of hair dragged this way and that, and curious, intense eyes.

'I keep trying, Tom, but it doesn't seem to like me.'

Reeve was a reporter for the *Leeds Mercury*, his days spent following up on stories. By late afternoon he was always here, sitting with his pencil, writing words then crossing them out again.

'I have a favour to ask.'

'That's never a good thing to hear from a copper.'

'There was a girl raped in the Arches a couple of nights ago. It's possible it had something to do with the murder down there, but I want to keep that part quiet for now.'

Reeve was attentive, pencil poised above the paper.

'I don't have much of a description.' The inspector told him what he knew. 'There's one more thing. He had a lisp.'

'That narrows it down.'

'Not enough, though. Can you print something? The usual – Police would like to talk to, and all that? With my name?'

'I can do that,' Reeve agreed. 'Do you really think it has something to do with the murder?'

'I've no idea.'

'Is it true what they said?'

'What's that?' He was surprised it had taken so long for word to spread.

'That the metal had melted on her.'

'You know better, Henry. I couldn't say, and you couldn't print it, anyway.' He rose. 'I appreciate it.'

If nothing else, he might be able to give Nellie Rider some justice. And maybe it would lead to more.

'Another meeting tonight,' Annabelle told him as she buttoned up her coat and hunted for her umbrella. 'Filthy out there, too.'

The rain had begun as Harper sat on the tram.

Now he stared out of the window at the growing puddles, hearing the water cascading down the drainpipes.

'You don't have to go,' he said.

'I do,' she said tenderly. 'There's a speaker from Manchester.'

'Where is it?'

'The old Assembly Rooms.'

'Then take a hackney. There and back.'

'I will,' she promised. 'Don't you worry, Tom.' She smiled at him. 'I'll look after myself.'

He kissed her. 'Make sure you do.'

'I have to. Especially now.'

She'd shown him the letter while they ate. A note from Miss Ford, asking if she'd consider becoming a speaker at the suffragist meetings. Annabelle had power, the woman had written, and even better, she had experience of life. She'd made something of herself.

He was certain she'd spent the whole day fretting about the note, pacing around the room until she'd worn grooves in the boards.

'I thought it was daft at first,' she said. 'Who'd want to hear me yattering? Then I thought maybe there was something in it, after all. Yes and no all day.' She laughed at herself. 'Like a yo-yo.'

'Are you going to do it?' he asked. She blushed and nodded. 'If it's what you want, I'm behind you.'

'I still don't see why she thinks I'd be any good.' She tied her hat under her chin. 'I'm nowt special.'

But he understood it very well. Annabelle had grown up poor and made something of herself.

She was an example of what women could achieve, no matter where they began. She was at home with people of all classes, men and women. She spoke her mind, no fear or favour.

'I think you're very special,' he told her.

'I should hope you do,' she grinned, 'or you'll be out on your ear.' She exhaled slowly. 'Seriously, Tom, I don't know that I can stand up and address a crowd. I'll be shaking.'

Public speaking was one thing she'd never done. But she'd never been slow to voice her opinion about things.

'You'll be fine.' Harper grinned. 'Just be who you are. No airs and graces.'

She snorted. 'Chance'd be a fine thing.'

Alone, he had time to sit and stare, thinking about life and death. Too many things were crowding him. The murder of Catherine Carr. Stanley Sugden escaped from the asylum. The rape of Nellie Rider. The dead baby.

Each of them pulled him in a different direction. Sometimes his job made him feel like a man on the high wire, simply trying to keep his balance as he crossed. One wrong step and he'd go tumbling down.

But he couldn't do anything about the baby until he knew where the Waites had gone. He was relying on the beat bobbies to gather information. And the piece in the *Mercury* should bring leads on the rape.

That left Sugden and Katie Carr. The man was the immediate danger. Armed and violent. With some luck, the inspector hoped, he'd wake in the morning to discover that Sugden was in custody and on his way back to Menston. But life was never that kind.

Catherine Carr. The possibilities just kept growing. The man outside her lodgings. The ones who watched the meetings. Patrick Martin. Robert Carr, the husband. Not himself, but he had the money enough to hire someone. And revenge on her for leaving, for belittling him, could be a powerful reason.

Too many. He hadn't been able to whittle them down yet. He watched the runnels of water slide down the window.

The knock on the door made him turn. He hadn't caught the footsteps on the stair. His hearing was growing worse. He should go back to that expensive doctor, but he already knew what the man would say: there was nothing he could do. It would only be a waste of money.

'That barman knows my face so he said to come up, sir,' Ash said as the inspector let him in. 'I'm sorry to disturb you, but it's on my way home.'

'Has something happened?'

'I thought I'd go out to Tramway Street again. Call at the houses where there was no one home before.'

'You found something?'

'Not much.' He pushed his lips together doubtfully. 'There was something. The man at number 35 was just going to bed when he heard someone running. He looked out of the window. There's a street lamp there, so he caught a glimpse.'

'Go on.'

'He says he saw someone with fair hair. Reasonably well-dressed, bowler hat. Big side whiskers. But he was gone in a moment.'

And they both knew how reliable witnesses were. Ten of them would see a dozen different things. The description fitted many men in Leeds . . . including Patrick Martin.

'Very good. Do you want a drink while you're here?'

'I shouldn't, sir, but thank you.' He smiled. 'The missus will be keeping my tea warm.'

After the constable left Harper made a cup of tea and sat in the chair. Pat Martin. They were going to have a long chat tomorrow. But first there was a funeral.

Ten

The day was grey. The rain had passed, but the sense of dampness lingered in the air. At the Chapel Allerton omnibus terminus, leaves were falling and scattering on the breeze. The three of them walked past the board school and crossed over the Harrogate Road.

Iron railings surrounded the cemetery, and a church that looked the worse for its years stood at the far end, close to a high brick wall. From inside they could hear a voice droning.

'We can wait out here,' Harper told them. 'Look around. Sugden could be hiding anywhere.'

'If he's even here,' Reed answered.

124

'There are supposed to be a couple of bobbies around, too. Just keep your eyes peeled.'

'No one,' the sergeant said when he returned. 'Mind you,' he warned, 'Sugden's a trained scout and a sniper. He'll be used to hiding himself and waiting.'

'Then we'd better stay very alert, Billy. They're coming out.'

The bell tolled, and the congregation appeared with the coffin. Robert Carr supported himself on his sticks, his son Neville on one side, a young man on the other. The grandson, Gordon, Harper supposed. Servants from the house. But not many others. And no Miss Ford. The suffragists wouldn't be welcome here.

The vicar read the service of the dead and the body was lowered into the open grave. Carr had reclaimed Catherine in death, making her into the loving wife he'd desired. The true history could be swept away, and the fiction would live on in the headstone.

He looked around. Ash stood close to the road, keeping a respectful distance away, hat in his hands. Reed was close to the church, eyes moving around.

It was time for the final blessing.

Then the shot rang out.

'Down.' Reed yelled. It was his training; he didn't even have to think. He crouched behind a gravestone. Waiting for the next shot. Looking around. No one seemed to be hurt.

The sergeant waved to Ash and dashed towards the wall. No more shots, just silence. The birds

125

had scattered. He pulled himself up and over, into a lane beyond, the constable close behind. Reed glanced both ways. One led back to the Harrogate Road. No, he thought, and began to run in the other direction.

A track led through the woods, down into the valley. He covered a hundred yards, Ash on his heels, and stopped. He tried to listen, but all he could hear was the blood hammering in his ears. His body felt like it was jangling. All around them the undergrowth was thick and wild.

'He could be anywhere in here.' No sign. No grass trampled or bushes moving.

'You said he was trained, sir.'

Reed nodded. 'If he remembers what he learned, he could be six feet away and we'd never know.' He looked around, frustrated. 'We might as well go back. We're not going to find him here.'

Harper stood up, brushing the dirt off his suit. He'd seen the others run after Sugden. Now he just had to hope they'd caught him.

The women were crying. Carr grasped his sticks tightly. He looked affronted, as if someone had stolen this moment from him.

'What the devil's going on?' he bellowed.

'You'll be fine now, sir,' the inspector assured him. Sugden had done what he came to do. Not kill. He'd been a sniper; he could have shot people if he'd wanted. A farewell to his sister?

Carr glared. His son gave Harper a disdainful look.

'He's gone,' the inspector said.

126

'How can I be fine when someone's trying to kill me?'

'I don't believe he was, sir. My men are after him.' He looked at the vicar. 'You can finish. You'll be safe now.'

'We should have been safe before,' Robert Carr shouted. 'That's your bloody job.'

Harper walked away. Where were the uniforms who should have been patrolling?

He waited at the top of the lane for the others to straggle back. The longer they were, the more chance they'd found Sugden. But they came back on their own.

'Not a chance in all those woods,' Reed told him. 'We looked around but there's nothing I can see.'

'I'll get some people to start hunting. Any sign of those uniforms?'

The sergeant shook his head.

'Do you think he's done now?' Ash asked.

'No,' Reed answered quickly. 'He'd have thrown down the gun and waited for us. If you ask me, he's just beginning. He wants to settle scores.'

It wasn't a comforting thought. A man who knew how to use a gun looking for revenge.

'I want to lead the search for him,' the sergeant said suddenly.

'What?' Harper asked in surprise. He thought Billy wanted to return to the fire brigade as soon as possible.

'I know how he thinks, Tom.' When there was no answer, he continued, 'I was a soldier too, remember.'

The inspector weighed it in his mind. There was no one better suited to the task than Billy. He'd served, he knew what it was like. He'd stared into the same darkness as Stanley Sugden. And with Reed in charge he'd be free to concentrate on the other things.

'Fine,' he agreed after a little while. 'It's yours. As long as Dick Hill allows it.'

'I'll talk to him.'

By the time they reached the churchyard, the mourners had all left. Only the two constables remained, and the gravediggers, filling in the hole.

'Where were you?' Harper snapped at the bobbies.

'On the Harrogate Road, sir. We came as quick as we could.'

He was a middle-aged man with a bland face. The other was younger, but equally empty.

'Breathe,' Harper ordered coldly, and smelt the beer. 'You too.' He noted down their numbers. 'I'll be reporting the pair of you for drinking on duty. Go back to the station, tell your sergeant. You're dismissed here.' He watched as they marched away, shoulders back. 'Bloody idiots.'

If they'd been here, doing their jobs . . . He shook his head and sighed. They had to make do with things as they were.

'I'll see you get a couple of bobbies to help you,' he told Reed.

'Try to find some who've been in the army.'

The inspector looked at Ash. 'You know anybody?'

'Stowe,' he answered. 'Maybe Meers. But he might have been in the navy.'

'I'll talk to the super.'

'I'm going to spend some time up here,' the sergeant said 'There are farms down in the valley. Someone might have seen him. Have them meet me in the station tomorrow morning.'

'What do you think, sir? Is the sergeant right? Sugden's not done yet?'

The omnibus had brought them back into the centre of Leeds, among the smoke and soot and the people coughing.

'Yes,' Harper answered bleakly. 'I think Mr Reed is probably correct.'

Eleven

Henry Reeve had done him proud; the article was on page three of the *Mercury*. When Harper walked back into Millgarth, Sergeant Tollman handed him ten slips of paper.

'That's what we've had so far, sir. I expect there'll be more. And there's a gentleman waiting for you.' He consulted the ledger. 'A Mr Martin. Arrived just after you left. Said you wanted to see him.'

'That's right. Bring him in.' He passed on the information about the constables drinking on duty. 'You know what to do.'

'Indeed I do, sir.' Tollman gave a grim smile.

Patrick Martin's expression was a curious mix of anger and resignation as he was led into the interview room. He held a small book in his hand and placed it on the table.

'I've been waiting a long time, Inspector,' he said.

'My apologies. There was a problem. Thank you for your patience.'

Martin seemed surprised by the courtesy.

'I brought my diary.' He pushed it across. 'It shows everything I do.'

Another diary. More words on the page. He wondered if that was how this would go, a case solved by reading. Before he could open it, a constable appeared with two cups of tea. It would make Martin feel more comfortable, and that might make him reveal more.

Harper glanced through. Every day was broken down and detailed. On the opening pages Martin had described the spiritual life of the Quarry Hill district:

> The prevailing vices are there – adultery, fornication, drunkenness, swearing and gossiping. The Lord's Day is awfully profaned – washing, baking, and sleeping in the afternoon, and in the evening, drinking.

He riffled through the pages, picking up on a note.

> Since I came to the district, eleven chil-dren have died from burning; and to me

it is no wonder, when I find so many houses left with the children, and the mothers 'throng' gossiping with their neighbours.

Every day Martin was rebuffed, but it didn't seem to discourage him. *Left a tract, and we parted friendly*. He was cursed away from doors, threatened. Still, he didn't give up.

Martin even wrote about standing and praying outside the suffragist meetings, and the names of the men he met. The night Catherine Carr died, he'd been visiting a family where the mother was dying, and stayed by the woman's bed until her last breath. That would be easy enough to check.

For the night before, when she'd seen someone watching her window from the street, there was no entry. Other evenings showed the same.

'What does it mean when you've written nothing?' Harper asked.

'I was at home.' He smiled. 'I'm allowed a little time off, Inspector. Even from God's work.'

Martin was dedicated, no doubt of that. Six days a week, usually from early to very late, then praying all Sunday. Only a few snatched evenings to himself. He read more, jottings here and there.

'Who sees this?'

'My superior. It's a record of what I do.'

'Do you know where Tramway Street is?'

'No,' Martin asked. 'Should I?'

'It's in Sheepscar. Mrs Carr lived there before she was killed.'

The man shook his head and Harper almost believed him. There was so much of the innocent about him. He truly believed everything he said about heaven and hell. And it seemed as if he did some good deeds. Food for a starving family, finding blankets for those who were cold.

But that didn't mean he couldn't commit murder.

'I wouldn't even know how to find it.'

'It's not far from Quarry Hill.' He paused. 'She believed a man was watching her.'

'It wasn't me, Inspector.' Martin's voice was soft, his gaze steady.

'He had fair hair, side whiskers, and a bowler hat.'

He saw something flicker across the man's face.

'There are plenty of men like that.'

'I know,' Harper agreed easily. 'But you can understand my questions. You stand outside the suffragist meetings . . .'

'I pray for them,' Martin corrected him and Harper shrugged.

'You're still there regularly. To me, that's a connection.'

'I've never harmed or killed anyone.'

They looked at each other. The inspector tried to read the expression in the man's eyes. Fear? Hurt? He couldn't tell. Finally he placed the diary in front of Martin.

'I'll need to follow up on some things, but you're free to go. For now.'

At the door Martin turned and opened his mouth to say something. Instead he just shook his head once and left.

He was convincing. But good liars were everywhere. He wasn't prepared to cross Patrick Martin off the list yet.

More tips on the rapist had arrived. He gave half of them to Ash and took the remainder. It was a waste of an afternoon. Trailing around from factory to shop, around poor streets where soot clung to the houses. The only good thing was the wind, fierce enough to blow the smoke away from Leeds. But even that brought grey skies and tiny needles of rain that stung his cheek.

He spent twenty minutes at the Garden Gate public house in Hunslet, where the coughing was louder than the conversation. A man with a lisp, but after a while he proved he'd been on the night shift when the rape happened. Ten minutes talking to a shop clerk in Armley who was forty at least; he'd been at home with his family that night.

Kirkstall, Burley. Two more and no one who resembled Nellie Rider's description. By six, his feet aching and mind too full of nothing, Harper gave up. The others would wait for tomorrow. And there'd probably be more to go with them.

On the tram out to the Victoria he gnawed at the problem of Catherine Carr. He wanted answers, something solid he could follow, but it all seemed out of reach. As if the answer was teasing him.

He'd get there in the end, but it was starting to feel like a long slog. In his mind he'd gone over everything, again and again. He knew he'd done everything correctly, turned over every stone. But so far no solution. Not even a suspect who felt right.

Harper stared out of the window, not seeing the pedestrians. Lost in his own head.

*　　*　　*

133

Reed had no better joy in Gledhow Valley. None of the farmers had spotted a stranger with a shotgun. Back at Millgarth, two coppers were waiting for him. Bob Stowe had served ten years in the artillery and still held himself like a soldier. Arthur Meers was a navy man, barely tall enough to become a copper. He explained to them about Sugden, watching as they nodded with understanding, then sent them off to Hunslet, to ask questions in the streets where the man had grown up and see if there were any relatives around.

He'd gone out to Carr's boot works to talk to the foreman, glad to see the policeman still on guard at the gate. Sugden had worked there a few years, he must have had some friends. The sergeant came away with two names, troublemakers who hung on to their jobs by the skin of their teeth, the foreman told him.

A few more questions and he discovered where they drank; they spent their evenings at the Royal Inn, close to where Sugden had grown up.

With time to kill he returned to town, and walked into the fire station. It felt strange, as if months had passed since he'd been there instead of no more than a few days. The engine stood there, just cleaned, puddles of water on the floor, and he could hear the men in the back room.

They were pleased to see him, gathering round, making tea, sitting and talking. They were his comrades. For months they'd looked after each other and worked as a team. A unit. He'd trusted his life to them.

But now he felt as if a wall separated him from them. He'd been gone less than a week, but somehow it seemed like a lifetime. There was a new sergeant, a face he didn't know, standing back quietly, holding a mug of tea in his hands.

'Missed us, Sarge?' Jem Hargreaves laughed.

'I've had holes in my head I've missed more.'

'We love you too, Sarge.'

It was easy, fun, but distant. He felt as if he was talking to people who were slipping away into his history. Finally, as the clock hands moved, he stood.

'I need to get back to work. We can't all spend our days sitting around.'

'You're just jealous, Sarge. When are you coming back?'

'Soon,' he promised. 'Once this case is done.'

He didn't mention the new job; Hill obviously hadn't told them. And he didn't say anything about the image that kept slipping into his mind, Catherine Carr, her body half covered in shining metal.

'Come home safe,' Reed told them as he left.

The Royal Inn stood on South Accommodation Road, a small building that looked up the hill towards Cross Green. The landlord stood behind the bar, a small man with broad shoulders, shirtsleeves rolled up to show thick forearms, his red waistcoat tight around a bulging belly. Reed introduced himself.

'I'm looking for Willie Tanner and Harold Carey,' he said.

'Oh aye? What have they done?'

'I didn't say they had.'

The landlord raised an eyebrow in disbelief.

135

He nodded towards two men sitting together, eating pork pies and drinking beer. 'Over there.'

They looked up as the sergeant approached.

'I'm Detective Sergeant Reed. Willie Tanner and Harold Carey?'

One by one, they nodded. Tanner coughed, then drank quickly. Carey glowered.

'What do you need?' he asked. His body was heavily muscled, the smell of leather ingrained in his skin.

'You both know Stanley Sugden?'

'What about it?'

'Have you seen him since he escaped from the asylum?' Carey looked away. Tanner began to cough again, covering his mouth with his hand. But neither gave an answer.

'He came to his sister's funeral today and fired a gun.'

'A man deserves to say goodbye to his kin.'

'Is that what you think, Mr Tanner?'

The man raised his head defiantly. 'It's right enough.'

He could feel the tension, the other men in the pub stopping to watch.

'I'll say this once: if you know where he is, tell me now. If I think you're lying, I'll take you down to the station and question you. Trust me, you won't like that. Are we clear?'

Carey stood quickly, fists clenched. But Reed stood his ground and smiled.

'Hitting a policeman is a sentence in Armley,' he said softly. 'Sugden's not worth it.'

Carey sat again, the squeak of his chair the only sound in the place.

'Well?' the sergeant asked. 'What's it going to be? Last chance.' Tanner leaned forward and muttered something to his friend. 'What?'

'I said he should tell you.' The man's voice was raw. He coughed again, bringing something up into a handkerchief. 'Go on,' he told Carey.

'He came to see me,' the man admitted. 'Early this morning.'

'What did he want?'

Carey shrugged. 'A wash and summat to eat. I couldn't say no, he's a mate.'

'You must have talked to him when he was there. Did he say what he was going to do?'

'He din't talk much. Never was much for that.'

'He must have said something.'

'Came for the funeral.'

Reed shook his head. 'There's more to it than that.' He placed his hands on the table and leaned forward until his face was close to Carey's. 'What else?'

'Revenge.'

'What kind?' the sergeant asked, although he could guess.

'He didn't say. Just told me it was the time to do it.'

'Time? What does that mean?'

'No idea,' the man answered, staring into his eyes. 'He didn't make any sense. Just that it was the right time to do it.'

'Where he is now?'

'Not at mine.' Reed stared at him disbelievingly. 'Go and look if you like.'

'I've not seen him,' Wheeler added.

'You two had better be telling me the truth. If

137

he comes back, I want to know.' He waited. 'You understand?'

They nodded.

'Revenge,' Carey repeated. 'That was all he said.'

Twelve

Harper finally climbed the stairs at the Victoria and turned the doorknob. He felt weary, drained.

Annabelle was pacing round the room. Her hair had come out of its clips, and hung loose on her shoulders. A nib and paper lay on the desk, words written and crossed out. She had a frantic expression, biting her lip as she looked at him.

'What is it?' he asked. He opened his arms as she came to him, trying to hold her close, but her fists grabbed at his coat. 'What's wrong?'

After a long time she pulled back, her fingers still clutching his sleeves. There was fear in her eyes, something he'd never seen before.

'Annabelle . . .' he began. 'What's happened?'

She took a deep breath.

'You remember I told you that Miss Ford wants me to become a speaker at meetings?' He nodded. 'She wants me to start the day after tomorrow. The woman they'd booked is poorly.' She began to pace again. 'I can't do it, Tom. I can't bloody do it.'

'Listen,' he said, reaching for her hand, but she snatched it away and pointed at the desk.

'You know what I've done all day? I've been trying to write. Then I crossed it all out. Over and over. I've got ten words. Ten.' Her face seemed to wither. 'I can't get up there and speak to them.'

'Yes, you can,' he told her. 'Listen,' he said again, but it was enough to make her stare accusingly. 'Listen to me. Why do you think Isabella Ford asked you in the first place?'

'I don't know. I wish she hadn't.'

'You run businesses. You've made them successful.'

'A pub and some back-street bakeries.'

'Yes, a pub and three bakeries,' he corrected her. 'How many people have done that? Forget those women who've had money all their lives.'

'I can't.' Her voice wavered. 'They're the ones who'll be listening. They'll be judging me.'

'Then let them.' He exhaled slowly, took her hand and led her to the settee. 'I mean it. What have they ever had to do? *Really* do. Not a day's work in their lives.' She opened her mouth to object. In the end nothing came out. 'I know they're fighting for something good,' Harper told her. 'But look at yourself. You're the one who's the example for women, not them.'

'I—' she began, but he cut her off.

'How many women do you know who don't have to think about where the next penny's coming from?'

'A few.'

'And how many who are always wondering how to stretch the wages until the next payday?' He looked at her.

'Most of them,' she admitted.

'And don't they need the vote even more?'

'We all do,' she told him angrily, pushing herself up and striding around the room again. 'Every one of us. And there are plenty who'd say it better than I can.'

'But they won't be up there. You will.'

Her dress rustled loudly as she moved. 'I'm petrified, Tom. I'm bloody terrified.'

'Then tell them that once you get up there. They'll understand.'

'It's at the Mechanics' Institute. In the Albert Hall.' The round lecture theatre. Room for a big audience; that was what she meant. All of them looking at her, listening to her.

'You don't have to be like them,' Harper said. 'Just be yourself.'

'They'll laugh at me.'

'No,' he insisted softly, 'they won't. Just tell them about yourself. Tell them why you support women having the vote. *Ordinary* women. That's all you have to do.'

'Do you really think that?' she asked doubtfully. 'Honestly? You're not kidding me?'

'Honestly.' He glanced at the paper and the pen. 'Don't worry about all that. Don't even write it down. Just get up there and speak. Tell them what you feel. You'll be fine.'

'Ten seconds and they'll be rushing out screaming.'

Harper smiled. 'You'll be fine. I promise.'

'I won't.'

'You will. Trust me, I'm a policeman.'

She chuckled and her mood brightened. 'Is that what you tell all the girls, Tom Harper?'

140

'It used to work.'

'Maybe when you were young.' She winked, then she looked at his hands. 'Those bandages are filthy. Let's get them off.'

She brought out a pair of scissors and cut them away. The skin on his palms was pale and wrinkled, but the blisters he'd received at the railway station fire were healing.

'Leave them like this,' he said. 'Let them breathe. I can always wear gloves.'

Annabelle nodded. 'There's something else, Tom. That hearing of yours. It's getting worse, isn't it?'

'A little,' he admitted reluctantly.

'I *know* it is,' she told him. 'Maybe we should go and see that doctor again?'

'Why?' he asked bitterly. 'Why spend a guinea to hear him say I'll be stone deaf in my right ear soon and there's nothing anyone can do about it?'

'Do you know where Sugden is yet?' the inspector asked. They were sitting in the office, the fire burning bright, and outside the window the sound of carts groaning past with their morning deliveries.

'No,' Reed said. 'I know where he was before the funeral, though.' He explained what he'd discovered. 'He said he's here for revenge.'

'Then find him before he has the chance,' Superintendent Kendall ordered. He was standing close to the hearth, listening intently as he puffed on his pipe.

'I have two men looking, sir,' the sergeant said.

141

'If he's been in Hunslet, let's have a sweep. I'll get on to the station there.'

'Yes, sir.'

'How are you getting on with the Carr murder?' Kendall asked Harper.

'No further. Suspects but no proof.'

'And that rape in the Arches? Is it tied in?'

'I don't know yet. We've had plenty of tips from that article.'

'I have one that looks good, sir,' Ash broke in. 'A chap called Peter Grady.'

'Go on,' the superintendent told him.

'He fits the description the lass gave. Gravedigger out at Beckett Street cemetery.'

'Have you been out to see him?' Harper asked.

'I tried, sir. He's not been seen there for a couple of days. Didn't show up to work.'

'Did you try his house?'

'He lives on the Bank, sir.'

They all knew what that meant. It was where the Irish first settled when they came to Leeds in the '40s. Many of them still lived there, generations of families living cheek by jowl on cramped, dirty streets. Loyalties ran as thick as blood and the police were hated.

'We'll go today,' the inspector said.

Thirteen

The houses on Spinner Street looked battered and beaten. Slates missing here and there on the roofs. A few broken windows covered by cardboard. Number seven was no better or worse than the rest.

The landlady eyed them with suspicion. Reluctantly she told them that Grady hadn't been there for a few days.

'Just as well, if he's been drinking,' she said. 'He gets a right temper on him.'

Harper felt a prickle at the back of his neck. Grady. It grew stronger when they persuaded the woman to let them search his room, as bare as a monk's cell. A cast iron bedstead, rotting mattress, a thick blanket, and a crucifix nailed to the wall.

'What about his other clothes?' All the man had was a change of underwear and socks.

'He has another suit, but it spends more time down the pawnbroker than it does here.'

'It's him,' Harper said as they walked back down the street.

'I think so, too, sir,' Ash agreed. 'Happen we'd better try the public houses, see if they'll tell us anything.'

The first couple of places gave them short shrift, a creeping sense of violence from the men sitting and drinking. Finally they found a landlord who was willing to talk to them in the back room. Grady had last been in on the night of the rape.

'He were in early. He'd had a skinful by then. I kicked him out when he tried to start a fight. I run a decent house here.'

Peter Grady. Straight to the top of the list, the inspector decided.

They all met back at Millgarth before dinner.

'Have they found anything in Hunslet?' Harper asked.

'Not yet. I was over there this morning,' Reed answered. 'Not a sniff of Sugden. I'm going back later.'

'Keep on it.'

Before the sergeant could say more, the door opened. Tollman, the desk sergeant, put his head around, his face grave.

'Just had a message from Burmantofts, sir. There's been some trouble at a bakery there. I thought you'd want to know.'

Harper looked at Reed. 'We'll get a hackney,' he said.

The front window had been smashed. Already a glazier was measuring it up, his assistant sweeping up the shards of glass on the pavement.

The sergeant jumped out of the cab and dashed into the shop. Harper lingered outside, surveying the damage. The policeman in him saw it as something minor, easily mended. But as a husband his anger boiled.

Reed was tending to Elizabeth. She had cuts on her arms and face, and her eyes still brimmed

144

with tears. Her wounds had been washed and cleaned but she still looked shaken.

Annabelle stood talking to the beat bobby. PC Waterhouse. Conscientious enough. Five years in this manor, the inspector remembered; he knew it very well.

Harper laid a gentle hand on his wife's shoulder and she turned, relief flooding her face.

'Tom . . .'

'What happened?' he asked her.

'That woman we sacked the other day. Her son came and hefted a brick through the window. Elizabeth was looking out when he did it. It's only scratches, thank God. It all happened just before I got here.'

'Do you know where they live?' he asked Waterhouse.

'Not two minutes away, sir,' the constable replied. He had a thin neck, Adam's apple bouncing as he spoke. 'I'll go round there and bring him in.'

'No,' Annabelle said firmly. 'Please. Not unless Elizabeth wants to press charges.' They all looked at her, wrapped in Reed's arms. 'Locking him up won't do a bit of good.'

'Billy and I can go and have a word,' Harper suggested. 'We'll put the fear of God in him.' Waterhouse opened his mouth to object, but the inspector continued, 'I know. This is your patch. Come along with us.'

'He can work off the cost,' Annabelle suggested. 'Clean up and do things here.' She paused. 'As long as Elizabeth agrees. She's the manager.'

'I want him here at five tomorrow morning,'

Elizabeth said. She tried to sound firm but her voice quavered. 'On the dot. And you can tell him he'll pay for that window with his sweat. If he doesn't show up, you can go and arrest him.'

Lorraine Chapman stood in the corner of the room, arms folded, trying to hide her fear. She was young, too thin, streaks of grey already showing in her hair. The only window in the cellar was high in the wall, the glass smeared with dirt. A bed of straw and two ratty blankets. The whole place smelled of mould and damp.

The boy was called Jemmy. He was seven, so skinny he could have been made of twigs. He stood at attention, fists clenched to try and hide the trembling.

'Do you understand what I'm telling you?' Harper asked. The boy nodded, turning from face to face and finally to his mother. 'Well?'

'Yes, sir.' His voice was soft, on the verge of crying.

'If there's a single day you don't go in to work, Constable Waterhouse will come down here and take you to the station,' Reed said. His face was set, eyes dark; it was Elizabeth who'd been hurt.

'I'll be there, sir. Every day.'

'He will,' Lorraine Chapman promised. 'I'll make sure he is. Thank you.' She stared at the inspector. 'Please tell your wife I'm very sorry, sir. So's he.' She put out a bony hand and placed it on her son's head. 'He doesn't know how lucky he is.'

'I'll be checking every day,' Waterhouse told the boy. 'Mind you do what you're told.'

146

'When he's paid for the cost of the window, it's over and done,' Harper said as the others left. 'Nothing on his record.' He reached into his pocket, picked out a shilling, and left it on the rickety wooden table.

They walked back into town. The rain had stopped, but the skies still threatened off towards the hills.

'At least Elizabeth wasn't badly hurt,' the inspector said gently.

'She could have been.' The anger was still there in Reed's voice. 'What if she'd been standing closer to the window?'

'We did the right thing.' He needed to calm the man down. 'You know that as well as I do, Billy. Slinging the lad in jail wouldn't have helped anyone. I'll bet you a tanner he spends half of tomorrow apologizing.'

'What if it had been serious?'

'Then we'd have dealt with it differently.' He sighed. 'It's done, just leave it be. We have crimes to solve.' He sighed. 'A pity they're not all as easy as this one.'

They parted on York Street, close to the gasworks. Harper walked out past St Saviour's, to Cross Green. He found Constable Williams on Spring Close Street, leaning against a wall and talking to a woman who was smiling broadly. The policeman came to attention as the inspector approached. He whispered something and the woman disappeared with a saucy glance over her shoulder.

'Afternoon, sir.'

147

'Keeping good relations with the locals?' he asked with a grin.

Williams had the decency to blush. 'Lovely woman, sir. Tells me what's happening. Things I don't see.'

'Something about the Waites?'

'Nothing yet, sir. Talked to some old neighbours, but they haven't seen them. If they're around, they're keeping quiet.' He looked along the street. 'That's hard to do here.'

Another day of nothing. Sugden had gone to ground, Reed thought grimly. No sign of him in Hunslet. Flushing him out would be nigh on impossible.

He hadn't been able to keep his mind on the job during the afternoon; he'd been too worried about Elizabeth. But when he arrived home she just waved away his concern.

'It's nothing,' she told him. 'Just a few scratches.'

He could see them on her face and arms where the glass had sliced her skin. Nothing serious. A few days and they'd be forgotten.

'I just . . .' he began, then couldn't find the words.

'I know, luv.' She smiled and put her arms around him. 'How do you think I feel when you go off to work as a fireman? I love you, you daft beggar.'

'Jemmy, the lad, he'll be there first thing in the morning. Don't go soft on him.'

'Don't you worry,' she told him. 'He'll work off every penny of that window.'

'Good.' He let himself relax against her body. Her warmth was comforting after a day out in the cold.

'I got some good tripe at the butcher. Kept it warm for your supper. And I can send John down to the pub if you want beer.'

'Just tea is fine.'

'Are you sure, Billy?'

He was certain. The times he really wanted a drink had grown further apart. What he did need was her and everything she gave him. Something certain in his life. Something worthwhile. Elizabeth and the children. If something happened to her . . .

Reed spent part of next morning at Hunslet police station, looking through the results of another sweep through the area. Still nothing. The only thing anyone had found was a relative of Stanley Sugden.

It wasn't far to Grape Street, but it was like walking into hell, surrounded by the glowing fires and the constant metal pounding of the foundry of the engine works. The air tasted of iron and the blast of the furnaces seemed to lick out on to the roads. Was it like this all night too, he wondered? How could anyone live in a place like this? The devil himself would have a hard time here.

The house was like all the others on the street: tired, worn, the glass covered by a film of powdered iron. The woman who came to the door had thick, wiry white hair and clear blue eyes, standing straight.

'It was my cousin Margaret who married James Sugden,' she explained as they sat in the kitchen. 'I remember the little ones clear as day. Sweet, they were. The Lord only knows what happened to Stanley to do what he did. In prison . . . The last I heard of the lass . . . must be years and years ago now . . . she went off into service. George died when Stanley was just a bairn. And the typhus took Jane when it came around again.'

The woman didn't have much more to tell. She'd never been close to the family, had only ever seen them at weddings and funerals.

'Not even much of that these days,' she said. 'The young ones now, they don't know what family's like.'

'Is there anyone else who might know about him?'

'Nay, luv, I don't know. I'm sorry.'

Dead ends. It was like that all day, bouncing from one address to another and finding nothing of any use. By evening all he felt was frustration, as if he'd lost all the hours of daylight. Sugden was still out there with his plans for revenge and Reed didn't have a clue as to where to find him.

'You might as well go home,' the inspector told Ash. They'd spent the day chasing Peter Grady and looking for anything else to help track down Catherine Carr's killer. The image of her had been in his head when he woke, the shining silver that had replaced her skin.

He hadn't been able to shake it from his mind as he trailed around town. But it wasn't the only thing. Annabelle's speech was tonight. She'd woken when he rose, bustling around, making tea. She hadn't said anything, but she didn't need to; everything was on her face. The worry, the fear. He kept his arms around her for a long time before he left.

'Happen we'll have better luck tomorrow,' the constable said.

'Let's hope so.' Grady was hiding somewhere on the Bank. He was certain of that. It was the perfect place to run, around friends and family. Finding him, and arresting him; that would be the tricky part. He remembered having to go in there once when he was in uniform. Six of them sent to arrest a burglar. They'd almost had to fight their way out while the prisoner laughed and kicked at them all.

'Something has to turn up soon, sir. Goodnight.'

Maybe something would. But he'd always believed in making something happen. He walked wearily up George Street. At least his hands were starting to return to normal. And the hearing was no worse; he'd only needed to ask people to repeat things four times during the day.

He didn't have many informers on the Bank. They were too tight-lipped. He met the ones who had information to sell in town, where no one was likely to recognize them. Harper had tried them all once about Peter Grady. It was time for a second round.

'Not hide nor hair of the man,' Seamus Reilly told him. He'd lived in Leeds all his life but there was still the melody of Ireland in his voice. 'Not that he'd be too anxious to be seen.'

'He's somewhere,' the inspector said.

'Probably,' Reilly chuckled. 'I doubt God spirited him away.'

'He raped a girl. Remember that. He threatened to kill her.'

'Drink can make a devil of a man. We all know that, Mr Harper.'

'I don't care what the hell it does,' the inspector said, although he knew the words were true. 'I want him. Ten bob as a reward.'

He didn't have the superintendent's approval for that. Not yet. But it was good money, enough to tempt people into telling tales.

'I'll see what I can do.'

Reilly had three fingers missing from his left hand. An accident with a power loom when he was a boy working at Bank Mill. There were no jobs for a lad who couldn't be nimble. Seamus was twenty-five now, with a sour face and ragged eyes. But his eyes still sparkled when he laughed.

'Ask around.'

'I know the score, Inspector.' He held up the empty mug and Harper signalled for another, dropping a coin on the table.

'I need him soon, Seamus. The sooner the better.'

Reilly raised the fresh glass in a toast. 'May you have warm words on a cold evening.'

He'd heard it before, an old toast among the Irish. But apt today, he thought. Very apt.

None of the other informers had anything for him. Grady had disappeared. But chasing each one down took time; it was almost seven o'clock when he finished, the street lamps shining through the autumn gloom.

Leeds was still busy, people passing to and fro, carters on their way home, the rumble of the iron wheels of trams. The hackneys hurried along, squeaking in and out of the traffic.

It was quieter on Cookridge Street, away from the bustle. The Town Hall loomed large, brooding over everything, the stone as black as if it had burned. The Mechanics' Institute stood halfway up the hill, an expanse of stone steps rising up to the building.

A few women were gathered outside the doors, talking in low, serious voices. Harper nodded to Hardaker, the union man, and noticed a copper standing across the street. About bloody time, he thought. The inspector made his way past them, inside the tall entrance with its tiled floor.

Most of the seats were taken. Women in expensive wool coats and elaborate hats decorated with plumes and feathers sat next to others wrapped in threadbare shawls, women they'd never know elsewhere. Voices came from the balcony upstairs.

The stragglers arrived, settling on to chairs and letting the atmosphere surround them. In just a minute it was as hushed as any church. A line of four wooden chairs was spread across the stage. Harper stood at the back of the room, close to the doors, keeping in the shadows where Annabelle wouldn't see him.

The speakers came out. She was there, looking pale and nervous, sitting primly, hands in her lap. She was wearing one of her favourite gowns, purple and blue silk that looked iridescent in the

153

light from the mantles. Her hair was pinned up, showing her thin neck. Harper watched her eyes search the audience for friendly faces, but he stayed out of view; he'd see her later, when she was done.

The first two speakers both had sharp, precise voices. Their crisp tones and words seemed to echo each other. Women needed a say in running the country. Men made the law for themselves. It might have carried more weight if the first woman's husband didn't run a factory where mill girls earned pennies a week and didn't know from one day to the next if there'd be work for them.

The voices boomed off the high ceiling. Harper moved until he found a spot where even his bad ear could pick out every word. He waited and fidgeted. Looked at his pocket watch every few minutes and scanned the crowd, alert for any possible trouble.

Finally it was Annabelle's turn. She moved tentatively to the front of the stage, peering out, and cleared her throat.

'Well,' she said with a smile, 'now I know what it must be like to be on the halls. I feel like I should sing a song or something.'

A few chuckles from the audience. Annabelle took a deep breath.

'You don't know me,' she continued. 'No reason you should, really. I run a public house in Sheepscar. It's nothing grand but it pays the bills. And I grew up on the Bank.' She lifted her head, as if she was challenging them to say something. 'I know what they say: grow up on the Bank and you'll never amount to anything.

I've heard it all my life.' She had a rhythm now, pacing back and forth along the edge of the stage. 'I started out in the mills when I was nine. It's a hard life, I can tell you that right now. Moved into service a few years later because it paid better and it wasn't as dangerous.' With a quick smile, she held up her hands, palms outwards. 'I'm still not above scrubbing a floor if it needs it, or giving something a cleaning. Most of the girls I played with ended up doing the same. Maids or mills. If I ever see them now, the ones who are married have five or six children and husbands who bring in next to nothing every week. They survive, and that's all they do. It's down to the pawnbroker with the good clothes of a Tuesday morning so they can last until their men are paid. Redeem everything Friday evening. Do you know what they wish for when they're walking down the street holding everything of value that they own? That their little ones will have something better. But they won't.' She stopped to stare down at them. The room was absolutely quiet. 'Do you know why not? Because there's no one to speak up for them. They live, they die. Probably half of the girls I played hopscotch with when I was in pinafores are in the ground now.' She paused. 'I'm not saying having the vote would put everything right. I'm not a fool. Men will still run things, same as they always have. There'll still be more poor people than you can shake a stick at. But at least we'll have a say. All of us. That's the women on Leather Street, where I grew up, as much as anyone here.' Annabelle shook her

155

head and a strand of hair came loose, hanging down on her cheek. She brushed it back quickly. 'Maybe they need it even more than us. I'll tell you something else. Every day, every single day, I see women with all the hope gone from their faces. It's been battered away long before they're old enough to work. And we *need* hope. That's why every woman needs the vote. Every man, too. The only way those men standing for Parliament will ever do anything is if they need our votes to win. Half their promises will still vanish into thin air. Of course they will, they always do. And they still won't do anything more than they absolutely have to.' She waited and looked down at the stage before raising her head again. 'But for the first time they'll have to listen to us.'

For a moment there was silence. Then the applause came. A few hands clapping at first, then more. Two or three women stood, and slowly the others joined them. Annabelle just stood, her face flushed and pink, not sure what to do.

Harper beamed, putting his hands together with everyone else. He'd hardly dared to breathe as she spoke. The meeting was over; nothing could top that. People had gathered around Annabelle, to congratulate her and talk to her. She gulped from a glass of water, trying to keep up with everyone surrounding her.

He stayed back until the crowd began to disperse. Annabelle vanished for a minute, returning with her favourite dark blue cape over her shoulders and her hat fixed in place. She made her farewells and moved towards the entrance, glancing around.

Harper came forward into the light and she began to smile.

'How long have you been lurking there?' She sounded hoarse, as if her voice might vanish at any moment.

'The whole time,' he answered.

'Well?' she asked. 'What did you think?'

'You were wonderful.' He couldn't think of another word. Up there, she'd been herself. No airs, no graces, just the woman he'd married, speaking her mind.

Annabelle looked at him doubtfully. 'I didn't make a fool of myself?'

'You saw what they did,' he told her. 'They were on their feet and clapping when you finished.'

'I know, but . . .'

'No buts. They loved you.'

'I just wondered if they were being polite.'

For a moment he thought she was fishing for compliments. But she meant it; he saw that when he looked into her eyes.

'They did,' he assured her. 'Honestly.'

She took his arm and they went out into the night, cold air coming in a rush.

'I feel like I could fall over and go to sleep,' she said.

'Let's take a cab.'

At the kerb, he raised a hand and the vehicle came clopping slowly towards them. She rested her head against his shoulder on the journey, not speaking, eyes closed.

'Do you know what one of them said to me

157

after? "The Queen doesn't think women should have the vote."'

'What did you do?'

She gave a soft, throaty chuckle. 'I told her that the queen already has an empire full of men who'll do whatever she wants. She looked like she was going to spit feathers.'

At home she was in bed before he'd finished locking up.

'Who'd have believed just talking could take it out of you?' she asked in surprise.

'I'm proud of you,' Harper said.

She shifted on the pillow, raising her head to look down at him. 'Are you? Do you mean that, Tom? I'm not just being daft doing all this?'

'I mean it.' He pulled her close so she rested against him. 'Every word.'

Fourteen

Barbara Waite, Nellie Rider, Catherine Carr. The names jangled through his head. One to find, two who needed justice.

His head ached. The air was bad, sulphur and soot that made his eyes water. People passed, coughing, spitting into handkerchiefs or on the pavement. This was only October; by January things would be much worse. When he'd been on the beat, he was called out every winter to discover bodies. Killed by the weather. But even that was better than a knife in the Arches.

158

'What are we doing today, sir?' Ash asked as they stood outside Millgarth. Carts dodged between trams and omnibuses. Pedestrians pushed along, men carelessly crossing the road as if there were no traffic.

What could they do? Keep digging. They could find Peter Grady and get one crime off the books, at least. And it was possible he'd killed Katie Carr . . .

'The Bank,' he said. 'Let's go back and ask some more questions.'

The constable raised his eyebrows but said nothing.

Going through St Peter's Square, a voice called out and Harper turned.

'Inspector.' Patrick Martin, coming across the cobbles, a smile on his face, hand outstretched. The inspector shook it. 'I owe you an apology.'

'Do you?' The remark took him by surprise. Those weren't words he often heard.

'After you questioned me, I wished you ill,' the man admitted.

'You'd hardly be the first,' Harper told him with a chuckle.

'It was wrong of me. I'm sorry. I hope you'll forgive me.'

'It's nothing,' Harper assured him. For God's sake, the man should be angry. He'd practically accused him of murder.

'Thank you.' Martin smiled again. 'I hear your wife spoke at a meeting last night.'

'How did you know that?' he asked sharply. 'I didn't see you outside.'

159

'Someone told me,' Martin replied vaguely. 'I hope she was well received.'

'Very.'

The man nodded briefly. 'I'm pleased for her, even if I can't approve of the cause. I hope you'll pass her my best wishes.' He tipped his hat and walked away.

'Odd fish, isn't he, sir?' Ash said as they watched him leave.

'He is that,' Harper agreed. 'There's something about him I don't like.'

'I know what you mean.' He thought for a moment. 'He's very oily, isn't he?'

That was one word. Sanctimonious was another. Harper didn't trust anyone who lived by his certainties. One thing he'd learned as a copper was that little was black or white. All too often the answer lay in the grey between them. Anyone who believed otherwise didn't understand people at all.

'Yes,' he agreed. 'Come on, let's see if we can find Peter Grady.'

They had some luck. On New Row, where the middens were piled against the houses, they found Grady's cousin, a young woman with five small children around her. Four ran like hellions or clutched at her thin skirt, the other in her arms, grabbing tight to the threadbare shawl around her shoulders.

'Is that what he's done?' she snorted when the inspector explained why he was looking for the man. 'I'd not put it past him. He was always a wild one.'

'Do you know where he is?'

'No,' she replied after a moment. But her hesitation told him it was a lie. She gazed up and down the street to see if anyone was watching. A pair of men hung around the corner, leaning against the wall, smoking. They'd waited on other corners while Harper and Ash asked questions around the Bank. Keeping an eye out, noticing who they talked to.

'Are you sure?' he asked gently.

She shook her head. 'No, I wouldn't know that.'

'Thank you.'

'You gave up too easily, sir,' Ash said as they walked away. 'She knows, I could see it.'

'She's scared. You can't blame her, with those men around.'

They'd barely gone round the block before small footsteps were dashing towards them. A little girl, barefoot, in a dress so large she almost tripped over the hem, her eyes wide.

'Me mam sent me,' she said breathlessly. 'She said to tell you he's on Surrey Street.'

The inspector smiled and squatted in front of her. 'What number, did she tell you?'

'Number eight, sir.' The girl's accent was a mix of Leeds and Ireland.

'Thank you. And thank your mam.' He put a halfpenny in her palm. 'Run home before someone sees you.'

Sergeant Reed went through all the papers on Stanley Sugden once more. Two sweeps in Hunslet had brought nothing; no one had seen him.

There was no point in going out to look; he

161

had no idea where to begin. With the skills Sugden had, he could make a camp anywhere and stay hidden.

What he needed was some little nugget. Just something, a clue to start him on the way. He'd asked for this case, now he had to solve it and arrest the man. Dick Hill had understood. He knew enough about the sergeant's past to see why he wanted this. But the approval had been limited.

'A fortnight,' Hill had said. 'After that, I need you back, no matter what. Sooner if you can manage it.'

'Yes, sir,' Reed had answered with relief. Now he was beginning to wonder if he'd bitten off more than he could chew. There was bloody nothing to latch on to in the files. He thought about bracing Sugden's two friends again, but he doubted that the man would have gone back. Word was out now. He'd be too visible, someone would say something.

The sergeant lit another Woodbine and picked strands of tobacco off his tongue. Revenge, he thought. That was what Sugden said he wanted. There were plenty of places for that. He'd been released from the regiment. He'd been sacked from Carr's and other firms. He'd been an armed robber who was caught. Too many possibilities to cover.

'How do you fancy a scrap tonight, Billy?' Harper asked as he walked into the office.

'What?'

'That rape suspect is hiding on the Bank.' He turned to Ash. 'We'll go in this evening. Find four constables. Big ones who aren't afraid of using their fists.'

'I'm sure I can find a few of those, sir.'

'Better find your truncheon,' the inspector said to Reed. 'You'll need it.'

'You think he's connected to the Carr killing?'

Harper threw his hat on the desk and sat down with a long sigh. 'I haven't a clue. Not until I can question him. How about you? Anything on Sugden yet?'

Reed shook his head. 'Probably the next we'll know is when he shows himself again. It's what he'll do then that scares me.'

'Do we still have a man at Carr's factory?'

'Yes.'

'Keep him there.' He glanced at the clock. 'Come on, Billy, I'll buy you some dinner.'

Wray's on Vicar Lane was close enough. The crowds were thinning out as men returned to work; they found a table away from the others. Pie and peas and tea, enough to warm the inner man.

'Annabelle's become a speaker at the suffragist meetings,' Harper said after they'd finished.

'Elizabeth didn't say anything about it to me,' the sergeant answered.

'I think she wants to keep it under her hat.'

'When's she going to speak?'

'She already did. Last night. She surprised me. I knew she'd be good, but they were on their feet clapping.' He beamed with pride.

'I'm not surprised. You know how she is with people.'

'She had them like that.' He held up his hand,

palm open. 'Didn't hold back, either. I'm just worried, that's all. I can't be at every meeting.'

They both knew the reason: whoever killed Catherine Carr might set his sights on her.

'He hasn't gone after anyone else.'

'Yet.'

'We don't even know it's connected with politics, Tom. It could be something else. Family. A random killing.'

'Christ, don't say that.' They'd never find the murderer then. He took his watch from his pocket. 'We'd better go back, they'll think we've deserted.'

A message was waiting, to meet the beat bobby for Cross Green at St Hilda's Church, three o'clock. Plenty of time to stroll out there and wait. There was a good view down the hill, looking over Hunslet, just high enough to enjoy a little clean air. He could see the smoke and grime below, clinging around the streets and houses.

The constable was prompt, arriving on the dot and giving a brisk salute.

'Williams, sir. I've got a lead on that Waite family you were looking for. Well,' he corrected himself, 'a bit of one, anyway.'

'Let's see what you have.'

It wasn't far, on a street that ran up the hillside at a steep angle. An end terrace, close to the block of privies, the stink strong enough to make him retch.

'You get used to it, sir,' Williams said with a chuckle and knocked on the door. The woman who answered smiled to see the constable and invited them in, looking up and down the road to see if anyone was snooping. 'This is Mrs Bradshaw, sir. She's related to the Waites . . . how is it again, Cissie?'

'Distant,' she replied. She was in her forties, hands red and swollen from work, hair drawn into a tight bun on the back of her head. She smelt of soap. A washerwoman, he guessed. 'I don't even rightly know myself.' The woman gave a full-throated laugh. 'Daft, isn't it?'

'Are they in Cross Green?' Harper asked.

'I've seen him,' she said. 'He was going in the pub. Couldn't believe it at first, he's not been round here in years.'

'You mean the father?'

'Aye, that's the one. I saw him when he came out again, too. He has a beard now but it was definitely him. Those eyes of his, I'd remember them anywhere'

The inspector looked at Williams. The constable shrugged.

'Do you know where he's living, Mrs Bradshaw?'

'Nay, luv, not an inkling. That's all I noticed, and no one else has seen him. Not that they'd remember him, most like. He moved away when he got wed, and that's a long time now.'

The family was here. Now it was just a matter of tracking them down. The area wasn't so large.

'What do you think, sir?' Williams asked when the door had closed behind them.

'I think you need to start asking some questions. Find out what families have moved in recently.'

'I've already asked about anyone called Waite.'

'They've probably changed their name. Talk to Mrs Bradshaw again, get a description of Waite.'

'Yes, sir.'

'Let me know when you have something.'

As he strode along East Street on his way back to Millgarth, he felt some small satisfaction. It was only a matter of time before he'd be questioning Barbara Waite about the dead baby.

The police station was hushed. It was the shank of the afternoon, towards the end of the shift, when the day men began thinking about going home. Harper made a cup of tea and settled at his desk. At least there'd been a little progress today.

Once it was dark they'd go over to the Bank and bring Grady out. It was going to be rough, but one crime solved. Maybe even two, if he was lucky. The inspector reached into the bottom drawer of his desk and brought out his truncheon. Good, solid mahogany. He slipped the leather strap over his wrist. A good blow from that would make anyone think twice. He needed gloves, though. The skin on his palms was still soft and tender where it was healing.

There was nothing more to do until nightfall and all the men were assembled. He picked up Catherine Carr's diary again. He'd looked at it so often that he knew half of it by heart, could almost recite it like the poems he'd had to learn in school.

If she'd just written a little more, he'd know exactly where to look and this business would be over. Right now he was flailing, simply hoping to stumble across the right answers.

166

Reed arrived a little after five, Ash a few minutes later. They sat, waiting. No need for talk. Harper could feel the boots moving in the station as the shifts prepared to change. At least he didn't have to hear all the banter and orders: that was the only good thing about losing part of his hearing.

He flexed his hands. Maybe everything would be smooth and simple. Arrest Grady and get him back to Millgarth before any trouble began. But it was wishful thinking. They'd be hurling stones and cobbles.

Somewhere, he could hear the bell of a telephone, loud and piercing. Then the night sergeant came in, the colour gone from his face.

'There's been a shooting, sir,' he announced. 'Out at Carr's boot factory. One dead, one wounded.'

Fifteen

Harper looked at Reed. The sergeant was already on his feet and reaching for his hat.

'Have them telephone for an ambulance. I want as many men there as you can find. We're on our way.'

'What about the constables you wanted for tonight, sir?'

'Never mind that now.' Murder trumped everything. 'Whistle up a hackney. We need to be out there quickly.'

He tipped the driver well; they'd made quick time. As they alighted the horse shook its head, flecks of spittle and sweat across its muzzle.

Sugden. It had to be. And he'd timed it well, the light gone, the shifts changing, plenty of men around. Easy targets, simple to escape quickly into the gloom.

But where the hell was the constable who was supposed to be standing guard?

Workers had gathered in the large yard, small groups clustered together in the dusk, the light of cigarettes and pipes marking them out in the darkness. A pair of bobbies were going around, taking statements. Someone had set up oil lamps around the body. A piece of old canvas covered the corpse, no more than a few yards from the gate. Harper walked over, knelt, and pulled the covering away.

The man's chest was a bloody mess. But his face was mostly intact, just small wounds and blood. Bald, with a heavy hawk nose and thin lips. Brown eyes that would never see anything again.

The inspector felt someone watching and turned. A young constable was watching him.

'I'm sorry, sir, but who are you?'

'Detective Inspector Harper. Who was on duty out here?'

'Simpson, sir.' He pointed to a figure standing off by himself.

'I thought two were shot.'

'They've already taken the other one to the infirmary, sir. Not sure if he'll make it, mind. It looked bad.'

Harper strode across to Constable Simpson. 'Where were you when the shooting happened?' he said coldly.

'I had to nip away, sir.' He hung his head. 'Call of nature.'

But his breath told the truth. He stank of whisky. 'Turn out your pockets.'

The last thing Simpson produced was the hip flask. Shamefacedly, he placed it on the ground.

'Go home,' he said. 'You're suspended. You'll be called in for a hearing.'

'Yes, sir,' Simpson said quietly. 'If I'd known . . .' he began.

'If you'd bloody well been where you were supposed to be, there might not be a corpse lying there now.' He stopped. 'Did you see anything at all?'

'I heard the shots and came running. Two of them were lying on the ground. I ran to the gate but I couldn't see anyone. They have a telephone here so I had them ring the infirmary for an ambulance and then the station, sir.'

'Get out of here.'

Dammit, he thought. Too many drunks and incompetents on the bloody force. Now it had cost one life, maybe two.

Plenty of men had seen Sugden. He hadn't tried to hide himself, striding into the yard with his shotgun. One of the witnesses, Mark Kidd, had been too far away to do anything as the man fired. He'd been the first to reach the bodies, yelling out for help.

'Who were they?' Reed asked him.

169

'Luke White.' He nodded at the corpse with a bleak expression. 'He was a foreman.'

'Was he the one who sacked Sugden?'

'That's him.'

'What about the other man?' Harper wondered.

'John Trevelyan.' His voice was flat and empty. 'Been here years, he had.'

'Did he have anything to do with Sugden's sacking?'

'John? No. Just in the wrong place at the wrong time, that's all.'

'Did you see the man with the gun?' the sergeant asked another man.

'Stanley Sugden.' He didn't even hesitate before answering. 'I'd know him anywhere with that bloody beard. He was a menace to himself with all the machines around. Mr White told him over and over, cover it or cut it off. Finally they got into it, started fighting. After Stanley hit him, Mr White didn't have any choice but to sack him.'

Reed stood by the gate, staring over to the far side of Meanwood Road. Plenty of woods along the valley. The perfect place to disappear. More constables had arrived and he'd sent four of them to start questioning the local residents. Someone must have noticed something.

'What do you think, Billy?' the inspector asked.

'If Sugden's a lunatic, he's the slyest one I've ever seen. He picked his time carefully. We don't have a hope in hell of tracking him now. Woods close by . . .' He shook his head.

'It's your case,' Harper told him. 'I'll be here, but you make the decisions. Do whatever you

170

need. Ash is taking statements.' He was about to continue when he felt a touch on his arm and turned. One of the clerks, pale and shaken, trying not to look at the body on the ground.

'Mr Carr would like a word, sir.' He gave a short nod and walked away. The inspector raised his eyebrows at Reed then followed.

Neville Carr's anger exploded as soon as the inspector closed the door. He was pacing around the room, face dark with fury.

'I thought you'd stationed a man out here to stop something like this happening,' he shouted.

'We did, sir. You know that.' He must have seen the constable every day. 'He had to leave his post for a minute sir.' He hated to cover for the man, but this time a lie was better than the truth.

'And now my best foreman's dead and another worker's in hospital.'

'Yes, sir.'

Carr exhaled. Harper knew he had no choice but to take all the abuse Carr could give him.

'What are you doing about it? It was Sugden, wasn't it?'

'It was.'

'Do you know where he is yet?'

'We're looking, sir.'

Carr pointed a stubby finger. 'I'm holding you responsible for finding him.'

'That's my job, sir.'

'I've lost one man. The workers have been standing idle for over an hour. I'm not going to get a damn bit of work from the night shift.'

171

'We're out searching.' Harper kept his voice calm and professional. All the man cared about was getting his money's worth out of his workers. 'And I'll make sure nothing else happens here.'

'Too bloody late now, isn't it?' Carr yelled.

'Yes, sir.' The inspector gritted his teeth. 'If you'll excuse me, I have work to do.'

'I'll be talking to the chief constable.'

He didn't bother to reply. Outside, even the air that stank of leather smelled cleaner than Carr's office.

Luke White's corpse had been removed. Ash was waiting in the yard, his heavy face grave.

'The infirmary sent a message. They couldn't save the other man.'

Harper took a deep breath. 'Right.' He looked down, seeing two broad patches of blood glistening in the failing light, flies buzzing around them. 'Have you told Sergeant Reed?'

'Yes, sir.'

'Let's see what help he needs.'

The sergeant was directing constables. A thin rain was beginning to fall, the bobbies hunched in their capes. He sent a group of them off.

'More house to house?' Harper asked.

'For what it's worth,' Reed sighed. 'We've not found anything so far.'

'Going to scour the woods in the morning?'

'As soon as it's light. God knows there's nothing more we can find here.'

'Keep at it. I'll go and see Dr King about the bodies tomorrow.' He smiled. 'I know it's not your favourite place.'

172

The sergeant grimaced. 'I'd rather be out here.' He glanced up at the sky. 'Even in this. I'll keep them out a little while longer. How did things go with Carr?'

'He tore a strip off me.' Harper shrugged. 'I can't blame him. But he doesn't care about the men, just the time lost. I'll leave it with you, Billy.'

As they waited for the tram, Ash said, 'If our man hadn't been skiving, he might have been dead, too.'

'I know,' the inspector replied. But he'd have been doing his job, and it might have given the workers a chance to escape. It was a disaster, a complete bloody disaster. Two murders. It would be in all the newspapers. A madman on the loose. People would be terrified and he could hardly blame them. Sugden wanted revenge. He'd already had that. But Harper felt certain that the man hadn't finished yet.

They were almost at Sheepscar when he spoke again. The tram was steamy, windows covered in condensation, the air full of the smell of damp wool.

'Tomorrow morning we'll go in and get Grady. When people are at work or getting up.' He grinned. 'We might leave with a few less bruises.' He stood. 'This is my stop. First thing tomorrow.'

The rain had turned steady, dripping off his bowler hat. Reed heard wheels turning and looked around, moving out of the way as Carr left the factory in his carriage.

'What next, Sergeant?' a constable asked.

173

'We've been around the area. The best we've got is someone who might have seen Sugden heading off to the woods. It's not much.'

It was bugger all, Reed thought. A hope and a wish.

'Keep two men asking around,' he ordered. 'And I want someone here. You never know, he might decide to come back for a second helping. You can stand everyone else down for the night. Have them back here in the morning and we'll beat the woods.'

The man nodded.

Even if Sugden was over on the hillside in a little camp, he'd be gone with first light. Maybe he was a lunatic. But he wasn't a bloody fool.

'I'm in the kitchen,' Annabelle shouted as she heard the door. 'I'll be done in a minute.'

Harper hung his mackintosh and hat on the coat rack, glad to be home again. The fire was crackling, the room warm, inviting him to sit.

'You won't believe what's—' she began merrily as she bustled through the door, wiping her hands on her apron. 'What's happened?'

He didn't realize his face was showing the strain of the day.

'We had a shooting. Two men dead.'

'My God.' She brought a hand up to her mouth.

'We know who did it. Catherine Carr's brother. Billy's in charge.'

She sighed. 'Poor Katie. It's like she was cursed, isn't it?'

He put his arms around her. 'We'll find him,' he told her, 'and the one who killed her,' although he had no idea how. Or even how he'd manage to get to the bottom of all these cases. 'Now, what were you going to say?'

She was quiet, reflective for a moment, then answered quietly. 'Miss Ford sent me a note. She wants me to speak again next week. She told me they loved what I had to say.'

'I said you were good.' He gave her a squeeze.

Annabelle blushed. 'I know you did, but . . . I never dreamed they'd want me to do it again. I thought it was just going to be the once, to be kind.'

'You've got something. They listen to you.'

'And now I have to do it all over again,' she said glumly.

'You'll be fine. It'll be easier the second time around.'

'We'll see.' She took hold of his hand, turning it over and examining the palm. 'I'm going to put some more ointment on that. It'll heal faster.'

He smiled, remembering his mother using the same words when he was a small boy.

'Sit down,' Elizabeth said. 'You're like a cat on hot bricks tonight.'

'I can't settle,' Reed told her. 'I keep thinking about Sugden. I need to find him.' He pushed the chair away from the table and stood.

'He'll still be there in the morning. All you're going to do is wear out the floor if you keep pacing like that.'

He nodded and lit a cigarette. She was right, he needed to calm himself. He had to be thinking straight in the morning.

'How was the bakery? Has that lad been showing up to pay off his debt?'

She cleared away the plates. A kettle of water was heating on the hob.

'Jemmy? He's a grand little worker. He was shy at first, but he tries hard. Puts in two hours before school.'

He came up behind her as she stood washing the pots at the chipped stone sink, and his arms circled her waist.

'You've got a soft spot for him, haven't you?'

'He spent most of the first morning saying sorry. I thought he was going to burst into tears. He tries hard.'

'Have you been feeding him?' He nuzzled against her.

'Of course I have. I can't send him off without any breakfast.' She paused. 'One way or another this case of yours will be over soon and you can go back to the brigade. If you still want to,' she added cautiously.

'What do you mean? Of course I do.'

Elizabeth gave a quick nod. 'It's just that you've been wrapped up in this. Is that what it'll be like when you're a fire investigator, too?'

'I don't know.' He honestly had no idea what to expect. He'd seen Inspector Hill working, the detail of his knowledge. It would take a long time to understand that much.

'Will you still be fighting fires as well?' she asked.

'Only the big ones, where they need everyone.'

'But not every day?' There was an hopeful edge to her question.

176

'No,' Reed assured her. 'I don't suppose so. There'll be too many other things.'

'I'm glad about that.' She turned, wiping her hands on her apron before putting them round his neck. 'I worry about you every time you go off to work.'

He'd heard it from the others on the crew; every fireman's wife was the same. Each shift was a gamble. All you could do was pray you'd go home again.

'It'll be fine. I promise.'

'You know, you haven't had a drink in a long time.'

'Yes,' was all he said. Sometimes it was a struggle. When he'd had a bad day. On his way home tonight he'd been tempted. One drink, it wouldn't hurt. Instead he'd waited for the omnibus, letting the feeling slowly pass. He wasn't about to sign the pledge, nothing as daft as that. No making promises he couldn't keep. He'd try. That was all he could do.

Sixteen

Ash had pulled together four bobbies from the night shift, all of them eager for some overtime. Big lads, older, hard men, used to dealing with some of the worst trouble in Leeds. It should be enough, Harper thought, even if the neighbours gave them a problem. In the morning the Bank shouldn't be too dangerous.

It wasn't that far from Millgarth. He led them out, hobnails singing on the cobbles. The men stayed silent as they marched. Not even full light yet. The morning shifts had started at Black Dog and Bank Mills, only a few stragglers taken aback to see them on the streets as they passed. Light from the gas lamps reflected on the cobbles where rain had fallen earlier.

Surrey Street was short, back-to-back houses, only one way in and out of each one. A church hall stood at the end. Harper kept his men standing there for ten minutes, waiting in case anyone was out using the privy.

Finally he led them down, truncheons drawn. A light was burning in number eight. He hammered on the door and took a step back. As soon as it opened, he dashed forward, barging past one man and into the parlour, two of the biggest coppers right behind him.

Four men were gathered around the fire, laughter caught in their throats. One had his hand outstretched, reaching for a bottle. Harper saw a man's eyes shift around, looking for a way out. He darted through, grabbing him by his jacket and pulling so hard that the man fell to his knees. He was young, with pale, wispy side whiskers and a cap on his fair hair.

'Peter Grady,' the inspector told him, 'I'm arresting you on suspicion of rape.'

Grady's friends stood, ready to square up to the police. It only took a few blows from the truncheons to make them think better of it. Harper kept tight hold of Grady, dragging him out into the chilly dawn.

Already a few people were gathering on their doorsteps, drawn by all the noise. Sweating, the inspector snapped the handcuffs on Grady's wrist, tight enough to pinch.

'Right,' Harper ordered his men, 'Let's go.'

They knew enough to move quickly. Around here things could turn ugly in a breath. They hated the police, especially when the coppers were arresting one of their own. The inspector looked up, staring ahead. Four men were standing at the top of the road.

'Keep going,' Harper said. 'Nice and steady.' He kept one hand tight on the chain of the handcuffs, pulling Grady along.

The first stone missed by yards, skidding away. The second was closer.

'You two. Get them.' A pair of bobbies ran and the men scattered quickly. Another stone came from behind, striking one of the uniforms in the back and making him stagger. 'Keep your order.' He kept his voice loud enough to assure the men, in control. A rock caught a constable on the neck. He went down, then stood straight back up again, dazed, blood flowing.

A flurry followed – pebbles, wood, a couple of cobblestones, anything that came to hand. The inspector turned his head and something grazed his cheek, stinging hard. A crowd was growing, men and boys, screaming insults. They were smart about it; close enough to cause some damage, far enough away to disperse if the police charged.

'Go faster,' Harper ordered. They needed to be out of here quickly, before things could grow.

The pace increased to a fast trot. Not running; bobbies never ran away.

It felt like cat and mouse all the way to Marsh Lane. They kept coming near enough to taunt, then quickly melted back. Missiles kept falling. Then finally it stopped, and the footsteps behind them faded away.

The policemen stopped, catching their breath and checking their wounds. Every one of them had been hit, even Grady, with a wound on his scalp, his mouth grim. Harper wiped the blood off his cheek.

Walking wounded. Cuts and bruises; nothing too bad. They'd escaped lightly. He took a tighter grip of the handcuffs.

'Good work,' he told the men, and started the procession back to Millgarth.

Sergeant Tollman delivered Grady down to the cells while the officers drank tea.

'A bit hairy there for a while,' one of them called out. There was nervous laughter around the room.

'We made it, though,' Harper praised them. 'Good discipline.'

'We should have waded in,' the man complained. 'Could have taken a few more of them.'

'Just broken some heads,' another suggested.

He left them to blow off steam. They deserved it. Another few minutes and it could have been much worse. He'd let Grady stew until afternoon before he questioned him.

'I have to thank you, Inspector,' Dr King said. The two bodies from the factory lay on slabs,

180

both covered with old sheets. 'You keep me in business.' He lit a cigar, filling the air with smoke. 'Two together this time.'

'It's not what I'd have chosen,' Harper said.

'None of us knows when we'll go, or how.' King examined the cigar as if he was surprised to see it there. 'It's why I keep on working. God knows I'd rather die in my traces than bored at home.' He raised an eyebrow. 'What am I going to do, raise chrysanthemums in Far Headingley?'

He was surprised to hear the man so reflective. Usually he was brisk and caustic.

'Is there much you can tell me about these two?' he asked.

'You already know they both died from gunshot wounds,' King answered. He stood behind his desk. Papers tottered in a dangerous, untidy pile on one side, the other taken up by a large glass ashtray filled with cigar butts. 'There's nothing more I can tell you.'

'How far away was he when he fired?'

'No more than ten feet,' the doctor replied after a little thought. 'If he knew what he was doing it was impossible to miss.'

'He'd been a soldier.'

King nodded. 'An armed lunatic who's been a soldier,' he mused. 'Not a pleasant combination. I hope you find him soon, Inspector.'

'That makes two of us,' Harper told him.

'Let me take a look at that cheek. Nasty cut.' He took a bottle from a shelf and a piece of cloth from the pocket of his coat. 'This will hurt a little,' he warned.

It did, enough to make him flinch.

'Don't be a baby,' King told him, moving away. 'It'll stop any infection.'

'Thank you.'

'One more thing, Inspector, since it's just the two of us here.'

'What?'

The doctor smiled. 'That hearing problem of yours is growing worse, isn't it?'

Harper raised his head in surprise.

'I'm a physician,' King continued gently. 'I know you think I spend all my time with dead bodies, but I keep an eye on the living, too. I'm right, aren't I?'

'Yes,' he admitted after a moment. 'But—'

'But what?'

'Who else knows?' He took a slow breath. He didn't want this on his record. It could lead to dismissal, unfit for duty.

'I've no idea. I haven't told anyone. I'm not about to, either, if that's what worries you.'

'Thank you.' He felt abjectly, stupidly grateful.

'Have you seen anyone about it?'

'Dr Kent. He said there's probably not much to be done.'

'Kent is good,' King said with a nod. 'You won't remember Charlie Graham, will you?'

'No. Who was he?'

'A superintendent with B Division. Must have been, what, twenty years ago now. Before your time. Stone deaf in his left ear.'

'What happened to him?' Harper asked.

'Nothing,' the man said triumphantly. 'He was good at his job. No reason to let him go just

182

because he couldn't hear too well.' He raised an eyebrow. 'Food for thought, Inspector.'

'Yes.' He turned to leave. As he placed his hand on the doorknob he heard King say, 'I wouldn't be surprised if the men you work with knew about your problem. It's hard to hide, you know.'

'You're Peter Grady?' Harper asked.

The man sat in the interview room, the handcuffs tight on his wrists. He was thin, a spare, bony man. Curly fair hair and an attempt to grow mutton chop whiskers, like fluff on his face. Something to make him look older

'Yes.' The s came out as *th*. A lisp. Just as Nellie Rider had described. Ash was going to escort the girl down here after her shift at Armley Mill. It would be confirmation. But the inspector was already certain he had his man.

'You've been hard to find. You haven't shown up for work, you've disappeared from your lodgings.'

Grady shrugged. 'I'd had enough.'

Harper paced, moving behind the man. 'I don't believe you, Peter.'

'It's the truth,' Grady protested.

'You vanished after you raped someone in the Arches.' He kept his voice even, sounding reasonable. 'When that happens they're usually guilty.'

'I never.' But there was weakness and defeat in his voice.

'You had a knife. You threatened to kill her.' The inspector brought a blade from his waistcoat pocket. They'd taken it off the man before they put him in the cell. 'Is that yours?'

183

'Yes.' That sibilant sound again. 'You know it is.'

'You threatened to kill her. Just like the other woman in the Arches.' He waited, but Grady remained silent. 'Well?'

'No.' He was looking down.

'It's not going to look good for you in court. You run away, almost start a riot when we try to bring you in. It's going to add a lot to your sentence. And if you murdered the other woman down there it'll be hanging for you.'

'What?' He started to rise and the constable standing guard at the door began to move forward. Harper put a hand on Grady's shoulder and pushed him back down.

'How was it when you killed her, Peter? Did you feel powerful? Did you get a taste for it? Is that why you went back to the Arches? You were going to kill that second girl, weren't you?'

'I never killed no one!' He shouted the words.

'Why was Catherine Carr down there? Did she say? How did you find her?'

The man shook his head.

'Did she struggle, Peter?' he pressed. 'Is that why you used your knife on her? How long before the fire was it?'

'I didn't,' Grady roared.

This was easier than he'd expected. The man had no fight in him.

'You did. And I'll see you in court for it.'

'I wan't even there that night.'

Harper leaned forward so his mouth was close to Grady's ear. 'Not a big leap from rape to murder. Or are you still going to deny that, too?'

184

'I . . .' The air had gone out of him. 'I raped that lass. If she's so bloody stupid she dun't ask for the money first, she gets what she deserves.'

Harper smiled. 'And the killing? How did you do that?'

Grady turned his head to look up at the inspector.

'I din't. Honest, I wan't there. All I knew was what people said.' He was almost in tears, desperate to be believed.

'Where were you the night of the fire?'

'Out.' His voice was low.

'Where?'

'Drinking.'

'You didn't go drinking alone, Peter.'

'Friends. Lads I know.'

'I need their names. And what happened later.' There was more, he could sense it.

'I went down to Butts Court.'

It was a small street running off the Headrow. A good place to find prostitutes. God, he thought, Nellie wasn't his first rape.

'What did you do there?' He wanted to hear the man say it.

'She was stupid.' Grady almost spat the words.

'That's not an excuse,' Harper told him coldly. 'You raped her.'

The man stared straight ahead, lips pushed tight together.

'Two rapes,' the inspector said thoughtfully, then paused for a heartbeat. 'How many more, Peter? How many more do you want to plead to?'

'None.'

'You'll feel better if you tell me, Peter. Get it off your chest.' He made it sound like an invitation. 'Are you sure?'

'Yes.'

They'd been searching the woods for two hours before they found the camp. It was a small bivouac, well hidden among the trees, branches carefully placed together to give shelter. There was no sign of a fire, but that was hardly surprising. It had rained, the wood was damp, and Sugden wouldn't have wanted anyone to know he was there. He'd been trained to make camp with no blaze, to live wild.

Reed knelt, feeling the ground. Still damp, although the grass was bent. He couldn't tell how long since someone had been here. The man could have left this morning or in the middle of the night. Whenever he'd gone, they were on a hiding to nothing looking around here. Sugden was wily. He was long gone.

There was no clue, not a trace of anything around. Steps through the grass led to a path, but from there . . . he couldn't even begin to guess. The sergeant took off his bowler hat and ran a hand through his hair.

Reed had wanted this case. He'd asked for it. When the man had shot off a round at the funeral, he believed he'd have the kind of understanding of Sugden's mind that other copper couldn't manage.

Now he knew just what a mistake he'd made. Two men were dead. He'd read the stories in the newspapers that morning. **Lunatic On The**

Loose. **Mad Killer In Leeds**. Guaranteed to terrify everyone and have them watching out.

How could he burrow into Sugden's mind and discover what he was thinking? Revenge, that's what the man had said. But who knew what he saw as slights, who he had grudges against?

The bobbies were waiting for orders. Their uniforms were sodden from the tall wet grass. They looked cold and unhappy.

'Carry on to the end of the woods,' he told them. It was only a couple of hundred yards. 'Call it a day here after that. Go and get yourselves warm.'

That cheered them. A few smiles, the will to work returning now the end was in sight. But where the hell did they look after this?

Harper stared out of the window of the omnibus, not even certain why he was travelling back to Adel. Maybe there was something more that Miss Ford could tell him. Something she didn't even realize. God knew he was running out of options.

And the journey gave him a chance to think about Dr King's words. Did the others know about his hearing? He thought he'd always concealed it well. Did Superintendent Kendall know?

Sooner or later he'd have to admit it. At least now he knew about an officer who'd kept his job even though he was deaf. It gave him a little heart. Once this was done and Catherine Carr's killer was in jail, he'd tell the super. Her face slipped into his mind and he shivered.

'Someone walk over your grave?' the man next to him asked jovially.

'I hope not,' he answered with a sad smile.

Miss Ford was in the library, going through her correspondence. A pile of letters waited for her attention, and her nib flew across the paper. It was a comfortable room, the fire roaring, shelves all the way to the ceiling, lined with books. The window looked out on a bare autumn garden of greens and browns, piles of dead leaves neatly raked.

As soon as she saw him she stood, hope in her eyes.

'Have you found him?' she asked, her face falling as he shook his head.

'I wish I had some good news.'

He told her what he'd discovered, wondering if any of it might jog something in her mind. But she just listened attentively.

'Tell me,' he said when he'd finished, 'have you received any threats?'

Miss Ford smiled. 'Me personally? Or the Suffragist Society?'

'Both.'

'You don't get change without annoying people, Inspector. And if you don't upset people, you're not trying hard enough.'

'What were they? Letters?'

'Letters, notes, all manner of things.'

'Have you kept them?'

'A few. Most are rants, not even worth the paper they're written on. If I thought they were important I'd have shown you before.'

188

'I'd still like to see them.'

She nodded and went over to a cabinet, digging through the files on a shelf.

'Have you told the police about them?' Harper asked.

'Why?' She handed him the folder. It was half an inch thick. Many of the notes were scrawled, a few well-formed. 'I've seen how effective your force has been at our meetings.'

He'd apologized for that before; he wasn't going to do it again.

'Can I take these?'

'If you like.' She shrugged. 'I wouldn't take them too seriously, Inspector. If they were real, they'd have acted on them.'

'Perhaps someone found an easier target,' he told her.

She was silent for a long time.

'I hope not,' Miss Ford said quietly. 'I'd rather someone had killed me.' She cleared her throat. 'But honestly, I've never paid too much heed to those.' She nodded at the folder. 'Let them get it off their chest if that's what they want. We'll win in the end.'

He didn't believe her. If she was so unconcerned, why had she kept them?

'I'll look into them,' Harper said as he stood.

'Your wife is a remarkable speaker,' she said.

He smiled. 'She's a remarkable woman.'

'Did she tell you I've asked her to speak again?'

'She did.'

'I think she's an excellent addition to our platform.'

'I'll tell her you said so.'

The woman returned his smile. 'Please do, Mr Harper. And I hope you find Catherine's killer very soon.'

'We're doing everything we can.'

She looked into his eyes and nodded slowly.

'I believe you.' She took his hand in her own. 'And I wish you well.'

Thirty letters. They ranged from barely legible, misspelled venom about women to pages of argument written in careful copperplate that still made no sense. Just reading them made his head reel. When he'd finished he put them all away then went and washed his hands. He felt dirty, tainted. Staring in the mirror he laughed. Every day he dealt with the worst people could do to each other. But it took words to make him feel unclean. Stupid.

Still, he understood why Miss Ford wasn't too worried. The men who wrote the letters might rage or feel they were right, but they weren't the type to act. No signatures, no addresses. They were scared little men, fearful of a changing world. But not killers. They'd only have courage with a pen in their hand, where they could stay anonymous. Compared to them, the men standing quietly outside the meetings were brave.

Another road that led nowhere. Just like all the others in this bloody case. After half an hour he took out his pocket watch, winding it as he glanced at the time, then stood.

'Tom!' the superintendent called.

The office was wreathed in smoke from

190

Kendall's pipe. He could smell the pomade from the man's hair.

'Close the door and sit down. What's going on about Sugden?'

'Reed and Ash are searching.'

'The chief constable wants me in charge of the investigation. It'll show we're serious.'

Harper nodded. Billy wouldn't be happy, but he knew it made sense. They'd never had anything like this in Leeds before. Two men shot dead. In cold blood, out in the open. It needed a senior officer. Kendall might spend most of his time behind a desk now, but he'd been a good detective; he'd taught Harper his trade.

'Every officer has Sugden's description,' the superintendent continued. 'We're running sweeps through each division.'

'He knows how to hide. Just ask Billy.'

'I will,' Kendall told him. 'I've talked to Dick Hill, we can keep Reed until Sugden's caught.'

'That's good.'

The superintendent sat back. 'You've looked for him. What do you think?'

Harper shook his head. 'He's smart. Cunning. You'll have your work cut out trying to find him.'

'What do you think he'll do?'

'I don't know. Billy might have more idea.'

Kendall nodded. 'What progress have you made on the Carr murder?'

'Nothing,' he replied in frustration. 'We caught the rapist from the Arches, but he's not the killer.'

'What leads do you have?'

They discussed the case for ten minutes, the superintendent taking notes.

191

'What are the chances of solving this?' Kendall asked finally. 'Be honest, Tom.'

He didn't want to answer. Each day he felt that the likelihood of finding the murderer was slipping farther and farther away. But the image of Katie Carr after they pulled the rubble off her body, half-skin, half-metal, wouldn't leave him alone. He woke in the night and saw it. He had to discover the person responsible for that.

'I'll find him,' he said finally and saw Kendall nod. He understood the way some cases wormed under the skin.

'And the dead baby?'

The inspector shook his head. 'I thought we had something but it hasn't panned out yet.' Like everything lately, it was trying to grasp clouds.

'Keep at it.'

'I will.'

There was noise in the office as Reed and Ash returned.

'Send the sergeant in, Tom.' Before the inspector could leave there was another question. 'Tell me, do you think Reed's heart is in this?'

'Oh yes,' he replied with no hesitation. 'No doubt about that.'

Boar Lane was busy. Men in bowler hats, top hats, a few trying to cling to summer with straw boaters. Buses and trams ploughed by and the hackney carriages tried to save time, dodging around the wagons, horses plodding under their loads or boys pushing small carts as they ran.

He crossed the road, trying to avoid the piles

of horse dung that littered the street. The Griffin Hotel seemed like an oasis, as hushed as a bank or library.

Barnabas Tooms sat at his usual table, a mustard yellow waistcoat stretched across his large belly, luxuriant whiskers combed out over his cheeks. He looked well-fed and self-satisfied. But he was a man with information. Harper took a deep breath before he sat down.

'Twice in just a few days,' Tooms said with a condescending smile. 'Should I be flattered or worried?'

'You said Neville Carr had a mistress.' He didn't want to exchange any pleasantries with the man. One day they'd find proof that Tooms was breaking the law and it would be a pleasure to throw him into a cell. Now, though, the inspector needed his knowledge. And he loathed himself for it.

'That's right.' The man moved a little more upright and took a sip from a glass of beer. 'What about it?'

'I'd like her name.'

Tooms took a cigar from the pocket of his suit jacket and made a performance of lighting it.

'What's in it for me?'

'A favour in the future.' Selling his soul, he thought.

The man rubbed a hand across his chin. 'All right. Her name's Bertha Davis. She lives in Headingley.'

Harper stared at him. 'Street?' If he had to be in debt to this man, it was going to be worthwhile.

'Bennett Road.'

The inspector nodded. He could find her from there.

'Will you have a drink with me, Inspector?'

'No, Mr Tooms. I won't.'

The man inclined his head.

'Your choice. I'll let you know when the bill is due.'

Reed trudged through the mud by the canal path. He was supervising the men scouring the area from the centre of Leeds out towards Armley. Three on each side of the water, slashing at the long grass and undergrowth with sticks.

He'd spent an hour with Kendall, going over the map of Leeds, answering questions about Sugden, making suggestions.

'He's not anywhere around people,' the sergeant said. 'I'm sure of that. Someone would have seen him and reported it. He's keeping his distance. We need to search every piece of woodland.'

The superintendent sighed. 'We don't have enough men for it. It would be impossible in the big parks, anyway.'

'Then let's do what we can,' Reed said urgently. 'We can flush him out.'

'He might come out shooting.'

The sergeant looked at Kendall. 'Which is better, sir? Shooting at us or at civilians?'

The superintendent grimaced and nodded. 'Go ahead, then. I'll send out squads to look.'

And now Reed was by the canal. Another group, led by Constable Ash, was heading down to Knostrop. There were coppers beating bushes

194

in Gotts Park, Gledhow Woods, out by Kirkstall Abbey. Maybe they'd get a glimpse and force him out into the open. Maybe not. But at least they were doing something.

A squall of rain passed and he ducked under the trees for shelter, his gaze shifting around the ground and finding nothing.

'Sarge! Over here!'

It was one of the men from the far side of the canal. Reed had to dash to the lock and edge his way across, water close on one side, a long drop on the other. The constable was standing by a camp, hidden from the towpath by bushes. It was the same type of bivouac he'd seen in Meanwood, quick to put up, easy to leave.

'It's this, sir. Caught the light.' He knelt and held up a shotgun shell.

'Very good,' the sergeant said. There were the remains of a small fire. He placed his hand on the ashes. Still a little warmth. Sugden hadn't been gone more than two hours. But where? 'Spread the line wider,' he ordered. 'He's been here. Maybe he's still somewhere close.' He looked at the men who'd gathered round him. 'Keep your wits about you. He's armed.'

Reed watched as they moved away. It wasn't success, but it was a small start. Everyone home safe, he thought.

Neville Carr had done his mistress proud, Harper decided. A decent through terrace house on a good street in Headingley. Bertha Davis. An actress. That was what the neighbours claimed, although no one had ever seen her perform in anything. The man visited her twice a week, Tuesday and Thursday afternoons, staying until early evening.

'Pulls up in a hackney and walks in, bold as brass,' the woman three doors down told him. 'Dun't even bother knocking on the door.'

'How about other callers?' he asked.

She folded her arms and smiled. 'Two who come regular. Gentlemen.' She pronounced the word with spiteful relish. She had little more to say about Carr, and nothing kind about Miss Davis.

'Right little madam, she is. Never a good morning or how are you. Acts like she's Lady Muck.' The woman glanced along the street. 'She ought to know better. There's always a time when you need your friends round here.'

He hadn't called on the woman. He wasn't even sure why he wanted to know about her. The way Carr had acted after the shooting, perhaps, his lack of concern for the victims. Something about the man rubbed him the wrong way. Or because everything was worth knowing on a case where he felt he knew nothing at all.

There was nothing to connect Neville Carr to Katie's murder. But there wasn't any evidence to tie anyone to it. The inspector was clutching at every straw and he knew it. And he prayed one of them might be the right one.

By seven he was exhausted, grateful to drag himself up the stairs at the Victoria. The living room was warm and welcoming, a fire burning in the grate, curtains drawn against the night.

'Tom?' Annabelle called from the bedroom.

'It's only me.' He place his palm against the teapot. Still hot. He poured a cup and slumped into an armchair. She bustled through, dressed in a elegant burgundy gown with a small bustle, fastening a bracelet around her wrist as she bent to kiss him.

'Is that dress new?' he asked. He couldn't recall seeing it before.

'I had a quick trip to the Grand Pygmalion.' She smiled and him, and twirled around. 'Do you like it?'

'It suits you,' he told her admiringly. 'What is it tonight? Another meeting?'

'Licensed victuallers,' she answered with a sigh. 'You know what that means.'

'A bunch of landlords drinking as much as they can.'

'I have to show my face. It's good for business. Just for a little while, though. I won't be late.'

'Do you want me to come with you?'

Annabelle grinned. 'You don't look as if you could move, let alone have a good time.'

'That's true enough.'

'Anyway, I need to make them all jealous when I announce we'll be on that first tram to Roundhay Park.'

'I hope it's worth it. All that food and drink's going to cost a fortune.'

'And the memories will be cheap at twice the price. How many will be able to say they rode the first electric tram, eh?' She came and kissed him lightly. He smelled her scent, something delicate with a touch of lemon. 'I'd better get going or they'll all be gossiping about me.'

The nudge on his shoulder woke him and he struggled to open his eyes. The cup of tea was still there, cold. Annabelle was unpinning her hat.

'Go to bed,' she told him gently.

'I will,' he mumbled. 'How was the meeting?'

She shrugged. 'Same as usual. Everyone talking and no one listening. Ducked out as soon as I could.'

He stood and stretched. 'Are you coming?'

'In a little while. I thought I'd read first.'

'I had an interesting talk with Dr King today,' he said.

'Interesting?' she asked in astonishment. 'I thought he only talked about dead people.'

'He'd guessed about my hearing.' She stared at him. 'He says he's probably not the only one, either.'

'No one else has mentioned anything?'

Harper shook his head.

'Not a word. But he told me about a superintendent who was deaf in one ear and kept his job.'

'That's good, isn't it?'

'I hope so,' he said. 'I'm going to have to tell the super sooner or later. Every time I'm out I miss something. A word, a whole sentence sometimes.'

'I know.' She took his hand. 'I know.'

Seventeen

Two days of searching for Sugden, and no more trace of him. Harper heard the complaints and grumbles from the constables who had to spend their shifts wading through mud and bushes on the hunt.

He saw it in the frustration and anger on Reed's face when he came in to the station, Ash trailing behind him, and sat talking with Kendall. It was like searching a hundred haystacks on the trail of a single needle.

The newspapers were hounding the police and demanding action. All they managed was to whip up fear. People sent in notes, saying they'd seen Sugden here, there, everywhere around Leeds. Constables were sent. But it was never him, just a waste of time they could have spent elsewhere.

And Harper's luck was no better. Still nothing in the Catherine Carr case. He'd dug into Neville Carr's family. It didn't take long to discover a few things about his son, Gordon. He was in his early twenties. Didn't have a job, seemed to spend most of his time with his friends, out drinking. He'd been arrested several times when he was eighteen and nineteen. Fighting, drunken behaviour, insulting a policeman. Once an accusation of rape that had been dropped. Harper was willing to bet that Tooms was behind that. There'd been

199

nothing in the police records for a couple of years, but the inspector doubted he'd suddenly become a law-abiding citizen. Tooms was just more efficient, heading off trouble early. All to help Neville Carr's political career.

The rumours about Gordon were easy to track. 'Fifty pound,' a man in Holbeck told him. 'A man come over, cash in his hand. That's how much he give us. Right there, as long as we said no more about it.' Behind him, in the house, Reed could hear a baby crying as a woman tried to soothe it. 'That's a lot of money.'

It was a year's wages for a working man. A fortune. Too much to resist. And there was more, like the man in Chapeltown who'd been beaten and dropped the charges.

'Ten pounds and they paid for the doctor,' he explained, looking down at the ground. There was a pale scar on his cheek.

Other sums paid to stop charges of vandalism and theft. Gordon Carr seemed like a spoilt child. Maybe he'd grow out of it in time, Harper thought. Marry and take on some responsibility. But most likely the man would never change. He'd seen it before. All he cared about was the moment, his own pleasure. Money could take care of the rest. The bills didn't matter.

Robert Carr the wife-beater, his son the ambitious man who cared little for his workers, and his grandson a wastrel. It wasn't an attractive family. He pitied Katie Carr. All she'd wanted was some security and she'd ended up with Carr. Then dead.

None of it helped him find her killer. But every

piece of information had its value. If not now, then later.

Another morning, grey and dismal with the threat of rain. Harper saw Reed and the super studying the map of Leeds, pointing at different areas. It was a wild goose chase and they both knew it. But what else could they do? Sugden had vanished. The only real chance was to catch him quickly when he came out again.

Sugden's revenge wasn't complete yet. That was what they all believed. They were waiting and hoping they were ready.

'Sir?' Williams, the constable from Cross Green, stood by his desk.

'Sorry, I was thinking.' It was true enough, even if he hadn't heard the man. 'Have you found something?'

'Maybe,' the copper answer slowly. 'There's a family moved into the manor a little while back. Call themselves Wilson. Mother, father, daughter.'

'That's interesting.' It fitted with the Waites. 'What else have you found out about them?'

'Nothing, really, sir. Keep themselves to themselves, the neighbours say.'

'Could be worth a visit.'

Williams smiled. 'I was hoping you'd think so, sir.'

It was an easy enough walk, heading up to St Hilda's like a beacon at the top of the hill.

'They're on Lucas Street, sir. It's a nothing place, blink and you miss it.'

'Show me,' Harper told him. He could feel it

inside, this was the one; he'd find Barbara Waite, the girl who'd bundled up her dead baby and put him in the post.

Williams was right. Lucas Street was barely there, a road of six houses off South Accommodation Road, running along the hillside. He stood for a moment looking down into Hunslet below, then followed the constable, waiting as he knocked on the door.

It took a long time until someone answered, then a girl was standing there. She was in her middle teens, thin-faced and dark-haired, with quick, nervous eyes. Her old dress was shapeless, faded and forlorn, her feet in woollen stockings, but no shoes.

As soon as he saw her, he knew. She did, too. Panic crossed her face and she started to close the door. Harper reached out and pushed to keep it open.

'Hello, Barbara. I've been looking for you. I think we need to have a talk.'

'I thought if I took him to the hospital, people would say I'd killed him.' Her eyes were pleading. It hadn't taken long to get the story, how her labour had started and her mother had come to help. The baby stillborn, not breathing even after they slapped him. 'I knew what they thought of me,' she continued. Once she'd begun it all came in a torrent. 'I could see it. And that bloody Holy Joe as come around, he was the worst.'

'Mr Martin?' Harper asked.

She nodded. 'That's the one. Always going on

202

about how I was a sinner when all I wanted was to make enough to live.'

He sat at the table and listened.

'Why did you think people would say you'd murdered your son?' he asked finally.

'Because that's how it is, in't it?' Mr Waite began. 'I've heard about it.' His thick arms were resting on the table, fists loosely bunched.

'If you'd gone to the infirmary they'd have looked after you. Plenty lose their children at birth,' he said gently. Mr Waite snorted. 'It's true,' Harper continued. He wasn't even sure how to ask the next question. 'What made you send him in a parcel like that?'

'Reckoned someone would find him and bury him, and no one would trace it back to our lass,' Waite told him bluntly. 'Look after your own, that's what you have to do. Even one like her.' He nodded at his daughter.

'What now?' Barbara asked quietly. 'Are you going to arrest me?'

What was he going to do? He'd heard her story and he believed it. She'd been scared. She was still terrified. What she'd done was a crime, but he understood her reasons. The child had been dead anyway; Dr King had agreed with that. What would anyone gain by putting her in court? What would she learn in jail?

'No,' he said eventually.

Barbara burst into tears, and her mother put an arm around her shoulders to comfort her.

'Thank you, sir,' she said, biting her lip.

Waite kept his expression straight, showing nothing as Harper stood.

'I think this will be one of those things that's never solved,' the inspector said. 'How about you, Constable?'

'Yes, sir,' he agreed readily. 'Pity we could never find the lass.'

Harper tipped his hat as they left. Outside, he sighed deeply.

'Would have been a shame to put her behind bars for that,' Williams said.

'Yes.' He shook his head. 'Best we forget we ever found them.' He winked.

'Fine by me, sir. Hope you enjoyed your walk around here. Shame it came to nowt.'

'God, Tom,' Annabelle said softly when he told her about the girl. They were sitting on the settee. Her head rested on his chest, legs curled up underneath her dress. 'Can you imagine what that poor girl went through?'

'I saw her face.'

She squeezed him gently. 'I'm glad you didn't take her in.'

'What would be the point? She's already suffered. Their only crime is ignorance.'

'And fear.'

He nodded slowly. 'That too. You know, it always surprises me when people are so scared of us.'

'Why?' She shifted, sitting up and looking at him. 'You enforce the laws, and they're made by the rich. Agreed?'

'Yes.'

'And those laws protect the rich.'

'They're meant to protect everyone. That's the

204

point. That's what I do.' He gave a brief smile. 'You sound like one of your books.'

Annabelle thought for a moment, going over the words she'd spoken. Then she threw her head back and laughed. 'Oh God, I do, don't I?' She shook her head, amazed at what she'd said. 'I'm sorry. But there's truth in it, you've got to admit.'

'Not in my work.'

'No?' she asked.

He thought about Gordon Carr, the family money buying him out of trouble.

'Sometimes,' he admitted. He was about to say more when she turned her head. He heard a knock on the door and Dan came in followed by Constable Stone. It couldn't be good news.

'You're needed down in town, sir,' he said seriously. 'There's a hackney outside for you.'

'What is it?' If they'd ordered a cab it had to be serious.

'A man on Briggate with a shotgun. He's been firing at people.'

Oh Christ, he thought. He'd been dreading something like this.

'Anyone hurt?'

'Three people injured,' Stone said seriously. 'They've been taken to the infirmary.' He glanced down. 'Two dead.'

Annabelle gasped.

'Sugden?' he asked.

'Sounds like it, sir. Long beard, looks ragged. He ran off into the courts. The sergeant said you know that area.'

'It was my beat back when I was in uniform.

I'll go straight there. I want messages sent to Sergeant Reed and Constable Ash.'

'Already done, sir. The superintendent is on his way.'

'I'll be there in a few minutes.'

He was pulling on the mackintosh when he felt her breath on his neck. He turned, and Annabelle held him tight.

'Just be careful, Tom. Please. This isn't sticks and stones.'

'I will.' He kissed her. 'Promise.'

Eighteen

He walked quickly, grim-faced. The night had turned cold, the scent of rain close by. Briggate was eerily empty, just the trams and omnibuses clanking by. No people walking. Just policemen crowded around the corner of Commercial Street.

Kendall was standing and directing his men, top hat shiny under the gas lamps. The smell of bay rum hair pomade wafted through the air. An ambulance stood on the road, the horse waiting patiently as two men placed a stretcher inside.

'Have they found him yet?' Harper asked.

The superintendent shook his head slowly. 'Ran off down Rose and Crown Yard. Some men took off after him but they stopped when he fired at them.'

Harper look around. Small dark pools of blood on the pavement, more spattered all around. Light glistened on tiny pellets of lead shot from the gun.

'What about the people he shot?'

'Carnage,' Kendall answered quietly. 'Two of them dead, three more wounded. No rhyme or reason to it. The witnesses said he just seemed to appear and start shooting.'

'Do we know who the victims are?' Maybe one of them had slighted Sugden long ago and the grudge had simmered until it boiled over.

The superintendent pulled a small notebook from his waistcoat.

'Michael Samuels. A jeweller. He's dead. His wife took some shot in her arm and leg. A piece in the eye, too. She might lose her sight. Seems her husband moved in front of her when Sugden aimed or she'd probably be dead, too. Bad enough as it is.' He sighed. 'The other one he killed is William Wright. A clerk in Holbeck. Nobody, just out for the evening. The other two he hit aren't too bad, thank God. Why, Tom? Do you understand it?'

He wished he did. He walked around. From the bloodstains on the ground, the people must have been close together. Taken by surprise, no chance to run. They hadn't stood a chance.

'Tom?'

He turned. Kendall was looking at him. He must have spoken; Harper hadn't heard.

'Sorry, sir.'

'Can you make sense of it?'

'No,' he answered. But how could you make sense of anything a madman did? 'How many do we have hunting him?'

'Six. It's all the sergeant could pull together quickly. I want you in charge of them. Search every court behind Briggate.'

'He could have cut through and run off somewhere else.'

'I know that,' Kendall said testily. 'But we're going to be thorough. I want him caught. And make sure no one else is killed.'

'Yes, sir.'

'Reed and Ash will be along soon and there are ten more uniforms on their way. Split them up, go through everything. Keep going until we find him. I'm off to the infirmary.'

Faces gawped through the windows as a tram passed. The bodies had already been taken to Hunslet. All that remained was the blood.

Harper beckoned to one of the constables standing guard.

'Are any of the witnesses still here?'

'One, sir. Over there.'

He pointed at a man leaning against the dirty bricks, a thin fellow with grey hair, a patchy beard, and a twitching mouth.

'Sir?' the inspector asked, and the man raised his head. Someone had brought him a glass of brandy from one of the public houses. He held it cupped in his hands, taking tiny, nervous sips. 'I'm Detective Inspector Harper.' The man gave a hint of a nod. 'Can I have your name please, sir?'

'Page.' The man's voice was a thin croak. 'Harold Page.'

'I'm sorry, Mr Page,' the inspector said quietly. 'I'm sure it must have been terrible, but I need to know what you saw.'

It took time, the man speaking in fits and starts, nipping at the brandy after every sentence. Sugden was striding down Briggate, carrying the gun. It seemed like he'd come out of nowhere. People moved away as soon as they saw him. Everyone was running and screaming. Page had ducked into the passage leading down to Whitelock's.

Sugden stopped at the corner of Commercial Street, raised the gun and shot, one barrel, then the other. He looked at the people he'd hit, then ran back up the street.

'Did he seem to be looking for anyone in particular?' the inspector asked.

'No.' Page took another little sip then shook his head. 'Not at all.'

There was nothing more to learn from the man. Harper thanked him and started up Briggate. It must have been crowded as Sugden began to walk. Then people noticed him, and started to flee. He could picture the terror on their faces, the desperate scramble to save themselves.

How could you know what a madman would do, he wondered? How could anyone even begin to understand? Kendall had been right: there was no rhyme to this, no reason. It had just been slaughter for its own sake.

A uniformed sergeant was organizing the new coppers as they arrived.

'Where do you want them, sir?' he asked.

'Have them work their way through all the courts towards Lands Lane,' Harper ordered. 'Groups of two. I want everything searched. I mean *everything* – every building, every pile of

209

rubbish.' He stared at the constables. 'Watch yourselves. He's armed and he probably has more ammunition.'

He was watching them leave when a hand tapped his shoulder.

'I came as soon as I could,' Reed told him. He was wearing an old jacket, no collar, and scuffed boots.

'It's bad.' He summed up what had happened. 'We've got uniforms searching.'

'You know what Sugden's like, he's probably vanished.'

'Very likely,' the inspector agreed grimly. Sugden might be a lunatic but he knew how to survive. 'He likes to hide where there are woods. There's nothing like that around here. Ash will be here soon. Work with him. This was his beat before he became a detective, he knows it as well as anyone.'

'What about you?'

'I'm going to see someone.'

He picked his way through the rubbish in Fidelity Court. Oil lamps still burned in some of the houses. He knocked on a door and waited until it was opened by a heavy woman holding up a lantern.

'Hello, Ginny,' he said. She raised the light higher to see his face and snorted as she recognized him.

'Mr Harper,' Ginny Dempsey said. 'Still Inspector, is it, or are you Chief Constable by now?'

'I've not made the dizzy heights yet. You heard what happened?'

'Course I did. Do you think I'm daft? You've been away from here too long.'

'There are two people dead, Ginny. I need the man who did it.'

'Only been two through here in the last hour.'

He smiled. If anyone knew all the business in this court, it was her. 'Who?'

'Arthur Brennan, just passing through on his way to the Leopard Hotel. And someone else, not seen him before.'

'What did he look like?'

'Can't see too well back here. We don't have the gas.'

No lamps to light the way, just the moon and hope.

'Come on, I know you.'

'Aye, well,' she said. 'Beard, carrying summat. About your height, I suppose.'

'How long ago?' Harper asked urgently.

'Half an hour, maybe more. I wasn't keeping track.'

The time fitted. 'Where did he go?'

'Out past old Clem's. Cutting through, most like.'

He thought quickly. That ginnel led to so many places, ending up on Swan Street.

'If he comes back, I need to know as soon as possible. There are coppers going all round here, just find one of them. But keep yourself out of his way.'

'I will, don't you worry about that.'

'He's dangerous, Ginny. I'm not joking.'

Harper moved on, going slowly through the narrow passage between the houses. There was no room there for Sugden to hide. He blundered on, tripping and steadying himself against a wall. A few years ago he could have followed the path wearing a blindfold. Back in those days this had been his beat and he'd known every inch of it. Every smell, every sound. Now it was half a memory.

The inspector came out into Swan Street, turning a corner to find bright lights and people moving around, the press of a crowd leaving Thornton's Music Hall. But no Sugden.

He walked back down to Briggate, then the hundred yards to the corner of Commercial Street. There was only one copper left there now, standing under the lamp. Everyone else was searching.

He rubbed his palms across his eyes, trying to push the tiredness away. When the men were done here, he'd spread them out. There was so much to cover. In his gut, though, he knew Sugden was already far away.

And it had begun when he went out to Menston to tell Sugden that his sister was dead. It was as if the news had turned some sort of switch. But it seemed a very long, twisted path from a woman whose skin shone like silver to a man killing at random with a shotgun.

He took out his pocket watch. Quarter past eleven. It was going to be a long night. They'd be out until dawn, poking into everything. Flickering lights through all the courts. Where would he go if he was Sugden? Somewhere well away from here, to leave the police flailing around.

But he wasn't a madman. There was no telling what someone like that might do. He could be waiting somewhere, the gun cocked, ready . . .

The constable was pulling at his arm.

'What?'

'Some shouting, sir. Back in there.' He nodded towards the courts hidden behind the shops.

Now he could just make it out, on the edge of his hearing.

'Thank you.'

Harper started to run. The sound grew louder at the end of a ginnel and he followed it, ducking through two more courts then moving quickly to a third. Two constables were holding a man, yelling at him.

'Who have you found?'

One of the coppers held up a lantern. 'Looks like it could be him, sir.'

But it wasn't. He had a long beard, but he was older, stooped. A man Harper recognized from years ago. He tried to dredge the name out of his memory.

'It's not. You can let him go.'

Willie Woods. It came to him. A drunk with no real home. He dossed in rooming houses when he had a few pennies, and anywhere he could when he had nothing. The inspector took two pennies from his pocket and put them in Woods's hand.

'Find yourself a bed, Willie. You'll be safer indoors tonight.'

Not the right man, but at least they'd found someone. That would give them some heart. He walked on, seeing coppers everywhere. Finally he caught up with Reed and Ash.

'Looks like all they've managed to dig up is old Willie Woods.'

'Must have scared him,' Ash said with a laugh. 'Once Willie's asleep, nothing can rouse him.'

'We've found nothing,' Reed said.

'Ginny Dempsey saw Sugden going through Fidelity Court. But there's no sign of him.'

'Gone,' was all the sergeant said.

'Time to spread out a bit, I think.'

There were miles of courts and yards. That was how it seemed. By first light, Billy Reed's feet ached. He'd been tramping around for hours and felt like he'd gone nowhere. He understood: they had to be thorough. Sugden had killed four people now, and wounded more. He was dangerous. Deadly. But he wasn't anywhere around here.

The sergeant thought about the way Elizabeth had looked at him when the constable knocked on their door. The fear. She'd never experienced it in the time they'd been living together. It didn't happen with the fire brigade; he was on duty or off. But as soon as he heard the sound, he knew what it meant, and he felt the buzz of excitement.

Now, after so many fruitless, frustrating hours it had all faded away. He felt exhausted

Finally he gave up. Sugden wasn't here. He walked slowly back to Millgarth. All he wanted was a hot drink and something to fill his belly. Kendall was still out directing the constables.

'He's gone,' Reed said, settling on to a chair. 'Must have.'

Harper nodded absently.

'Why?' the inspector asked. 'Why would anyone do that?' He had the report from the hospital on his desk. The dead man's wife would be out of hospital later, but she'd lose the sight in one eye. A husband gone and half her vision, and for no reason at all. 'What's going on in Sugden's mind? This isn't revenge.'

'He's a lunatic, sir,' Ash said with a grave sigh.

'Something must have snapped in him,' the sergeant offered.

'Go on.'

'He showed up after his sister's funeral and shot at no one. At Carr's factory he had his revenge. He killed the man who sacked him.' Harper and the constable nodded. 'There's a kind of reason in what he did.'

'What are you thinking?'

'We had someone like him when I was in Afghanistan. Andrew McCormack. He was in one of the other platoons. A good enough soldier, but his sergeant was always finding fault with him. Made him into a wreck. The sergeant just enjoyed being a bully. When they were out on patrol Jones had his revenge. Shot the sergeant in the back then turned the gun on the others before he ran off.'

'Did you find him?' Ash asked after a long silence. Reed shook his head.

'The tribesmen got him first. They had a ritual when they caught one of ours.' His voice trailed away bitterly. 'We could almost understand what he did, shooting at his NCO like that. But his mates? That's what I thought about when I was looking for Sugden tonight. The army hushed it all up. Bad for morale.'

'How do you explain tonight?' Harper asked.

'He's snapped,' Reed repeated.

The superintendent had entered; he stood quietly in the doorway, listening.

'I don't care if he's snapped or if he's as sane as me,' Kendall said. 'We need to find him.'

His face was drawn, the dapper clothes dishevelled, hair rumpled when he took off his top hat.

'I want a plan,' he continued. 'Right now, every copper in Leeds is looking for him.' He gestured towards his office. 'Tom.'

Harper closed the door and sat, watching Kendall. The man looked tired as he sat back and rubbed his hands down his face.

'You heard about the dead man's wife?'

'Yes,' he said, nodding slowly, then stirred. 'How's the Carr investigation? Be honest.'

'Stalled.'

'I want you on Sugden, then.' He was quiet for a few seconds. 'Nothing else matters at the moment. I need to know if any of the victims had anything to do with Sugden. Dig deep. Even if it's tenuous, I want to know.'

'Yes, sir.'

'It'll be just you. I need Ash out searching.' He thought for a moment. 'Do you still have someone guarding Carr's house?'

'Since the funeral.'

'Make sure he's alert. We don't want a repeat of the mess at the factory.'

'For what it's worth, I think Billy's right. Sugden's snapped.'

216

'It doesn't matter. We *have* to find him. The pressure's going to be on us now. Can you imagine what the newspapers are going to say in the morning? People will be scared to go out.'

'More bobbies on the streets?' Harper suggested.

'How?' The superintendent gave a deep sigh. 'We'll have everyone out searching. I can pull in a few men from Bradford and Wakefield, but not for long.'

'Maybe we'll catch him quickly.'

'We'd better,' Kendall said darkly.

The painted sign read M. Samuels, Jeweller, in ornate script. But the window display of the shop had been removed, in its place black funeral crepe and a notice that simply said *Closed for Bereavement*.

Harper knocked on the door and waited. People passed along Lower Basinghall Street. Walking over from Millgarth through the early crowds he could feel the tension, thicker than smoke in the air. Boys had been selling the morning editions of the paper, shouting out horror headlines. **Two Shot On Street! Madman Kills Two!**

Finally a clerk emerged from the back room of the jeweller's and opened the door.

'I'm sorry, sir . . .' he began but Harper introduced himself and the man nodded quickly. 'Of course, come in.'

It seemed unlikely that Sugden could ever have been a customer in a place like this. It felt as sacred as a church. The glass display cases gleamed, the carpet on the floor so thick he felt

217

himself sink into it. Everything resonated with luxury and money.

The office at the back was sparser, just a desk and battered wooden chairs, the door open to a workshop with vices and tools on the bench.

'What can I do for you, Inspector?' the clerk asked. 'As you can imagine, it will be several days before we reopen.'

'May I offer the condolences of the force?' Harper began. 'It's a terrible thing. But we need to look into it all. I'm sure you'll understand that.' He waited as the man nodded. 'The man who killed Mr Samuel was called Stanley Sugden. Does the name mean anything to you?'

'No.'

'He has a very long beard. Not a rich man, by any means.'

'I'm certain he's never been here. I'd remember a customer like that.'

'How long have you worked here, Mr . . .?'

'George Wall. I've been here for ten years.'

'Who runs the shop with Mr Samuel?'

'His brother-in-law. Mr Payne. It was Mr Samuel who made most of the pieces. He spends most of his time in there.' He inclined his head towards the workshop then his face dropped. 'Spent, I mean. Didn't often see customers unless they wanted something special. Mr Payne and I work the shop.'

'Could Mr Samuel have had an argument with Sugden over something?'

The man pursed his lips then shook his head.

'Not that I ever heard about.'

'Thank you.'

William Wright had been a clerk at Tetley's Brewery, just a few minutes' walk from his home in Holbeck. As the inspector approached, the thick smell of malt took him back to the years he'd worked at Brunswick's, rolling barrels of beer. Too many bad memories.

Wright had been employed there for almost twenty years, rising to senior clerk. But Sugden had never been employed at Tetley's. There wasn't even any record that he'd applied for a job at the place.

There didn't seem to be any connection between Sugden and his victims. Wright's wife, sitting behind closed curtains in the small house, had never heard of him. Neighbours and relatives crowded around, offering consolation and food.

Mrs Wright was distraught. She didn't understand what had happened. Why it happened. She looked at the inspector for an explanation, but he had none. How could he? How could anyone explain it?

The Samuel house was in Headingley, standing by itself at the end of a short drive, surrounded by trees whose leaves had fallen into large russet piles. A black wreath hung on the door. It seemed to be surrounded by silence.

The maid let him into a parlour where John Payne and his wife sat with the three Samuel daughters. A tea tray sat on a low table, all the cups untouched, a plate of sandwiches uneaten.

Payne led the inspector into another room, away from the women. He had a pinched face with prominent teeth, most of the hair gone from his head, neck bulging against a tight wing collar.

'It's not a suitable subject for the ladies,' he announced gravely. 'They're upset enough as it is. Poor Michael, and what happened to Hannah. What I want to know is how you explain it, Inspector. How can something like that happen in the middle of Leeds?'

'That's what we're trying to find out, sir. Do you know of any connection between Mr Samuel and a man called Stanley Sugden? He's the one who fired the shots.'

'No,' he answered shortly.

'I have to check, sir.'

'If the police were doing their job, he'd have been caught before any of this could happen,' he fumed.

'We were already searching for him.'

'Well, you damned well didn't catch him, did you? And now my brother-in-law is dead and my sister's lost her husband and an eye.'

'I'm sorry, sir.' It was easier to let him rage than try to calm him. He was lost in his grief, pacing around the room.

'What are you going to do about it? Is he still out there?'

'Yes, sir, he is,' Harper admitted. 'And we'll find him.'

'It's too late for Michael. And for Hannah.'

'We'll find him,' the inspector repeated.

Payne's eyes blazed. 'When you do, you won't need to pay the hangman. I'll do the job myself. I just hope you find him before someone else dies.'

There was nothing to say to that.

'Is there anything else, Inspector?'

220

'No, sir. Once again, my condolences.' He shook the man's hand, feeling the force of his grip, and left.

Reed stopped and stretched. His legs ached, his feet ached and he could barely think. He'd been awake for a day and a half, and all the fire and the fury of the night before had drained out of him. Darkness was falling; the day had turned chilly, and a fog was beginning to rise.

He'd been all over Leeds, supervising the teams of coppers searching for Sugden. Nothing, of course. Now he needed to go home, have a hot meal and then to sleep for hours. He was too old to work this long. With the fire brigade you worked your shift and that was it. He lit another cigarette, coughing as he drew down the smoke. Millgarth was in sight, lights shining through the growing mist. He'd see how things stood, then go back to Elizabeth and the children.

Ash was in the office, talking to a weary Kendall. The superintendent raised an eyebrow in question.

'No, sir.'

'Right. Go home. Get some rest. We'll start again in the morning.'

'Any news at all?' the sergeant asked.

'As far as we know, there was no connection between Sugden and the victims. The shooting seems absolutely random.' He ran a hand through his hair and the faint perfume of his pomade floated around the office. 'What's going through his mind? Do you have any idea at all?'

'No, sir. I wish I did.'

221

Kendall gave a tired smile.

'You're probably wishing you'd gone back to the fire brigade, aren't you, Sergeant?'

'I'm fine, sir.' A small lie didn't hurt.

'Good. God knows, I can use everyone I can get right now. Go home, the pair of you.'

'Sir,' Reed said, 'you could use some rest yourself, if you don't mind me saying so.'

The superintendent nodded. 'When I can, Sergeant. When I can.'

Outside, Reed tasted the fog, sharp and sulphurous.

'Where have you been today?' he asked Ash.

'Hither and yon. Feels like I've seen all of Leeds.'

'I know the feeling. Nothing?'

'Not even a sniff, sir. The bugger's gone well to ground.'

'The problem's going to be when he comes out again.'

'You're not wrong there, sir.' He sighed. 'I'd better go and see if my missus has forgotten what I look like. Maybe we'll have more luck in the morning, eh?'

'You look all in,' Annabelle said.

Harper flopped into the chair, glad to be off his feet at last.

'I feel it.'

She stood behind him, slowly kneading his shoulders.

'I read about it in the *Post*. Was it really this Sudgen fellow?'

'Oh yes,' he replied, feeling his muscles ease under her hands. 'No doubt about it.'

222

'Those poor, poor people.' She stayed silent for a few moments. 'I had Ellie pop your supper in the oven to keep warm.'

It wasn't hot, but there was ample food to take the edge off his appetite. Steak and kidney pie. He set the plate aside, letting the warmth of the fire wash over him. She settled on the chair across from him, gathering her skirt around her legs and folding her hands in her lap.

'I've been thinking,' she began, and he cocked his head, waiting. 'About your hearing.'

'It's no worse than it was a few days ago.' He heard the edge in his voice and regretted it. But he didn't want to talk about it. Not now. He was bone-weary and not in the mood for raking this over.

'We could go back to that doctor.'

'Why? He told us last time that it's not going to get any better.'

'See someone else then. London, maybe.'

'Why? It won't do any bloody good. We'll just be throwing good money after bad.' He gave her a wan smile. 'I'm sorry. Let's just leave it.'

'If you're sure that's what you want.'

He didn't know what he wanted. As he'd gone around during the day he'd thought about the superintendent Dr King had mentioned. Deaf, but he'd carried on working as a copper. He'd thought about the other comment, too, that everyone probably knew about his hearing problem. It rubbed at him like a burr under his clothes.

'For now,' he said finally. 'I know you're trying to help.' He remembered something. 'It's tomorrow night you're speaking again, isn't it?'

'Yes.' There wasn't any pleasure in her voice.
'I still don't know why I told them I'd do it. I've
spent all afternoon thinking of what I'm going
to say.'

'Just be the way you were last time. Say what
you're thinking.'

'That's the problem, Tom. I don't know what
I'm thinking. I get an idea, start to follow it, then
there's another and another and I get all tied up.'

'You were fine before.'

She dismissed it. 'Beginner's luck.'

'No,' he assured her. 'It was a lot more than
that.' She shook her head, exactly the way he
knew she would. 'A lot more,' he told her and
reached out a hand. 'I'm jiggered. Come on, let's
go to bed.'

Nineteen

Another fruitless day. By five o'clock, worn and
frustrated after tramping around Leeds for hours,
Harper sat at his desk. Reed was writing up his
report. No more than a few lines: where they'd
searched, the fact that they'd found nothing.

Suddenly the inspector sat upright. 'The suffragist meeting tonight.'

'What about it, sir?' Ash asked. He had his
hands wrapped around a mug of tea, warming
himself.

'Sugden might be there.'

'He could be anywhere,' Reed said bitterly. He

took out a handkerchief and coughed phlegm into it. 'Bloody fog.'

'His sister was involved, she went to the meetings.'

'You're clutching at straws,' the sergeant told him with a shake of his head.

'We don't have any better ideas. It's worth a shot.'

He saw Reed glance at the constable and roll his eyes. But he had their interest. The possibility of finding Sugden.

Harper stood in the Albert Hall at the Mechanics' Institute. The crowd was filing in slowly. Women for the most part, one or two accompanied by long-faced men who looked as if they'd rather be anywhere else.

He'd spotted Annabelle a few minutes before. She'd been pacing around, unable to settle, dressed in a royal blue gown that caught the light, an elaborate bustle at the back, with her hair piled high, topped with a small military hat.

'You look a picture,' he told her.

'I don't feel like one.' She chewed on her bottom lip. 'What am I going to tell them, Tom? I said my piece last time.'

'Then say it again. Some of them won't have heard it.'

She shook her head quickly, hands nervously brushing invisible specks on the front of the gown.

She looked at him, eyes wide. 'I'm going to stand up and open my mouth and nothing's going to come out. I know it. In front of them all.'

Harper stroked her shoulder. 'You'll be fine,' he told her gently. 'I promise.'

She shooed him away so she could fret. Harper glanced out of the glass doors at the front of the building. The people standing in the darkness were nothing more than faint shapes.

Reed and Ash would be out there, and Will Hardaker, the union man, would be looking after things. If Sugden appeared, this time they'd be ready.

There were just a few stragglers, hurrying along on their way inside, their faces lit for a moment by the gas lamps along the street. A copper stood on the other side of the road, looking bored.

Reed huddled into his overcoat. The night had turned cold, a sharp breeze coming down Cookridge Street and slicing at the back of his neck. He glanced at Constable Ash, standing twenty yards down the road, hands deep in his pockets, no expression on his face. A few men stood at the edge of the pavement, faces half-hidden by the mist. None of them spoke; they just gazed sullenly at the building.

But no Sugden. Just the crowd of silent men, standing, looking, the ones they'd seen the time before.

Reed had spent a little while with Hardaker earlier. They'd shared a cup of tea before the evening began. Now the man looked at him and shook his head. No sign of anyone with a gun.

They were waiting, hoping and scared that Sugden might appear. The sergeant stamped his feet, glad he'd worn his heavy boots and thick

226

socks. Times like this, all those years on the beat paid off.

One of the silent men shuffled away, head down. Over the next half hour another two arrived. He stood and watched.

Annabelle was the first speaker, standing at the front of the podium, hands by her sides, fists clenched. For a few seconds she'd simply stared at the people in front of her, and Harper held his breath, waiting for her to begin.

Once she started, she was full of passion, the words spilling out of her mouth. And then, suddenly, she stopped and laughed.

'You know what?' Anabelle looked around the faces. 'We can talk all we want, but there are only two things that'll make them down in London get up on their hind legs and give us the vote. *Give* us, like it's a special gift. And that's if they realize it's in their own interests, or if we scare them enough that they can't say no.' She stopped for a moment as they applauded loudly. 'It won't happen soon. Not this century. But it *will* happen. We'll make it happen, and so will all those who come after.'

They stood and roared. She'd given them exactly what they needed. Hope and anger. He clapped along with the rest of them, then turned away. There'd be another hour of speeches yet. Inside the room was safe enough. He needed to see what was going on outside.

'He's not bloody coming,' Reed complained. As the temperature started to fall, the fog was thickening. He coughed. 'You know he's not, Tom.' He wanted to be home, sitting with Elizabeth in front of the fire.

'We'll wait until they've all gone,' Harper said. Better to spend a little longer here and be safe. Ash raised his eyebrows but said nothing.

It was quiet. The mist drifted around, muffling sound. The gas lamps seemed to hang in the air, little blurred spots of light. Time passed slowly. The sergeant's eyes felt gritty from trying to peer through the murk.

Finally the doors of the Institute opened and the crowd started to flow out.

'Let's get down at the bottom of the steps,' the inspector said. 'Keep your eyes open.'

'We know what to bloody do, Tom,' Reed said quietly.

Harper knew. He trusted both of them. But it was his wife in there and he wanted her safe.

A few minutes passed, and only one or two were still left inside. Reed walked in small circles, trying to keep warm. The standing men had wandered away, the union guards were standing together, talking. The uniformed constable had vanished into the night.

'Let's call it a night,' Harper said, watching Reed and Ash amble away.

He climbed the stone steps, thanking Hardaker and his friend for keeping watch. Annabelle was still in the hall, talking to Miss Ford. He stood aside as workers cleared away the chairs and swept the floor.

They were still talking when the gas lights dimmed. Isabella Ford gave a small laugh, took

Annabelle by the arm and led her into the vestibule. The inspector followed. The woman's coach was waiting outside.

'Think about it, please,' Miss Ford said as she waved goodnight.

'What was that about?' he asked.

'I'm not sure.' She seemed stunned, out of words. 'I'll tell you on the way home.'

Twenty

The hackney passed the Grand Theatre and took the curve from New Briggate on to North Street, through the Leylands. The lights in the houses round here were already doused, the people in bed early. Only street lamps glimmered through the fog.

'Well,' Harper asked finally, 'What did she say?'

Annabelle had been silent since they left the Institute.

'Miss Ford asked if I'd join the committee of the Suffrage Society.' She said it slowly, as if she couldn't quite believe the words.

'Isn't that good?' He didn't understand; for the last six months or more she'd lived and breathed votes for women.

'It took me by surprise. I've only been involved with them for two minutes.'

'She asked you to speak.'

Annabelle turned to look at him. 'There are

229

people who've been there a long time. They've done a lot more than me.'

'She wouldn't ask if she didn't think you'd be good at it,' he pointed out. 'And look at the way they reacted to your speech. They loved it.'

'Did they?' She wasn't fishing for compliments, she really wanted to know.

'You got a standing ovation again.'

'I know, but . . .'

'But what?'

She shook her head. 'I wasn't speaking. Not really. I was just mouthing off.'

'They loved it.' The cab pulled up in front of the Victoria. 'Sleep on it,' he told her. 'See how you feel in the morning. I think they'd be getting a jewel in you.'

'You have to say that.'

He grinned. 'I know. But I mean it.'

Reed wrapped the scarf around his mouth and nose to keep out the taste of the fog. It was clammy, cold, foul in his mouth.

'We'll never find Sugden in this,' he said.

'It must be worse for him,' Ash answered. 'He's sleeping out in it.'

'He knows what he's doing.' He tried to peer through the gloom, dodging past someone on the street, no more than a faint shape. 'And he'll be able to have a fire.'

'If he can find any dry wood.'

'I've seen those scouts in Afghanistan. I don't know how they did it. They'd vanish for days.'

'Let's hope Lady Luck fancies us today.'

'We could pass him on the bloody street and

never know it.' He stopped suddenly and put a hand on the constable's arm. 'Hunslet,' he said.

'Sir?'

'This is the perfect weather for him to go back there. No one would see him.'

Ash pursed his lips. 'I'm not so sure, sir. What's there for him?'

'Those friends of his. We'll go and find them.'

'Might as well, I suppose,' the constable agreed. 'Makes as much sense as anything else.'

'More than standing outside that meeting last night.'

'With respect, sir, I think that was a good idea. Sugden could have appeared.'

Reed shook his head firmly. 'Bloody waste of time.'

Harper knew he should have been out searching for Sugden. But there were already enough men looking; one less would make no difference. Not that he had any idea where to go, anyway. And Catherine Carr wouldn't give him any peace. He'd struggled awake that morning to the memory of her in the Arches as they pulled away the rubble.

There was something else that nagged at him: would Sugden have escaped from the asylum if he hadn't gone to give him the news of his sister's death? Was he responsible for all the deaths that had followed?

He'd probably never know the answer.

But he was damned if he'd give up on Katie Carr. No one deserved to end up that way. In his gut he didn't feel it had anything to do with her politics. And with Annabelle so involved with the suffragists now, he hoped to God he was right.

If not politics, though, it had to be family. As far as he could see, the only one who could profit from her death was her husband. It was time for another talk with Mr Carr.

In Chapel Allerton the fog seemed even thicker. At the tram terminus he could scarcely make out the sign for the Mexborough Arms, not fifteen feet away. He picked his way along the pavement, trusting he was going the right way.

Finally he arrived at Carr's gate, and the constable on duty came close to peer at him.

'Any trouble?' Harper asked.

'Hardly seen a soul, sir. Just one of the lasses going off to do the shopping.'

'Is he in?'

'Hasn't stirred in days.' He wiped a hand across his mouth. 'Can't blame him in this.'

'Any visitors?'

'That son who runs the factory. Been here every day, like clockwork. That's it.'

'Just keep your eyes open. Sugden's still out there.'

'Never you mind, sir. He won't get past me.'

Carr was in the parlour, gazing morosely through the window into the whiteness outside. He was in the same chair he'd occupied on the inspector's last visit, the two walking sticks close by. The whisky decanter sat on the side table, a half-full glass beside it.

'Bringing me good news?' he asked. His voice was a low, dry croak. 'Have you found him?'

'No, sir. Just a few more questions.'

Carr turned his head. He looked older, as if his skin had grown thinner since his wife's funeral. Now it seemed stretched tight over his face, so pale that Harper believed he could almost see the skull beneath. Dark spots stood out against the flesh on his hands.

'Well? Ask them, man, and you can get back out there.' His eyes flashed. 'You can't find my wife's killer. You can't find her lunatic brother. What bloody good are the police?'

'We're doing all we can, sir.' The inspector paused. 'Tell me, did you change your will after your wife left?'

'What?' Carr looked up sharply. 'Of course not. I thought she'd come back.'

'What would she have inherited from you if you'd died first?'

'Everything.'

'The house, the money, the factory?'

'Every bloody thing. I just told you,' the man snapped.

'Who knew that, sir?' He could feel the first twinge of excitement inside, that he'd found something.

'Everyone, I suppose.' Carr's bony shoulders shrugged inside his jacket. 'It wasn't a secret.'

'What about your son? He runs the factory.'

'I know what he bloody does.'

'Why didn't you leave it to him?'

'He'd get it after she died.' Carr picked up the whisky glass and took a nip. It was how he survived the days, Harper imagined. Sitting, thinking, regretting, the alcohol to dull the edge of whatever pain he had.

'She couldn't sell the factory?'

'Why would she want to do a daft thing like that?' he snorted. 'She knew what made the money. I told her that the factory stays.'

'Was it in the will? Specifically?' the inspector pressed.

'Yes.'

'Now the factory will go to your son when you die.'

'That's right.' He took another sip of the whisky then looked up with a weary gaze. 'If you're trying to say that Neville might have killed her, that's the stupidest thing I've ever heard.'

'I'm not trying to say anything, sir.'

'He knew where he stood, that it would be all his in time,' Carr said.

'Thank you.'

'Was that it?' he asked caustically.

'What else was in the will?'

'Nothing. A few bequests.' He allowed himself another small drink. 'Nothing important.'

'I see, sir.'

'You'd better not go after my son, Inspector.'

'I was just asking, sir.' He paused. 'Was your son guaranteed his job at the factory?'

'Why would he need to be?' Carr's voice rose. 'He was going to inherit it all, anyway. Don't be so bloody stupid.'

'Of course, sir.' The room was hot, the fire burning bright. Harper was sweating in his coat, but another minute and he'd be leaving. At least this time he was going away with something, even if he wasn't sure what to make of it. 'I appreciate the information.'

Carr's face lost all its bluster. He looked like a sad, sick old man.

'Just catch my wife's killer, Inspector.'

'I'll do my best, sir.'

'And Sugden. You can kill him for all I care.'

Outside, the fog was damp and cool on his skin, refreshing after the overheated parlour. The constable saluted as he left. Slowly, he groped his way back to the Harrogate Road. He needed to think about the information he'd been given.

They were somewhere in Hunslet, Reed knew that. But one street blended into another, the mist swirling and obscuring the street signs. People passed three feet away and they were like ghosts, faint silhouettes.

'Where are we?' he asked. 'Do you know?'

'No idea, sir,' Ash answered with a quiet chuckle. 'Not a million miles from a brewery, going by the smell, but I'm jiggered if I know which one. Not my part of town.'

Somewhere in the distance a cart passed, a rumble of wheels over the cobbles. Coming over here had probably been a stupid decision, the sergeant thought. They'd be lucky to find the end of the road, let alone Sugden.

He was about to suggest they find somewhere warm for their dinner when they heard the sound. It was unmistakeable. The piercing shriek of a police whistle. It cut through everything.

'Come on, sir,' Ash said as he began to run.

All Reed could do was follow the footsteps, trying to stay close.

The man seemed to know just where he was going, changing direction a little with every blast of the whistle. How in God's name did he do it? Soon enough the sound was louder. They turned a corner. Halfway down the street a constable had the whistle raised to his lips again.

'What is it?' Reed asked as he tried to catch his breath.

'I think it's Sugden, sir. I glanced through the window as I passed. Saw someone with a long beard and something that could have been a gun.'

The sergeant looked at the house. It was a respectable through terrace, a handkerchief of garden at the front. The curtains were drawn back to show the parlour, empty now. There'd be a yard at the back, the privy, and a gate that gave on to the ginnel.

'What's your name?'

'Peters, sir.'

'You know this area well?'

'Been my beat for eleven years, sir.' Good, Reed thought; he needed someone familiar with the district.

'Who lives here?'

'Mr Ellis, sir. He's a widower, on his own. But he should be away at his work right now and I haven't heard he's poorly.'

'Have you tried the door?'

'No, sir.'

'You're sure someone was there?' He needed to be certain.

'Positive, sir. I saw him clear as anything.'

The sergeant thought for a moment.

'Go round to the ginnel,' he told the constable. 'Grab him if he comes out. We'll go in this way. And for God's sake don't give him a chance to shoot.'

'Don't you worry, sir.' The bobby grinned. 'My missus would kill me if I died.'

'I'll give you thirty seconds to get in place, then we'll go in.'

The sergeant looked at Ash as they waited. It was the same feeling as dashing to a fire, that surging mix of excitement and fear. Finally he nodded and tried the doorknob. Locked.

'Let me, sir,' Ash said, raising a large foot and bringing it down on the lock. Once, twice, three times and it splintered. He barged in quickly, Reed on his heels. They'd barely made it three paces inside when they heard the shot.

Constable Peters was lying in the ginnel, blood leaking on to the cobbles. Reed knelt, cradling the man's head. No hope, he could see that.

'Get after him,' he ordered Ash.

The shot must have been at close range. Half of Peters's chest was gone, and his face was peppered.

'Hold on,' Reed said softly. 'We'll get someone for you.'

The constable tried to smile. Blood leaked out of his mouth and trickled down his jaw.

He saw the moment when the man died. A last soft breath, then nothing. How many times had he gone through this with comrades in the war? Too many to count. Very gently, he lowered

237

Peters's head to the ground, took off his coat and covered the body with it.

His hands were shaking as he lit a cigarette. He wasn't used to this any more.

Ash came back shaking his head. 'Vanished. And this fog just swallows sound. He's got away.' He looked down and sighed. 'Sugden must have taken him by surprise.'

'Poor sod. I'll stay with him. Go to Hunslet station and bring some help.'

By the middle of the afternoon every copper in Leeds knew. Harper heard when he returned to Millgarth. The building seemed subdued, the conversation in whispers.

'Have you heard, sir?' Tollman asked from the desk.

'What?'

'Sugden's shot someone else. One of ours.'

'What?' He could feel his stomach lurch. 'Who?' he asked urgently.

'Constable Peters. A beat man over in Hunslet.'

The inspector closed his eyes. He'd met Peters a few times. He could picture the face, earnest but open. Someone who loved his work and did it well. Another to be buried with full honours. He let out a slow sigh.

'Sergeant Reed and Mr Ash were there. They're in with the super now,' Tollman told him.

He joined them in Kendall's office, listening as Reed recounted it all. The superintendent's face looked grey in the light, lines etched deep into his skin as he sucked slowly on his pipe.

'There was no hope of finding him?' he asked.

'We didn't know which way he'd gone, sir,' Ash replied. 'I tried one end of the ginnel but I couldn't hear anything. I didn't even know exactly where we were. It was like being blind in all that.'

'Five,' Kendall said. There was an age of exhaustion in the word. He looked around the faces. 'Five dead now. Do you have any idea how we can find him?' There was just silence. 'Sergeant? You were an army man.'

'He'll head for somewhere more open now. Somewhere he can hide. Where he can't be trapped.'

'How long can he survive like that?' Harper asked. 'He's already been out there a while.'

'I don't know.' He looked out at the fog beyond the window. 'With this, I don't see how we have a chance of finding him.'

He caught up with Reed just outside the station as the sergeant stopped to light a cigarette.

'Billy . . .'

'Don't.'

He'd seen it on the sergeant's face: he was blaming himself. All the things he might have done differently.

'I should have taken the ginnel myself.'

'Then you might be dead now.'

'I told him to be careful.'

They began to walk, vanishing into the fog, crossing the square of the open market, all the traders gone for the day. The lights of the café ahead were a small, blurred glow.

'He died while I was holding him.' The words seemed empty of all hope. 'He was married, wasn't he? Did he have children?'

239

'I've no idea,' Harper answered softly. 'But I knew him a little. He was a good copper.' It was the best accolade anyone on the force could have. A good copper. 'Sugden must have taken him by surprise.' He could only guess.

'I should have had him and Ash in the front and taken the back myself.'

The café was closing, but they could still sit, the owner bringing over two cups of tea. The sergeant ground out his cigarette.

'I was the one in charge there.'

'And you're not God,' Harper told him. 'Things happen. You didn't do anything wrong.'

Reed looked at him. 'I just didn't do enough.'

'I stopped for a drink,' Reed admitted when Elizabeth opened the door. He hadn't been able to fit his key in the lock and had ended up hammering on the wood. He saw her looking up at him with a mixture of concern and anger.

'Get yourself inside before all the neighbours come out,' she told him as she walked through to the scullery, arms folded tight across her chest. She filled the kettle and banged it down on the range. 'What's that on your coat?'

'Blood,' he told her and saw her face change.

He'd tried to scrape it off with a fingernail, but it had soaked deep into the material. That was when he knew he needed a drink. The first brandy in the public house soothed him a little. It burned sharply in his throat and warmed his stomach. The second went down more smoothly. The third hit him hard.

'I was with that copper who was shot,' he

continued. Reed held up his hands. 'I was holding him when he died.'

'Oh, Billy.' Elizabeth stood next to him, pulling him close and stroking his hair.

He told her as he drank the tea she made for him, long gaps between the sentences until it was done.

'I know it's a terrible thing to say,' Elizabeth told him, 'but thank God it wasn't you. I know that's selfish and I'm sorry for his family, but I don't know what I'd do if you weren't here.'

He nodded. It was all he could manage.

'But Billy.' He glanced up at her tone. 'Please, don't start drinking again, luv. Please.'

'I won't. It's just . . .' Just that the hunger had been too alive and the guilt too strong.

'I know. But next time come home. We can talk about it.'

'Yes.' He gave a small, fretful smile.

'What do you think we should do, Tom?' Kendall sat behind his desk, his voice bleak. 'Any ideas?'

'I think Billy's right,' Harper answered. 'We're never going to catch Sugden in this fog. Too easy for him to give us the slip. It sounds like blind luck that Peters spotted him.'

'Bad luck,' the superintendent said soberly. 'I'd rather he got away than lose one of ours.'

'I know.'

'When we do catch Sugden, if he resists arrest and ends up dead, I won't turn a hair.' The words hung between them; he'd never heard Kendall say anything like that before. 'I knew Charlie Peters,' he continued after a while. 'We started

241

out on the force together. He was the best beat bobby I've ever seen. Absolutely right for the job. He knew everyone and he cared about them.'

'I'm sorry, sir.'

'I was an usher at his wedding.' Kendall's mouth twitched into a smile at the memory. 'All of us in our uniforms. I'll go and sit with his widow tonight. We're a family in the force. Don't ever forget that.'

'I won't.'

'What would you do if you were leading the hunt? I'm meeting the other division heads in—' he took out his pocket watch and snapped it open '—three quarters of an hour at the Town Hall, and it's going to take me the better part of that to find my way there. I need ideas, Tom.'

'I don't have any. I really don't.'

Twenty-One

The fog had gone during the night, simply vanished, replaced by a wind from the west that brought cold, slicing rain.

'At least it's worse for Sugden out there,' Reed said, shaking out his mackintosh. 'He's going to be freezing.'

'Don't get too comfortable,' Harper warned him. 'We're all going to be out in it.'

He'd still been in the office, writing up his conversation with Robert Carr, when Kendall returned the night before.

'We're going to do everything,' the superintendent told him grimly.

'Everything?'

'Uniforms on house-to-house, everyone else beating the bushes. Including the detectives,' he added pointedly.

'Yes, sir.'

'The chief constable's taking charge of the investigation himself.' Before Harper could say anything, he continued: 'I know what you think, but he's a good policeman, Tom. He came up through the ranks, same as everyone else. He knows what he's doing.'

'Yes, sir.' It was safer to keep his mouth shut.

And now he was enjoying the fire before going out into the cold and wet.

'As soon as Ash arrives we'll get started.'

'Where are we going?'

'I hope you're wearing stout boots. We've drawn Roundhay Park. There have been men out there since first light.' He stared at the sergeant. His eyes were red, skin pale. 'Are you all right?'

'I'm fine. Why?'

'I just wondered.'

'Don't worry,' he said brusquely. 'How the hell are we supposed to search the park?'

'We'll do what we can.'

The door opened as Ash arrived, taking off his bowler hat and shaking the rain from it. 'Bit damp out there, sir.'

'You might as well get used to it.' He reached for his coat. 'We're going to spend the day in it.'

The horse tram trundled slowly along Roundhay

Road. He watched people walking, holding their umbrellas like shields against the driving rain.

'There'll be the electric tram along here soon, won't there, sir?'

'End of the month,' the inspector said. 'Annabelle's wangled us seats on the first one.'

Ash raised his eyebrows. 'She's resourceful, isn't she, your missus?'

Harper laughed. 'She can be when she wants something.' He glanced across at Reed, his head against the window. He looked the way he had when he used to drink. Drawn, silent. For a moment he thought about saying something. But it wasn't his problem. Nothing he'd said had ever made a difference, anyway.

From the terminus they marched across the field, the dampness creeping up their boots. The wind pushed hard, rain like shards of ice in their faces. Down the hill to meet a uniformed sergeant outside the café by the lake.

'Anything?' Harper asked as the man saluted.

'Not yet sir.' He held up a map and pointed with his finger. 'I've got men looking here and here. We've already been all around that castle.'

'Where do you want us?'

'We haven't started on the Gorge yet, sir,' the sergeant said hesitantly. 'You could take there if you like.'

It was thickly wooded, a steep valley. Almost impossible to search. The inspector sighed.

'That's fine.' The three of them would hardly make a dent there.

'I'll send more men as soon as they report back,' the sergeant offered.

The park was quiet. Not a day anyone would be walking for pleasure. The path to the Gorge took them past Waterloo Lake, the water grey, whipped up by the wind. Mud clung to their feet. Harper turned up the collar on his coat.

The Gorge began at the head of the lake, close to the folly. The castle, the sergeant had called it. A stream fed through the bottom of the valley. Bushes clung to the steep hillsides.

'Right,' he said. 'Who wants where?'

'I'll take the bottom, sir,' Ash offered. 'I don't mind getting a bit wet.'

'Billy?' The sergeant shrugged. 'All right, then. You take this side, I'll take that.'

At least the cold air had settled his stomach, Reed thought. He breathed deeply. But his head was still pounding, he wasn't thinking well. His own fault, and he knew it. Worse because he'd hardly drunk in months.

He'd seen the disappointment on Elizabeth's face. He'd felt ashamed; he'd let her down, chipped away a bit at the trust between them. Reaching out, he slashed at a bush with the branch he'd picked up. His feet slid in the dirt and he had to grab a tree limb to stay upright.

Water dripped off a leaf, down the back of his neck. This was a waste of time. You could hide whole platoons here. Finding one man was going to be impossible. They needed a line of coppers, a yard between each, working their way along the whole length of this place. That was the only way.

He'd been weak last night. He'd given in. Reed

poked at another bush and moved on, head down. That was going to be the last time.

They went up the valley and back, ending up at the lake again and coming out into a short, heavy squall of rain. Nothing. All they had to show was the dirt that clung hard to their boots. A squad of coppers, snug in their waterproof capes, was marching over the grass.

'Let's give them the pleasure of going over it again, shall we?' Harper said wearily. 'I don't know about you, but I need a cup of tea and somewhere warm to sit.'

'I wouldn't say no,' Ash agreed. 'A chance to dry out would be good, too.'

But the café was closed up tight for the winter, and nowhere within a mile to get out of the rain.

'You can try the Mansion, sir,' the uniformed sergeant suggested, gesturing towards a large house at the top of the hill, 'but I think it's empty.' He shivered, pulled out a handkerchief and blew his nose. 'I'll be rubbing myself with liniment for weeks after this.'

'Where next?' the inspector asked. There wasn't going to be a break. They might as well get on with the bloody job.

'If you've a mind, go along that road there.' He nodded towards the winding street that led down to the park. 'Anyone could hide in the gardens there.' He winked. 'Takes you all the way back to the tram stop, too. Happen you gentlemen might make it home in time for your supper.'

Harper laughed. The man was doing him a

favour. He glanced at the others. They both looked as miserable as sin.

'Thank you, Sergeant. We'll gladly do that.'

'We'll find him,' the sergeant said. 'I worked out of Hunslet for almost ten years. I knew Charlie Peters. There was no one better. This bastard isn't going to get away.'

'Where in God's name have you been, Tom? You're filthy,' Annabelle said when she saw him. She stood, hand on hips, glaring at him as he stood in the parlour. 'Take those boots off. You're tracking mud everywhere.'

Sheepishly he obeyed, telling her about the fruitless day.

'You'd better get changed, too. You look like you brought half the park home with you.'

In clean clothes he felt better. The fire was blazing, the tea warm in his belly. He settled back and closed his eyes. Just for a minute, he told himself.

He woke, trying to climb out of sleep as she shook his shoulder.

'You were dead to the world,' Annabelle told him with a smile. 'Supper's ready. Come and get something inside you.'

'What have you decided about the suffrage committee?' Harper asked as they ate.

'I haven't,' she answered quickly. 'I'm still thinking about it.'

'Is something wrong?'

'No.' She shook her head. 'I just need to think about it, that's all. It's a big step. I'd have to go to meetings all over the country. Things like that.'

There was more, he was certain of that. He knew her well enough by now. She'd never been hesitant or reticent about things. She was always one to plunge into things. He looked at her for a moment. She was toying with her food, not really eating. If she wanted, she'd tell him. Better to leave her to make the decision alone.

Harper was still thinking about it the next morning as he walked out to Cross Green. Someone had claimed to have spotted Sugden peering out through an upstairs window on Easy Road. Just the one report, but it was enough.

'What do you think the odds are, sir?' Ash asked. The rain had blown away during the night but the chill remained, a reminder that they were deep in autumn now.

'Eh?' His mind had been elsewhere. Or maybe he simply hadn't heard.

'The odds of Sugden being here, I mean.'

'It's probably not him.' They couldn't be that lucky. Not when most of the force was hunting the man all over Leeds. 'But we'll be very careful, just in case.'

No one was going to forget what had happened to Peters. A photograph of him, proud in his uniform, had gone up in the entrance to every police station in Leeds. Fallen in the line of duty. The notice had circulated: the funeral was set for the following day. Everyone in their best uniform. For once, Harper would put on the top hat and black coat without complaint.

'Yes, sir,' Ash said grimly.

Constable Williams met them by the bridge

248

over the railway cutting. The tracks below stood out as bright metal lines among the greens and dull browns.

'Morning, sir.' Williams gave a crisp salute. 'I've been asking around. If it's Sugden, no one else has seen him.' There was an eagerness under his words, as if he hoped the killer was in the house.

'Who lives there?' the inspector asked.

'That's the thing. It's old Mrs Mayhew and her daughter. Never been a man in the place that I've seen.'

'Will they be at home?'

'I don't even know the last time the old lass set foot outside the door, sir. Her daughter does all the shopping and that. Keeps everything neat as a pin.'

'Any connection to Sugden that you know?'

Williams shook his head. 'Nothing anyone seems to recall.'

But it wasn't far from here down to Hunslet, where Sugden had been raised. Ten minutes' walk, no more than that. Close enough to the streets he knew well. Maybe he'd been wrong. Sugden could be hiding out there.

'Softly, softly, then,' he said. 'Do you know Mrs . . .'

'Mayhew, sir. I pop in once a week, and I often see the daughter out and about.' He stopped, suddenly thoughtful. 'I didn't notice her anywhere yesterday.'

'Tell me how the house is laid out.'

There'd be no repeat of the last time. They'd go in ready, with a plan. Fast and forceful. Wright used a stick to draw a plan of the place in the dirt. Nothing unusual: parlour at the front, scullery behind, two bedrooms upstairs. A back door leading to the yard and the privy. The inspector stared at it for a moment.

'Who else has a key?' he asked.

'Annie Bates at number thirty-three,' Wright answered.

'Here's what we'll do . . .'

Constable Williams rapped on the door. Harper stood to one side, out of view, waiting. Ash was at the back, in the ginnel.

No answer.

'Try again,' he whispered.

But there was nothing.

'Use the key.'

It clicked quietly. Harper moved, pushing his way into the parlour. A fire had been lit in the grate, but it had burned low. Someone was here. Where?

The inspector turned to Williams, a finger to his lips. Then he peered around the doorway into the scullery. Empty. That left upstairs. His heart was beating so hard he thought the sound must fill the house. At the bottom of the steps Harper paused for a moment. His throat was dry, his head filled with silence. He took a deep breath and started to climb, alert for any shadow or movement, moving softly.

Gently he pushed open one door, letting it swing all the way back to the wall. Grey light came through the window. Empty. There was only one room left.

His palms were sweaty. He stood to one side of the door, reaching out, his fingers closing on the doorknob, the metal cold against his skin. This was it. Nowhere else he could be.

He waited. Sugden had to know he was out here.

Ten seconds, twenty. Thirty. He counted them off in his head. All the way to sixty. He closed his grip on the knob. In one movement he turned it, threw the door back and dashed into the room.

The pair had been bound with twine, wrists and ankles, rags stuffed into their mouths to keep them quiet.

'God,' he heard Williams say. They freed the women and helped them up. Miss Mayhew was crying, hands over her face. Her mother's expression was hard, a concentration of fury.

'Get Ash inside,' Harper ordered the constable. 'Make some tea, I'll help them downstairs.'

It took half an hour to piece the story together. The women sat together, Mrs Mayhew with an arm around her daughter, rocking the younger woman back and forth.

'I knew his mam years and years back,' Mrs Mayhew told them. 'He was just little then. She'd bring him with her when she came to visit.' Hot tea had brought some colour back to her cheeks. Her knuckles were gnarled and twisted around the cup. 'He was a lovely lad then. Good as gold.'

He'd come the evening before last, just after dark. Not long after he'd killed Constable Peters, Harper thought. When the daughter answered the door, he'd pushed his way in and held the shotgun

251

on them both. He wanted food, a place to wash and somewhere warm to sleep.

'Did he speak at all?' the inspector asked. Sugden had been silent when he'd seen him at the asylum. And he'd said nothing when he killed people.

'Course he did,' Mrs Mayhew said dismissively. 'He's not had his tongue cut out. Polite, he was, too. Kept apologizing for what he had to do. Said he didn't have any choice.'

He'd put them both in the back bedroom and locked the door. The next day the three of them had sat by the fire.

'I asked him why he did it,' Mrs Mayhew said. 'All them people.'

'What did he say?'

'Just that it was his revenge.'

The same thing he'd said before. But he hadn't even known two of the people he'd murdered.

'Did he explain that at all?'

She shook her head, pulling her daughter close as the younger woman began to cry again, making the soothing noises only mothers knew.

'What else did he talk about?'

'His sister. Kept calling her poor Katie. How he loved her when he was small, then she went off to be a servant and he hardly ever saw her any more.' She paused, staring straight ahead, then raised her gaze. 'Said he was going to kill the man who'd killed her.'

Harper's head jerked up. 'Did he say who that was?'

'No,' she answered simply. 'I asked him. He just said it would be the last thing he did.'

The silence seemed to grow large in the room.

'How long ago did he leave?' the inspector asked eventually.

'He come into the bedroom first thing. It was still pitch black outside.' He waited for the rest. 'He had that gun, I could make out the shape of it. I thought he was going to kill us.' But he hadn't, Harper thought. Why? Because of kindnesses he remembered from childhood? Because he'd had food and shelter there? God only knew. 'He just said he had to tie us up.' She snorted. 'He made sure it wasn't too tight. Said someone would find us soon.'

He left Constable Williams with the women. He could take their statements. Outside in the cold, the inspector looked at Ash.

'What do you make of that?'

'A bit strange, really, isn't it, sir?'

'Very.' Sugden hadn't harmed the women at all. He hadn't even threatened them by the sound of it.

'I'll tell you what worries me, sir. It's like he knows who killed Mrs Carr.'

'Or he imagines he does.'

If Sugden had really known, he'd have gone after the murderer first. Wouldn't he? It was impossible to know all the things tumbling and swirling in the man's mind. He'd shot innocent people with no compunction, but let two women live. No rhyme, no reason.

'Who do you think he means, sir?'

'I don't know,' Harper admitted with a sigh. They had a man keeping guard on Carr's house. There was someone at the boot factory. The superintendent had posted one more at Neville Carr's home. He glanced up and down the street. 'He's long gone from here. Let's go back to the station.'

'Cross Green?' Kendall asked in astonishment. 'That's just a stone's throw from here.'

'He'll be somewhere else by now,' the inspector said. 'You can bank on it. But he's after whoever he thinks killed his sister.'

'Who?'

All Harper could do was shake his head. 'Just that it would be the last thing he did.' He waited a heartbeat. 'The *last*,' he repeated.

The superintendent rubbed his palms slowly down his face. He looked weary. Haggard. There were bags under his eyes and his usually immaculate suit was rumpled. His tie sat slightly askew, his shirt collar grubby.

'Who do you think he means?'

'I've been racking my brains all the way back here. Beside the Carrs I can't think of anyone.'

'We have men on them.'

'Maybe there's someone from her past that we don't know about, someone he blames,' Ash said slowly. Harper turned to look at him. 'Some old sweetheart of hers that Sugden remembers. He can't know who really killed her, sir, can he?'

'Of course not.' It had to be in the man's imagination.

'Make sure the bobbies on the family stay alert,' Kendall said. 'Get back out there and keep looking.'

254

But Harper didn't leave. He closed the door and waited.

'What is it, Tom?'

'How long since you slept, sir?'

'I'll go home tonight and look fresh for the funeral tomorrow, Inspector,' he answered coldly. 'I suggest you make sure you dress your best, too. Is there anything else?'

'No, sir.'

'Then go and do your job and leave me to do mine.'

Harper walked behind the hearse with the other detectives, head bowed, top hat cradled in his hands. His boots gleamed, his cheeks were pink from the razor. Alongside him, Reed wore his fire brigade uniform.

The long procession marched under a slate sky full with the smell of rain. Just let it hold off until Peters was buried, he thought. Then the deluge could come.

Crowds lined the street, heads bowed, silent as they passed. There were hundreds of people, everything coming to a halt. The only sound was the slow clop of the horses' hooves and the rumble of the hearse's wheels on the road. The second time in just a few weeks. First the fireman who lost his life in the blaze at New Station and now a copper murdered as he did his duty.

At the cemetery on Beckett Street, the chief constable stood next to Peters's widow, a short, stout woman with a black veil covering her face.

'Keep close to the back,' Harper ordered Reed

and Ash. 'Keep your eyes peeled for Sugden. I wouldn't put it past him to show his face.'

'He'd be mad with all these coppers here,' Reed said.

'He bloody well is, remember?' the inspector hissed.

But it all passed calmly. The vicar's voice was clear and resonant. An honour guard of men from Hunslet police station were the pall-bearers, lowering the coffin slowly into the grave. Finally, as the first heavy drops of rain arrived, it was done. People scuttled away, eager to stay dry.

The inspector stayed. Sugden could still be close, ready to appear. He was willing to wait, just in case. He took out his pocket watch, checking the time as he sheltered under a beech tree. Leaves lay in piles by his feet.

Ten minutes. Twenty. He flipped the cover off the watch again. Half an hour. He nodded to the others and they marched out of the cemetery, leaving the gravediggers to do their work.

Twenty-Two

Two more days and still no sign of Sugden. Out on Holbeck Moor some men found an abandoned camp. It could have been his; there was no way of knowing.

The police searched everywhere, but there weren't enough of them. Volunteers joined the hunt. But wherever he was, Sugden stayed a step ahead of them. There hadn't even been any sightings.

'I told you,' Reed said. It had been a long, cold day outside. Now the fire was blazing in the office as they tried to warm their bones. 'He was an army scout. He knows how to hide and forage.'

'Begging your pardon, sir,' Ash pointed out, 'but he's surfaced twice. First that time when he killed poor Charlie Peters, then with those women in Cross Green.'

'He's right,' Kendall agreed. He stood in the doorway, puffing thoughtfully on his pipe. 'And he'll probably show himself again very soon.'

'We've talked to everyone we can find who knew him,' Harper said. He'd spent the last two days knocking on doors and asking questions. 'We're keeping a quiet eye on people.'

'Then let's hope it pays off.' The superintendent sounded exhausted. He seemed to be living at Millgarth when he wasn't dashing off to meetings. The strain showed on his face. He looked thinner, paler, with dark, heavy circles under his eyes.

But every copper seemed dead on his feet. In the days after Peters's death they'd raged through Leeds. Now it was more difficult; day after day of nothing had left them dispirited. They needed something to give them heart. Anything at all.

Sugden wanted the man who'd killed his sister. But, Harper wondered, who the hell did he believe was the murderer? And there was something else in there. He'd said the revenge would be the last thing he did. Was he planning on killing himself afterwards?

They had to find him.

'Tom.' Kendall's voice cut through his thoughts. 'Are you deaf?'

'Sorry, sir.' He felt himself colouring. 'I was miles away.'

'The connection to the Carr case. How can we use that to find him?'

'I've got two men covering Carr's house now, another two on his son's place.'

'Who else?'

'I've no idea,' the inspector answered with a sigh. 'Not unless Sugden knows something we haven't been able to find. The killing doesn't seem to have anything to do with Catherine Carr's politics. She didn't really have any friends. No lovers.'

The image of her slipped into his mind, her arm when they lifted off a chunk of the concrete. The metal shining in the light where her skin should have been.

'Keep digging,' the superintendent ordered, shaking his head in frustration.

They were just about to leave Millgarth, buttoning coats against the cold and damp, when Tollman lifted a hand to stop them. He was talking urgently on the telephone, his mouth close to the instrument, receiver pressed against his ear.

'Yes,' he said finally and turned. 'Someone claims he's seen Sugden in Headingley.'

'Where?' Harper asked.

'Bennett Road.'

'Christ.' The word slipped out. Reed and Ash stared at him. 'Neville Carr's mistress lives there.'

'Woodhouse has men on the way, sir,' Tollman said.

'Tell the super,' Harper ordered. 'We'll be there as soon as we can.'

Policemen blocked both ends of the street. The noise from the Otley Road was just a few yards away, but it could have been miles. Here things were deathly quiet.

'Who saw him?' Harper asked the sergeant in command.

'A man on his way to work, sir. Glanced along and saw a man with a beard and a gun.'

'He's certain it was a gun?'

'I questioned him myself. He's sure.' The man paused. 'You said he might be after a woman here.'

'Number twenty-seven.' The inspector kept his eyes on the street. No one moving anywhere. No curtains twitching. 'Through terrace. I want men stationed at the front and in the ginnel.'

'Yes, sir.'

'I'll go in through the back door. Just be ready, I don't want another copper killed.'

'Won't be one of us who ends up dead,' the sergeant promised.

His mouth was dry. The bricks felt cold against his cheek as he pressed himself against the wall. Ash stood behind him, two constables waiting

259

outside the yard. Reed and four more coppers waited by the front door.

This wasn't a time for knocking and hoping someone answered. They had to go in swift and hard. Harper could feel his heart thumping against his chest. Last time he'd done this he'd found two women alive and unhurt. This time? He daren't even guess.

He raised his hand and Ash moved to stand in front of the door. The inspector nodded and a heavy boot came down against the wood. A second kick splintered the wood, and a third sent the door crashing back.

Inside the curtains were closed, as if morning hadn't arrived. But he could smell it immediately. The iron tang of blood. He dashed through, into the parlour, then up the stairs. She was in the bedroom, already dead. The sheet around her was flooded with red.

A single cut across her throat. A sharp knife, blood on the blade that lay beside her head. Her skin was still warm, still flexible; she hadn't been dead for long. By the time he'd covered her face, Ash was in the room.

'No one else in the house, sir. I checked downstairs, the kitchen window's been forced.'

'If Sugden did this, he's changed his style.'

'Who else could have done it?'

'Neville Carr, maybe. She was his mistress. I don't know. Other men came around, too. That's what one of the neighbours told me the other day. Go through this place and start a house-to-house.'

'Yes, sir.'

The inspector rose to his feet slowly, eyes on the corpse.

'I'll go and see Carr.'

The boot factory was busy, the copper at the gate alert and suspicious. In the office the clerks worked, heads down over their ledgers. He had to wait, sitting on a hard chair and staring into space until the office door opened.

'What is it?' Carr asked as soon as the door closed. His starched high collar was crisp white, his tie perfectly knotted. 'I hope it's important.'

'It is, sir.' The quiet, serious tone made the man look up. Harper had checked with the clerks; Carr had arrived just after seven, too early to have killed the woman.

'Well?'

'I believe you know Miss Bertha Davis, sir.'

'What?' A first there was a lack of comprehension on his face. Then Carr took a breath. 'Yes,' he admitted. 'I do.'

'I'm very sorry to tell you, sir, but she's dead.'

'But—' he began, then shook his head as if he could remove the inspector's words. 'I saw her yesterday . . .'

'I've just come from there,' Harper said with slow certainty. He paused. 'Someone killed her. We think it might have been Sugden.'

'My God.' Carr seemed to deflate. Maybe he'd really loved her, the inspector thought. Or perhaps he was just considering all the scandal if word got out about his mistress.

'I need to know about Miss Davis, sir. Whatever you can tell me.'

'I . . .' Carr began, then stopped, rubbing a hand across his mouth. 'How?' he asked eventually.

'I really can't say at the moment, sir.' Harper kept his voice soothing. Better if the man didn't know the details. 'How long had you known her?'

'Two years. As of last Wednesday. I don't want—'

'Anything you tell me is in confidence.'

All Carr's bluster had vanished. His eyes looked hunted and the colour had drained from his face. His fingers fidgeted, needing something to do. He seemed fragile, as if a heavy gust of wind could blow him over.

'You know about the relationship I had with her?' he asked tentatively.

'Yes, sir.'

He teased out more details. She was an actress. They'd met at the Grand Theatre when she'd had a small part in a play. The story would have been sad if he hadn't been so earnest. He'd rented the house for her, visited two or three times a week. Harper didn't mention her other callers. There was no need to rub salt into Carr's wounds.

'Inspector,' he finished, 'it would be embarrassing for my wife and children if word of . . . got out.'

'I won't say anything,' Harper promised. But too many people already knew the truth. One way or another it would leak out.

'Thank you. Did she . . . did she suffer?'

'No, sir. It was quick.' The cut had been, at least. What happened before that, he couldn't tell.

Carr nodded. 'Are you close to finding him?'

'We've got every man looking.'

'Why Bertha? Why would he go after her?'

'To hurt you, sir. I think you're next on his list.'

'Me?' He blinked. 'Why?'

'I'm not sure sir, but somehow he might think you're responsible for his sister's death.'

Carr gave a nervous laugh. 'That's ridiculous. I never . . .'

'I'm increasing the number of men guarding you, sir. I don't want you going anywhere without a policeman accompanying you.'

'Why? Why would he think that?' There was an edge of desperation in his voice.

'I honestly don't know,' Harper told him. 'He's unbalanced.'

'You truly think he wants to kill me?'

'Yes, sir, I do.'

Carr sat in stunned silence.

'I want to put a third man on your house, too, sir,' the inspector continued.

'Of course,' he agreed.

'We'll find him, sir. And we'll keep you safe.'

'Do you really think it was Sugden?' Superintendent Kendall asked. Millgarth was deathly quiet, every copper out searching. Only Tollman was left, standing in his place behind the front desk.

'It has to be,' Harper answered. From the corner of his eye he could see Reed and Ash nodding. 'There's just one thing. How the hell did he find out about Carr's mistress? I only knew because I forced it out of Barnabas Tooms.'

263

'But he did know and he killed her.'

'I've put more men on Carr and his home.'

'More on his father's house, too,' Kendall ordered.

'Already done.'

Silence fell for a few seconds, then Ash said, 'I've been doing a little digging, sir. There's something that never sat right with me.'

'What's that?' Kendall asked sharply.

'Those people he shot on Briggate. Everything else Sugden's done has had a purpose, it's all been to do with his sister's death.' They nodded. 'But that was just out of the blue.'

'Go on,' Kendall told him.

'Turns out that twenty years ago that jeweller Samuel had a servant he dismissed. Accused her of theft. No reference.'

'Catherine Carr?' Harper asked.

'Yes, sir. Well, Sugden as she was back then. Circumstances like that, she was lucky to ever get another job. I had to find the housekeeper who worked there at the time. She remembered it.'

'Was she guilty?' Reed asked quietly. 'Was she a thief?'

'Turns out she wasn't, sir,' the constable answered. 'They found the goods on another lass a few weeks later. Too late by then. I think Sugden has a list in his head. Everyone who wronged him or his sister.'

'That's good work,' Kendall praised him.

'It doesn't get us any closer to Sugden, though,' Reed pointed out.

'Have you found any connection at all between

264

the Carr family and Catherine Carr's murder?' the superintendent asked Harper.

'Nothing. There was a motive, right enough. If the old man died first, Catherine would inherit everything. After her it would go to Neville. But I can't dig up anything connecting him to the killing.'

'If Sugden's gone after Neville Carr's mistress, he could go after his son, too,' Ash said.

'I'll talk to him,' Harper said. 'And get someone on him.'

'Let's see if we can find Sugden today,' Kendall said wearily, taking the watch from his waistcoat. 'We'll meet here at five. If there's anything at all, let me know.'

From Kirkstall, to Meanwood, Headingley then out to Adel, Reed moved between the groups of policemen searching the open spaces and woods. They found signs of camps, some recent, some older, but nothing to show it was Sugden who'd been there.

There was just one site he could pick out as likely: a bivouac in the army style in the woods just beyond Meanwood. Only a short distance from the boot factory. But it had been empty for a few days.

The ground was hard under his boots. The night had brought a heavy frost; the grass in the shade was still covered in white. Sugden would have a tough job surviving out here.

'Keep looking,' he told the men who'd gathered round, hearing them grumble. He didn't blame them. This wasn't what they'd joined the police to do. It wasn't what he wanted, either. As soon as this was over he'd be glad to get back to the fire brigade and his training as an investigator.

At least he hadn't had another drink. He hadn't even wanted one. His head had pounded for a whole day, and he'd felt like he couldn't keep any food down for half of it. But more than anything, it was the look of disappointment and hurt on Elizabeth's face that stopped him. He couldn't do that to her again. He didn't want her staring at him with eyes full of pity. He wanted to see hope and love.

In Adel he paid close attention to the area around the Ford house. If Sugden blamed Isabella for his sister's death, she'd make an easy target. But there was no sign anyone had made camp up there. That was something, but just a single, meagre crumb.

By four, feet aching, legs sore, he caught the omnibus back into town.

Harper had never been to Neville Carr's house before. It was just a stone's throw from his father's in Chapel Allerton, looking down on the Harrogate Road. New enough that there was still a sandy glow to the Yorkshire stone.

A constable guarded the gate; another was patrolling around the back of the house. Carr himself was at the boot factory, and his wife was out on her morning social calls. He had to wait for Gordon Carr. Ten o'clock and he wasn't up yet.

But there was a warm fire in the parlour and a comfortable chair. A maid brought a pot of tea

266

and some biscuits. He'd waited in far worse places. By the time the man appeared he'd almost brought his notebook up to date.

Gordon Carr wore his clothes well. His suit was expensive, soft grey wool that fitted him closely. A shirt of fine linen with a fresh celluloid collar. The tie and handkerchief in his pocket were deep red silk. He smelt of pomade and bay rum. Pale side whiskers clung to his cheeks. He had the self-satisfied look of a young man who believed the world was his to take.

'What do you want, Inspector?' No handshake, no apology. Just an irritated tone as if this was some chore to be done before he could move on to something more pleasant.

'We have reason to believe someone might target your family, sir. I'd like to have a policeman watch you when you're out.'

'You mean Sugden?' There was amusement in his voice. 'He killed my father's slut, didn't he? I saw it in the newspapers this morning.'

'Yes,' Harper answered coldly. 'He did. I found the body.'

'And you think he might come for me or Mama?' A smile played across his mouth.

'I think it's possible. My job is to keep you safe.'

'How many has he killed so far?' Carr asked tauntingly. 'Four, isn't it? Or is it five? And one wounded? You haven't been doing your job very well, Inspector.'

Harper felt the sharp bubble of anger rise and pushed it back down. It would be too easy to hate Gordon Carr. He had to keep him alive.

'It's six now. And I want to make sure he doesn't kill *you*, sir.' He almost had to clench his teeth to be polite.

'No,' Carr told him after a few seconds' thought. 'I don't want one of your ugly men traipsing around with me.'

'Sir—'

'I had a nanny when I was young. I hated her. I'm not going to have another. It's as simple as that.' He turned to leave the room.

'It's better than being dead, isn't it?'

The man didn't even turn his head. 'Didn't you hear me, Inspector? I said no.'

Carr didn't bother to close the door behind him. His footsteps trailed back up the stairs.

Harper waited a moment, then left. Outside, his breath bloomed in the cold air.

'Any luck, sir?' the constable at the gate asked. His face was ruddy from the chill and he stamped his feet to keep them warm.

'You've spent time here. What do you think?'

'Honestly, sir? I wouldn't give you tuppence for the lot of them, and that's the truth.'

The inspector smiled and winked. 'Just between you, me and the gatepost,' he said, 'I think you're valuing them too highly.'

Twenty-Three

'You're very quiet tonight,' Annabelle said.

He'd sat and brooded for the last quarter of an hour, staring into the flames of the fire without seeing a thing.

'Just thinking,' he apologized.

None of it would let him be. The faces of the dead, one after another, Catherine Carr's at the top. How could they stop Sugden? He'd been steps ahead of them all the way. And no matter how many men they had on Neville Carr, the truth was that they couldn't guarantee his safety. Sugden was fast and he was sly.

She put down the book she was reading and stared at him. 'It's not like you.'

'I'm sorry,' he said and sighed. 'This is . . .'

'It's fine,' she told him with a smile. 'I've seen the newspapers. Is he really a monster?'

'No,' Harper answered slowly. 'I don't think so. He believes he's doing the right thing, the way he sees it.'

'You'll hang him in the end.'

'Oh yes,' he said with certainty. They'd catch him, sooner or later. But it needed to be sooner, before anyone else died.

'How's your hearing?' Annabelle asked.

He grimaced. 'No better, but not any worse, thank God.'

'I meant what I said before, Tom. We can go

to London and see someone there. They might be able to do something.'

'No.' He knew the truth. It was exactly the same as it had been months and years before. Bit by bit, the hearing in his right ear was going. Soon it would vanish completely. And people knew. They had to. He thought he'd been clever and hidden it well. 'When this is all over I'm going to talk to the super about it.'

He'd made the decision the day before. Better that he say something before anyone else did. There was the tale Dr King had told him about the officer who'd done his job perfectly well when deaf. And there'd been deaf beat bobbies. He had to grasp the nettle.

'What if he says you have to leave?' Annabelle asked.

'I'll face that when I come to it.' He turned to look at her. It was time to change the subject. He'd made his decision, he didn't want to talk about it any more. 'What about you? Have you decided about being on the suffrage committee yet?'

'No.' She took a cushion, placed it in front of her and hugged it. A small gesture, but it made her seem like a child, vulnerable. 'I don't know that I want to be travelling all over the place.'

'Would you have to?'

She nodded. 'Manchester, London. And they'd want me to talk a lot. Give more speeches. I don't think it's me.'

There was something else. He was certain of it.

'Are you sure that's the real reason?'

'I never wanted to be a speaker. You know that, Tom.'

'Miss Ford's very persuasive.'

She chuckled. 'Very.'

'Are you going to refuse?'

'I don't know yet,' she sighed, crushing the cushion against her. 'Let's bank the fire and go to bed. We're not going to solve anything tonight, are we?'

'What else have you managed to find out about Sugden and his sister?' Kendall asked.

Ash opened his notebook and they all waited. Reed lit a cigarette.

'There's not a lot to tell, sir. That's the problem. Sugden was in and out of jobs after the army. Couldn't seem to settle at anything. Sometimes he left, sometimes he was dismissed.'

'I want a man guarding everyone who sacked him,' the superintendent interrupted.

'I've already given a list to Sergeant Tollman,' the constable continued. 'The longest time he spent was at Carr's. Then he did the robbery and went off to jail. The place he robbed isn't in business any more. Proprietor moved away, somewhere down south I was told.'

'So there's nothing more on him?' Reed asked.

'That's the lot.'

'What about his sister? If she was dismissed for theft, how did she manage to get another job?'

'The best I can tell, she must have lied, sir. I can't find any trace of her between that and working for the Carrs. I went back out there but

271

all the correspondence about her has gone.' He shrugged. 'It's a bit of a mystery.'

'I still can't come up with a connection between any of the family and Katie Carr's murder,' Harper added. He'd gone back to see Isabella Ford once more, but she'd already told him everything she knew. By the end of the day he'd worked his way through to Tilly, the mill woman. She seemed to be the closest to a friend Catherine Carr had in the last months of her life but she hadn't known much.

Katie's landlady had cleared the room and let it again. All her effects only filled a small box. He'd pored through it as she watched over him. But there was nothing. And what she knew about her tenant wouldn't have filled the back of a postage stamp.

They knew nothing about her.

He was back to square one.

'We've searched everywhere for Sugden,' Reed said. 'But it's easy enough for him to give us the slip.' He looked at the others. 'You know that. We've found some places where he might have camped, but that's it. There's simply too much to cover.' He sounded frustrated. 'He's gone to ground. We're not even getting any tips from people who've spotted him. We're just banging our heads against a bloody brick wall.'

'There's nothing else we can do for now,' Kendall concluded after he'd listened to them all. 'Unless one of you has a bright idea. Just keep hunting for Sugden, and make sure everyone he might go after is safe.' He paused. 'That was very good work, Ash.'

'Thank you, sir.' He beamed under his thick moustache.

'Where today, sir?' Ash asked the sergeant.

'You might as well stick a pin in the map and take your chance,' Reed told him.

'But perhaps we have him on the run. Moving from one place to another.'

'If we can't find him, that doesn't help.'

'Chin up, sir. Maybe we'll get lucky today.'

'See how you feel after a few hours out there.'

Reed was home early, not long after night had fallen. Elizabeth was in the scullery, mixing something in a bowl, smiling when she saw him.

'I didn't expect you for hours yet.'

'I'd had enough,' he answered as he hung his overcoat and hat on the peg.

'Still nothing?'

'No,' he said, kissing her on the cheek as he passed and sitting heavily on the chair before taking off his boots. 'That's better. What are you making?'

'I thought I'd do us a cake. A little treat.'

'You could have brought one from the shop.'

'Never the same as homemade.' She sniffed. 'Doesn't have that touch.'

He laughed as he lit a cigarette. 'But they're good enough to sell.'

'That's different,' she said defensively. 'If you want to be useful, put the kettle on. You look like you could do with a cup of tea.'

'You mean you need one.' He grinned. Just being at home cheered him. Away from all the frustrations of the hunt. With the woman he loved. And he still hadn't had a drink since that night. He'd wanted one but he hadn't given in.

She rubbed butter into a cake pan and spooned in the mixture.

'I do,' she said. 'But I'm busy and you're not.'

'How's that lad getting on? The one who broke the window.' He poured water into the kettle and settled it on the range.

'Starting to get cheeky sometimes.' She wiped a strand of hair off her face with her wrist. 'Open the oven door for me, will you?'

'He must be starting to feel comfortable there, then,' Reed said with a grin. 'How long until he's paid the cost of the new window?'

'A while yet.'

'You think he's learned his lesson?'

'Oh aye.' She chuckled. 'I tell you what, the girls in the shop could take a leaf from his book. As soon as he finishes one job he's back for the next.'

As the kettle steamed, he warmed the teapot, poured the water down the sink then spooned in the tea leaves. Pot to the kettle, the way his mother always did it, then leave it to mash.

'At least you're trained,' Elizabeth said wryly.

'I'm trying,' he told her, and they both knew he meant much more than the words he'd spoken.

'I know, luv.' She put her hand over his. 'And I'll help you all I can.'

It was cold outside, but the rain had stopped and the fog hadn't returned. Soon enough it would be back, clinging to Leeds all winter. There'd be

274

people coughing up their lungs, and the poor and the old would die when they couldn't afford to heat their rooms. No respite for the weak, Harper thought.

As he crossed St Peter's Square he heard someone calling his name.

'Mr Martin,' he said, waiting for the man to catch up.

'I'm glad I caught you,' Martin said. His back was straight, Bible in his hand, face bright with the light of certainty. What did he want, the inspector wondered? Another confession of guilt? A sermon on immorality?

'I'm in a hurry.' It was a lie, but it meant he could get away quickly.

'Where are you going?' Martin asked. 'I'll walk with you, if I might.'

'Is there something I can do for you?'

The man reached into his coat and brought out a pamphlet. 'I was hoping you'd give this to your wife.'

Harper glanced at the title. *The Wife and the Home.*

'I don't think this is going to change her thinking.'

'God moves in strange ways,' Martin said earnestly.

'Maybe,' he allowed. 'Was there something else?'

The man's face turned serious. 'I talked to a man yesterday. He was very troubled. Burdened.'

'Go on.'

'He told me he'd done something terrible.'

'What was it?' Harper asked. 'Did he say?'

275

Martin shook his head. 'I asked several times, but all he'd say was that it was terrible, over and over. He'd been drinking.'

'I'm not sure why you're telling me all this, Mr Martin.'

'It's just . . .' he began hesitantly. 'When you took me to the police station, you said you were looking for a man with fair side whiskers and a bowler hat.'

Suddenly the inspector was attentive. 'What's his name?'

'John. That's all he told me. No surname.'

'He had a bowler hat?'

'A very battered one,' Martin said. 'But yes, he did.'

'Where did you see him?' It was a lead, a thread. More than they'd had for days.

'He was outside the Palace Hotel on Kirkgate. He seemed to know who I was.'

'Thank you,' Harper told him and turned on his heel.

It was no more than a hundred yards to the Palace. The place was already busy, loaders from the wharves taking a break from their work. All the gas mantles were lit, the inside much brighter than the gloom out on the street. He pushed through the crowd and found the landlord behind the bar, busy filling orders. It was a well-kept house, the wood-work gleaming in the light.

He tried to remember the landlord's name. Ben something-or-other. The inspector had only been in here twice before, only for a few minutes each time.

'I'm sure I know you,' the landlord said once the rush had passed. 'I never forget a face.'

276

'Detective Inspector Harper, Leeds Police.'

'That's right.' His face creased into a broad smile. 'I used to have one of your lot in here regular like.'

'Billy Reed?' It was a fair guess.

'That's the one. Not seen him in months now.'

'I'm hoping you can help me, Mr . . .'

'Palmer. Ben Palmer.'

He'd remembered some of it anyway. 'I'm trying to find someone who drinks in here. All I know is that his name's John. He has a bowler hat that's seen better days, and fair hair. Big mutton chop whiskers.'

'I've seen him,' Palmer agreed with a nod. 'Don't know him, though. He's not really a regular. Sits off by himself and drinks brandy till he's out of money.'

'When was he here last?' Harper asked urgently.

'I don't know.' He ran a hand across his chin. 'It could have been last night. I'm not right sure.' He paused. 'No, wait, he was here, I remember now.'

'Does anyone know him?'

Palmer pursed his lips and shook his head. 'I don't think so. Like I said, he's not in all the time. Probably from one of the rooming houses.'

But there were hundreds of those in the streets around, beds for working men and the poor. Too many to check on a wild hunch.

'If he comes in again, I'd like you to send word to me at Millgarth.'

'Aye, all right. But he's never been in before evening, I can tell you that.'

'I'll be there,' the inspector promised.

* * *

277

There was nothing more he could do there. He started along Kirkgate, pausing at the union office when a hand waved at him through the window.

'Bearing up, Inspector?' Tom Maguire asked. For once he was smiling and looking happy.

'You're looking very bright today,' Harper said. 'Had some good news?'

'All's fine with the world, nothing more than that. I hear Miss Ford wants Annabelle for the suffrage committee.'

'Yes.' Maguire seemed to hear most things that happened in Leeds. Not just the news but what went on behind the scenes.

'She's going to take it, of course?' He'd grown up a few streets away from Annabelle on the Bank. She was a few years older, but the connections remained.

'You'd have to ask her.' It was the safest thing to say. 'She hasn't made up her mind yet.'

'Why on earth not?' Maguire asked in astonishment. 'She'd be perfect for it.'

'I don't know. It's her decision.'

'Of course,' Maguire agreed. 'I'd have thought she'd jump at the chance.'

All he could do was shrug in reply. Whatever was troubling Annabelle, she didn't want to talk about it yet.

'And how's your search?' Maguire continued.

'You probably know the answer to that,' Harper said with a sigh. 'If you have any information . . .'

'If I did, I'd tell you.'

'We need all the help we can get.'

'I haven't forgotten Mrs Carr.'

278

'Or all the ones Sugden killed.'

'May they rest in peace,' Maguire said quietly.

'Do you ever drink in the Palace?' Harper asked. It was worth a try; the public house was just down the street.

'Not often. Why?'

'I just wondered. There's someone I want to find who's been going there.'

'I'm sorry, Inspector, I can't help you.'

Never mind, he thought. There would be tonight.

'I need to go.'

'Of course,' Maguire said. 'And good luck. Should I stop by and talk to Annabelle, do you think?'

'Better to leave her to make up her own mind,' Harper advised.

'Fair play to her then. Good hunting, Inspector.'

Back at Millgarth he waited for Ash to return. The constable arrived with Reed a little before five. The sergeant tossed his hat on to the desk and sank into his chair.

'Another day wasted.' He reached into his jacket and took out cigarettes and matches. 'I'm starting to think we'll never bloody well find Sugden.'

'We will,' Harper said. He turned to Ash. 'I want you to go for a drink.'

The constable raised his eyebrows. 'Sir?'

'Go down to the Palace.' He pulled coins from his pocket. 'You have my permission to drink on duty.'

'Thank you, sir,' he said, mystified. 'Is there a reason?'

'I want you to keep your eyes peeled for someone.'

The others listened closely as he explained.

'If the landlord's going to send someone when this John fellow comes in, why do you need me there?' Ash asked.

'Insurance,' the inspector answered. 'And if they forget, you can bring him in.'

The constable smiled. 'Yes, sir. And my father always taught me never to turn down a free drink.'

'Do you want me tonight, Tom?' Reed asked.

'Not unless you fancy spending your evening in a pub.'

The sergeant shook his head. 'I'd just as soon go home.'

'You might as well get off, then. The super's at a meeting.' He glanced out at the darkness beyond the window. 'I doubt we'll be catching Sugden tonight.'

Time passed slowly. After an hour the inspector had caught up with his reports and read the newspaper. He settled back in the chair and closed his eyes. One thing he'd learned on the job was to take rest where he could. The next break might be a long time coming.

He was woken by the night sergeant shaking his shoulder.

'There's a lad out here, sir. Says Constable Ash sent him. The man you're after is at the Palace.'

'Thank you.' He fumbled in his pocket for a farthing. 'Give him that.'

The walk across the open market woke him. The square was empty, only the sound of his footsteps ringing, the air cold enough to sting his cheeks.

The lights of the Palace shone bright, the babble of voices loud even on the other side of Kirkgate. Someone was thumping a piano, and a few people sang along drunkenly. Harper slipped through the door and looked around the crowd for Ash.

He had a table close to the front window, a half-empty glass of beer on the table in front on him.

'I think that's your man, sir,' he said as the inspector sat. He followed the gaze. Sitting by himself, head bowed, hands cradling a glass of brandy. The worn bowler hat was still on his head, and thick blond sideboards covered his cheeks.

'Looks like him.'

'I'll go and brace him. You stand by the door in case he tries to run.'

'Right you are, sir.' Ash stood, swallowed the rest of his drink and went to wait just outside the pub.

'John,' Harper called out as he approached the man, seeing his head jerk up. 'You're John?'

His eyes didn't focus too well; he peered to try to make out who was talking to him. But he was able to nod.

'I'm Detective Inspector Harper. I'd like a word with you at Millgarth if you don't mind.'

He was prepared for the man to bolt, but didn't expect he'd be so fast. In one movement the man was up, knocking over the table and pushing him out of the way. He squeezed through the crowd and out through the door.

By the time Harper arrived, Ash already had the man on the ground, arms pinned behind his back as he fastened the handcuffs.

'He won't be going anywhere, sir,' the constable said with satisfaction.

'Take him to the station. I'll be there in a minute.'

He walked back into the stunned silence of the Palace. Faces stared at him then looked away quickly. They parted as he walked, giving him a clear path to the bar. Ben Palmer stood there, hands on hips, a cloth in his hand.

'I thought you were going to tell me when he came in.'

'If I'd seen him, I would have.' His face was grim. 'We're that busy, I never even noticed. You know there's never any trouble here.'

'Just see you keep it that way.'

Twenty-Four

The room was cold but the man was sweating. The drops stood out on his forehead as he sat shaking.

'What's your name?' Harper asked again. So far all he'd got was a few coughs and grunts. 'What have you done that's so bad, John?'

Ash stood by the door, out of the way but watching intently. They'd been in here for a quarter of an hour with no answers. John's bowler hat sat on the table. Impatiently, the inspector picked it up and threw it across the room.

'You'd better understand this. You're going to tell me what I want to know, and I'm running out of patience. Now: what have you done that's so bad?'

He waited and saw the man's mouth open.

'I killed someone.' He spoke so softly that Harper wasn't sure he'd heard him properly.

'You killed someone?'

John nodded.

'Who?' the inspector pressed.

'A woman.' He bent forward. Harper grabbed his collar and pulled him back.

'Who? Where?'

John slowly turned his head to face him.

'In the Arches.' His voice seemed empty, flat.

Catherine Carr. It had to be. He drew in a breath. This was what he needed, what he'd been waiting for. He could feel a current running through his body.

'When was this, John?' he asked, forcing his voice to remain calm. He wanted to grab the man, to shake the confession out of him. Patience, he thought. Softly, softly. He had to calm the tingling he felt inside. Let him take his time.

'The night of the fire.' The words seemed to stumble out of John's mouth. Harper looked over at Ash, but the constable's face remained impassive.

'Who did you kill?' He kept his eyes on the man, watching him. But it was as if John wasn't quite here, as if some part of him was lost, off somewhere. 'Who?'

'I don't know.'

'You must know,' Harper said in a lulling voice. 'You killed her.'

'Yes,' John answered dully.

'Who was she? Why did you kill her?'

'He paid me.'

The inspector stayed silent for a few seconds, thinking furiously.

'Someone paid you?'

'Yes.'

'Why did he want the woman killed?'

'I don't know,' he answered. 'I didn't ask.'

John was still sweating, his hands shaking a little.

'Who was she?' Harper asked again.

'I don't know. He pointed her out.'

'You didn't ask?'

'No.' John seemed to return to the room, looking at the inspector. 'He paid me ten guineas. Just kill her, he said.'

'How did you do it?'

'Knife.' He paused. 'I left it by her.'

They'd never found the weapon, but with all the debris and damage . . . He needed to be careful with his questions, to draw out all the information.

'You killed her in the Arches, you said?'

'Yes.'

'How did you persuade her to go there?' He couldn't imagine Katie Carr going to the Arches willingly.

'Knife.' John's mouth curled into a cruel smile.

'She didn't scream?'

'I told her what would happen if she tried.' The life died from his eyes again. He might have earned his ten guineas but he'd taken on a ghost that would haunt him until he died.

Harper wanted all the details, needed them, but they'd come in time. There was one urgent question.

'Who was it? Who paid you to kill her?' Time seemed to stop while he waited for an answer.

'Tooms.'

Harper let out his breath slowly. Well, well . . . all debts were cancelled now.

'How do you know him?'

'My brother.'

The rest could wait. He'd talk to John again soon. He had enough to arrest Barnabas Tooms.

'Have someone take him down to the cells,' the inspector ordered Ash. 'We'll get everything else tomorrow.'

'Yes, sir.'

'You and I have a visit to make.'

The people had faded away from Boar Lane with evening, just a few moving along in the chill. Omnibuses and trams clanked past. The displays in the shop windows were lit, the Grand Pygmalion, the butcher across the road. Gas mantles glowed bright above the pavement.

Harper strode quickly, Ash easily keeping pace beside him. They hadn't exchanged a word since they left Millgarth. He was thinking of the best way to approach Tooms. Deception wasn't going to work; the man was a master of that. But head on, brute force. That might scare him.

The bar at the Griffin Hotel was busy, men in frock coats, others in newer, shorter styles. The smell of damp wool and cigars. The look of money and self-satisfaction. But no sign of Tooms.

He kept a room here, Harper remembered. At the desk the clerk told him the number, protesting when he turned towards the stairs.

'You need to be announced, sir.'

The inspector turned, his face hard. 'I'm with the police. I'll announce myself.'

The corridor on the third floor was dark wood and thick carpet. His boots didn't make a sound as he walked towards room 306.

As he hammered on the door he could hear quick movement and voices inside. Tooms had a woman with him. Good, he thought, that would make things easier. He waited a few seconds and brought his fist down on the wood once more.

A key turned in the lock and the door opened an inch, enough to see Tooms's eye.

'You'll have to wait, Inspector. I'm busy.'

Harper pushed hard. The door opened wide and Tooms stumbled back into the room, barely staying on his feet. He had a towel wrapped around his waist, showing thin legs, a round belly and a hairy chest. In the bed a girl pulled the covers up to her chin.

'I'm not waiting, Barnabas.' The inspector turned to the girl. 'Get dressed and go.'

'You can't do this,' Tooms warned.

'I can.' With the flat of his hand he pushed Tooms. Once, twice, until he was sprawled on a chair.

'I'll talk to the chief constable. You know he's a friend of mine.'

286

'He used to be. You don't have any friends now.'

For the first time he saw some fear in the man's eyes.

In the bed the girl was scrambling, trying to put on her clothes without being seen. Finally she scuttled out, smoothing down her dress and carrying a pair of brown button boots into the corridor. Ash shut the door behind her.

'What's this about?' Tooms demanded. He'd had time to gather his thoughts, smiling, thinking he was in control.

'Constable,' Harper said without turning his head, 'put the handcuffs on Mr Tooms.'

'What?' the man asked as Ash stepped forward.

'You arranged the murder of Catherine Carr.'

'I never!' Tooms stood, his face red with anger.

'Sit down,' the inspector told him, waiting until he was back in the chair. 'I have the man you paid. The one who murdered her.'

'I never,' Tooms repeated. But the bluster had gone from his voice.

'You're going to jail, Barnabas.' The pleasure with which he said it surprised him. 'And so is Neville Carr.'

'Neville?' Tooms asked. 'What does he have to do with it?'

'You were doing what he wanted.'

The man threw back his head and began to laugh.

'Inspector,' he said when he finally caught his breath. 'It wasn't Neville who wanted her dead. It was Gordon Carr.'

287

Twenty-Five

'Gordon Carr,' Harper said to the constable on duty at the gate of Neville Carr's house. 'Is he at home?'

'Went out in the carriage about two hours ago, sir. The driver's been back a while.'

'Find out where he dropped him and if he has to pick him up again.'

'Yes, sir.'

The inspector hammered at the front door until a breathless servant answered it. He waited in the hall for Neville Carr. When the man emerged, his face was bright red with rage.

'What the hell do you think you're doing here? This is my home.'

'I'm looking for your son, sir.'

'He's not here. What do you want with him, anyway?'

'Do you know where he's gone and when he'll be back?'

'He's of age,' Carr replied coldly. 'He lives his own life. Why do you want him, anyway?'

Harper squared his shoulders and looked at the man.

'I'm going to arrest him for the murder of Catherine Carr.'

'What?' Carr shouted. 'Don't be so bloody stupid.'

'I have the evidence.'

'You've had a grudge against this family since you began.'

'You can think what you like,' Harper told him. 'But I'm going to arrest your son.'

'You can't even catch that bloody Sugden.'

'I'll ask you again, Mr Carr. Do you know where I can find your son?'

'No,' he replied. 'And if I did I wouldn't tell you.'

'Very well.' He turned on his heel and walked out. The constable was back at his post. 'What did you find out?'

'Dropped him on Albion Street, sir. No orders to pick him up. He often takes a hackney to get home.'

'Keep a good watch. If he comes back I want you to arrest him.'

'Sir?' the constable asked in astonishment.

'For murder.'

'Yes, sir.'

At Millgarth he gave Gordon Carr's description to the night sergeant. Soon enough everyone on the beat would be looking for him. But Harper was going to search, moving from public house to clubs all over the middle of town.

No sign of the man. A few places where he'd been earlier in the evening, but he'd moved on. By eleven he still hadn't found Carr and he'd tried everywhere. He was so close to victory that he could taste it. All he needed was the man.

He went around everywhere once again, passing the word to everyone he knew. Finally, long after the church clock had struck midnight, he gave up and returned to the police station. No going home tonight, he'd wait and hope that someone would spot Carr. There were places that remained open very late, the clubs and dens that catered to the rich who wanted their pleasures to last into the small hours.

He tried to settle at his desk, closing his eyes and hoping for sleep. But it wouldn't come. After two minutes he was up and walking around the office, wide awake, mind sparking. Two, three o'clock came and went. At six he heard the shift change, the parade of boots and the barked orders from Sergeant Tollman.

Half an hour later Ash and Reed arrived, Superintendent Kendall close behind them. Harper told them what had happened the evening before, seeing smiles cross their faces.

'Good job, Tom,' Kendall told him.

'Gordon Carr's not behind bars yet,' the inspector cautioned.

'You'll catch him today.'

'I've put men on the railway stations, just in case.'

The superintendent nodded his approval and turned to Reed. 'Sugden?'

'Nothing,' the sergeant answered quickly. 'Not a sign of him since he killed that woman in Headingley.'

'Do you think he's still in Leeds?'

'Oh yes,' Reed replied. 'He's not done here yet, I'm certain of that.'

'Then keep pressing. Let's see if we can finish everything today.' Kendall stood. 'I know it's been hard, but we'll get them both. Sergeant Reed, a word in my office, please.'

'You've done some excellent work on this,' the superintendent said once Reed was seated.

'Thank you, sir.'

'I'll be telling Inspector Hill that.' He paused. 'Do you still want to go back to the fire brigade when everything is done here?'

There was a long silence before the sergeant replied, 'I do, sir.'

'I'd like to persuade you to stay if I could. I know there's been bad blood between you and Inspector Harper.'

'I think that's all in the past, sir.'

'I'm glad to hear it.' Kendall brought his pipe from a jacket pocket and filled it, then struck a match. 'I've been thinking that you'd make a good inspector with CID.'

'Sir?' The idea ambushed him. He'd never imagined something like this.

'Johnson over at B Division is going to retire. They're going to need someone with experience in charge.'

'I . . . I don't know, sir. I don't know what to say.'

'Nothing's signed and sealed yet,' Kendall told him. 'Take a little time to think about it. Talk it over with your . . .' He let the sentence go, not sure what to call Elizabeth.

'I will, sir. And thank you.'

'I've seen the change in you while you've been back here, Sergeant. You've impressed me. It seems as if you've ironed out whatever problems you had before. I think you'd be an asset to us.'

'Yes, sir. Thank you.'

He wandered out in a daze. Elated. Confused. First the chance to be a fire investigator and now this. A promotion, more responsibility. More money, and God knew they could use that.

'You look happy, Billy,' Harper said.

'A funny life sometimes,' was all he replied.

'It is,' the inspector agreed. 'Now let's go and find our men, shall we?'

Twenty-Six

The information came from a tip.

Gordon Carr hadn't gone home the night before; Harper had received a message from the local station. He was still somewhere in Leeds. He didn't know the police were seeking him. It was just a matter of time.

But the inspector didn't want to wait. He wanted Carr in custody, to have it all wrapped up. By late morning, though, he still had nothing. No sign of the man.

He stopped at a tea stall to put something warm in his belly. The skies were grey and threatening, but at least the fog hadn't returned, though every-where people were coughing. Winter was settling in, cold and killing.

Harper stood, drinking his tea, when he sensed someone standing next to him. He turned and saw Davy Piper. He was a short man, not much more than a midget, but always smartly dressed in a spotless suit and overcoat, his bowler hat neatly brushed. Anyone seeing him would have thought him prosperous, a senior clerk, perhaps, or a businessman.

But he'd never held a job. His money came here and there, selling information, doing small jobs.

'Are you still looking for Gordon Carr?' He didn't look at the inspector, but stared down Briggate, watching a train cross the bridge above the street in a cloud of steam.

'I am,' Harper replied.

'How much?'

'Ten bob.' A lot of money, but the force could find that much. And worth every penny.

'Holbeck,' Piper said, so softly that the inspector had to turn his head to catch the word.

'Where?'

'Siddall Place. There's a pub. He's upstairs. Paid for the night with someone.'

'I'll see you get the money,' Harper told him and the man nodded his agreement.

The inspector finished his tea in a single gulp and wiped his mouth with the back of his hand.

Reed and Ash were both at Millgarth, back from another search of the courts and yards behind Briggate.

'Get your coats,' Harper ordered. 'We're going to Holbeck.'

'Sugden?' the sergeant asked hopefully.

'Carr.'

The route took them through the Arches, passing under the railway station, a uniformed bobby from Hunslet accompanying them. Scaffolding was up, and men were laying bricks and building the thick walls that would hold the new platforms. It was hard to believe the fire had been so recent. Everything was covered in dust, and the soft smell of mortar filled the air.

Harper tried to pick out the spot where they'd discovered Catherine Carr's body. But it was impossible. It might have happened somewhere else. Another town, another country. The only image left in his head was the silvered skin in the dim light.

The public house had a few lunchtime drinkers who stared as the policemen entered. Harper had told the uniform to stay outside. Just in case. When the inspector turned his head again, half the customers had quietly disappeared. The landlord bustled out of the back, face dropping when he saw them.

'I don't like coppers in here. I don't want trouble.'

'Then we'll make sure there isn't any,' Harper told him with a smile. 'You've had a man spending the night upstairs.'

'What the lasses do is their business,' the landlord said. 'Nowt to do with me.'

'Then it won't bother you if we go upstairs, will it?' He paused. 'Which room is it?'

'Third door along on the left,' he answered reluctantly. 'I don't want no trouble,' he repeated lamely.

They climbed the stairs quietly. Reed stood on one side of the door, Ash on the other as the inspector knocked. Silence, then the pad of bare feet on the boards and a girl turned the key.

Without waiting, Harper forced his way in, the others right behind him. Carr was still in the bed, awake and naked.

'What the hell . . .' he began, sitting up.

The inspector grabbed him by the hair, dragging him out of bed to stand white and exposed.

'I'm arresting you for the murder of Catherine Carr,' Harper told him. 'Get yourself dressed.'

Without a word, Carr obeyed, each action fast and deliberate until he sat to lace his boots.

'Handcuffs,' the inspector ordered.

Carr glared as Ash snapped them on his wrists, and they marched him out into the daylight.

'I didn't kill her,' Carr said haughtily.

'You arranged it,' Harper told him. 'Barnabas Tooms has admitted it and we have the man who used the knife on her.' He put a hand on the man's back and pushed him so hard he almost stumbled.

'Can I have a cigarette?'

After a brief hesitation, the inspector nodded, and Carr stopped, moving his hands awkwardly towards his pocket. Then, as they were standing, he began to run. Just a few yards' start.

'After him!' Harper shouted. But Carr had already turned the corner.

Before they'd gone two paces the shot boomed. Then another. Both barrels of a shotgun.

He saw Carr face down on the pavement, a lake of blood already spilling from his chest, and Sugden sprinting down the street, the weapon still in his hand.

'Stay here,' the inspector ordered the bobby. If Carr wasn't dead yet, he would be very soon. It was too late to help him.

He ran, hearing Reed and Ash just behind him. They sprinted along Sweet Street, footfalls echoing off the brick walls.

They followed Sugden around to Marshall Street, towards the big mills. Gaining ground. Only a yard or two, but getting closer.

The man swerved out into the road and ducked behind a cart; the driver raised his whip in astonishment. Next to him, Harper could hear Reed breathing hard.

Marshall's Mill lay ahead, but Sugden turned once more, dashing up the steps in front of Temple Mill.

He hadn't had time to reload, Reed thought. His eyes were on Sugden as the man pulled back the heavy doors and vanished.

The sergeant had passed the building hundreds of times in his life. Someone had once told him that the front of the place, with its pillars and strange carvings, was copied from an Egyptian temple. Now he hardly noticed as he pounded up the stairs and dragged back the door.

He heard Harper shout, 'Round the back,' and Ash's heavy footfalls disappearing.

Inside, the room was huge, vanishing into the distance. Shouting and the constant clack of machines filled the air. His eyes looked around for Sugden. Nothing. Then a woman at one of the looms raised her arm and pointed to the stairway off at the side.

The sergeant nodded and began to run. He'd only lost a second. Not long enough for the man to put more shells in the gun. One flight, two. He could hear the echo of boots above him, and the inspector close behind, panting heavily.

He looked up. Another flight and that was all. A wild shriek of metal as a door was dragged open. Reed pushed harder. He had Sugden on the run. This was the best chance he'd ever have.

He came out to a shock of sky, a cold wind scouring his face and making his eyes water. It was a landscape he'd never imagined. Far away the hills vanished into the low clouds.

The roof was filled with cones of glass, dozens of them. Light for the factory below. Each one was wide at the base and as high as his waist. For a second he had to stop and stare; it seemed so unreal, as if he'd stepped into another world.

'I'll take the far side,' Harper told him breathlessly. 'You go down this one.'

Then he was moving. Slow, cautious strides, scanning everywhere for Sugden. The movement caught his eye. The man had ducked down, trying to hide. The shotgun was broken open, and he fumbled inside a pocket for more ammunition.

'There,' Reed shouted and began to run, dodging between the cones. His mouth was dry, excitement surging through his body. Quick enough and he'd take Sugden before he could slip the shells into the weapon.

The man looked up and for the first time Reed could see him. The empty, flat expression. The hate in his eyes as his fingers moved. The long beard, matted and dirty.

He was too far away. Sugden would have time to reload, to close the breech and take aim. One round for each of them. A hell of a thing, Reed thought. Survive Afghanistan and die on a rooftop in Holbeck. No glory there.

But he moved ahead. This was his job.

Sugden stood. He held the barrel of the shotgun tight in one hand. Quickly, he glanced over his shoulder. Then he turned and began to run.

The sergeant looked across at Harper, picking his way along the other side of the roof. The inspector nodded. They were going to take him. Here. Now.

A low wall ran all around the edge, a few courses of brick capped with stone. Sugden halted there, his gaze off somewhere on the horizon.

Reed slowed. He could feel the blood pounding in his neck. He felt he was aware of everything, the way it had been in Afghanistan, the way it was during a fire. His eyes were locked on Sugden.

The man was standing at attention, his back straight, head back. His hands moved, a quick series of shifts, one, two, three, until he held the gun at port arms.

'Drop it!' the inspector shouted, but the wind seemed to tear his words away. Sugden didn't turn. He didn't even seem to have heard. They were close now, no more than ten feet away. He could see the heavy streaks of grey in Sugden's long hair. The dirt caked on his coat and trousers.

Nearer, step by step. Reed took a deep breath.

In one swift movement, Sudgen stepped on to the wall and jumped.

They dashed to the edge and peered down. The body was sprawled on the ground, the shotgun a few feet away. Ash was already there, his fingers on the man's neck. He looked up and shook his head.

The sergeant took out a cigarette, surprised to see his hands shaking. The wind extinguished three matches before he gave up.

'I saw his army record,' Reed said emptily. 'He was a good soldier. One of the best.'

'Things happen, Billy. Something snapped. You said that yourself.' But he knew what the sergeant was thinking.

There was nothing more to say. It was over, all of it. Carr dead, Sugden dead. The only thing that remained were the reports. Then the recriminations.

'Come on,' Harper said quietly. 'We might as well go down.'

Twenty-Seven

Workers had gathered in the yard, staring at the body but keeping their distance as they talked in low voices. As they walked between them, Reed managed to light the cigarette, drawing the smoke down greedily then kneeling over Sugden's body.

He reached down and turned the head. The sightless eyes. A trickle of blood from the mouth. It wasn't a great distance down from the roof. Just far enough. He stood and sighed. Harper was talking to Ash, their heads bowed as they concentrated. The inspector made small hand gestures, pointing up to the roof, then the arc down.

It was over. The biggest hunt in the history of Leeds. And no satisfaction in the ending. No one to try, or hang. Just a bag of broken bones lying on the dirt behind a mill in Holbeck.

Who knew what Sugden had seen in Afghanistan? What had he done that turned his mind? They could only guess.

The sergeant dropped the cigarette and ground it out under his boot. He felt deflated, empty. The only thing he wanted to do was go home and wrap his arms around Elizabeth. If he didn't do that he'd sink to the bottom of a bottle of brandy.

'Stay here until they take the corpse,' Harper said when they were done. Ash nodded.

He walked away, putting a hand on Reed's shoulder. 'Let's go back to Millgarth.'

They walked slowly, not talking, across the Victoria Bridge, letting the city wrap itself around them. The air stank of smoke and soot.

'We couldn't have stopped him,' the inspector said as they crossed by East Parade.

'I know, but . . .'

He understood. Such a small word but so, so big.

'Maybe he thought it was better than anything else. He said it would be his last act. He knew. He made his choice.'

They'd just passed Holy Trinity Church when Reed asked, 'How do you think Sugden knew Gordon Carr had murdered his sister?'

'I don't know that he did,' Harper replied slowly. 'We didn't until Tooms told us. My guess is that he was going to kill them all. Neville, the old man.'

'But he knew where to find Gordon.'

'Did he? No idea, Billy. He'd been an army scout.'

'Yes.'

'Maybe he used that skill.' He shook his head. 'It doesn't matter any more. They're both dead. Good riddance to the pair of them.'

'There'll be an inquiry,' Kendall told them after he heard the tale. 'How could you let Gordon Carr be killed? He shouldn't have got away from you for a second, never mind try to escape.'

Harper stared at him. He expected nothing less; it was procedure. But he already knew the conclusion. The police would have quickly recaptured Gordon Carr if it hadn't been for Sugden. And no one could have predicted he'd be there.

Neville Carr might complain, but probably not. His son might have been acting on his behalf, and Tooms had plenty of secrets to spill if he chose. If a few of those came to light, any political career for Carr would be over before it started.

And the old man, Catherine's husband? He'd have to live with the knowledge that his own grandson had arranged it all. Soon enough he'd have to explain all his failings to his maker.

Reed and Ash stood. It was done. But the inspector remained seated. As the door closed, Kendall said, 'What do you need, Tom?'

It was time to bite the bullet. If he didn't do it

now, he'd only put it off longer and longer, until it was too late. He could feel his heart racing.

'It's about my hearing, sir.'

Kendall took out his pipe, filled it slowly, then struck a match and filled the air with smoke.

'Your right ear, isn't it?' he said.

'Yes,' he replied, trying to keep the shock off his face.

'Tom, it's not a secret.' The superintendent smiled. 'We've all known for a while.'

'I see.' He wasn't sure what he felt. Relief? Fear? Both?

'Why do you think I haven't sent you for a medical?'

'What would happen?' He didn't want to hear the answer but he needed to know.

'You're good at your job.' Kendall pursed his mouth. 'Very good, although I don't want you getting a swollen head over it. The force isn't going to lose a good copper over something so minor. Your other ear's fine?'

'Yes.'

'Then I don't see it as a problem. It hasn't stopped you doing your work, has it?'

'No, sir,' he agreed.

'Don't worry about it. People know. It doesn't matter. I've had a bad back for years but it doesn't prevent me doing my job.' He chuckled. 'Not that there's much to do these days, beyond sitting at a desk.'

'Thank you.' Harper didn't know what else to say. Whatever he'd feared wasn't going to happen. As long as one ear worked well, he'd have his job.

302

'Tom,' Kendall said, 'just a quiet word of advice. You've told me. That's enough.'

The inspector smiled. 'I understand, sir. Thank you.'

'He offered you that?' Elizabeth asked. 'An inspector?'

Reed nodded. He'd left Millgarth after talking to the superintendent. His work was finished there, and he could go back to the fire service if he wanted. Or he could take up Kendall's offer.

He spent more than an hour just planting one foot in front of another, and kept seeing Stanley Sugden jumping off the roof, walking into the air. It could so easily have been him. Just the way the dice rolled. He stopped outside a pub, his hand on the door, aching for something to take away the taste of the day. But in the end he turned without going in.

'What are you going to do, Billy?' Elizabeth asked.

He held her for a long time. No words, just the feel of her in his arms. Of life. Then, finally, he sat down and told her everything.

'What do you think I should do?'

She stared at him. 'What do you really want to do?'

'I don't know.'

'Forget about the money and the rank,' Elizabeth said. 'What do you really want?'

That was the question. As a detective inspector he'd be giving orders instead of taking them. Cases would be his. He'd have the responsibility, the weight. With the brigade he'd be trained as a fire investigator; Dick Hill had promised him that. He'd be using everything he'd learned. And in time, there'd be promotion.

Reed sighed. 'The fire brigade,' he replied, and realized that he didn't regret saying it.

'That's your answer,' she told him. 'It was simple in the end, wasn't it?'

He laughed. 'What would I do without you?'

'So you're in the clear?' Annabelle asked. 'He really said that about your hearing?'

'Every word.' Supper had been cleared away, devilled kidneys and mashed potatoes. Warm food for a cold night. Harper sat, a cup of tea beside him on the arm of the settee. For the first time in weeks nothing was worrying him. Catherine Carr and her silver skin had finally been laid to rest. His job was safe.

For once, he felt content. Weariness was slowly rising through his body, the warmth of the fire making him sleepy. Soon he'd go off to bed, but he was too comfortable to move yet.

'I'm glad you found out what really happened to Katie,' Annabelle said, curling against him. 'She deserves that.'

And it had all been because a young man feared he'd end up with nothing. He'd spent the afternoon questioning Tooms and the man had given up everything. All in the hope of avoiding a hanging.

Gordon Carr was afraid his inheritance would vanish if his grandfather died and Catherine Carr received everything. There'd been no love lost between them. She'd made clear what she thought of him and his life. Having her murdered was his insurance. Once she was gone, life would be easy again. He'd gone to Tooms to arrange it, the way the man had fixed every other problem in the past.

Had Neville Carr known? It was the only point where Tooms hesitated. Was it loyalty or did he really not know? The inspector had pressed and pressed, but never got an answer.

'She never deserved what happened. Any of it,' he said, placing his arm around her shoulder. It was done, everything bar the court appearances. 'Did you make up your mind about the suffrage committee yet?'

He felt her body stiffen a little. 'I went out to see Miss Ford today.'

'What did she have to say?'

'I wanted to know just how much time I'd have to put in if I became a committee member.' She shifted her head to glance up at him. 'All the ones already on there, they don't have any other jobs. They have money.'

'So do you.'

'And a pub to run. The bakeries.'

'Elizabeth looks after those,' he pointed out.

'I still need to keep an eye on everything.'

There was something else. Something she wasn't saying. She was raising objections when there wasn't even a problem.

'What did you tell her in the end?'

'That I'll carry on speaking at meetings if she wants me to. But I couldn't give them enough time to be a committee member. Not properly. I don't want to be traipsing all over the country.

They have it all mapped out. London, Manchester, Birmingham. I'd spent half my life on trains.'

'How did she take it?'

'I think she was disappointed. But she said she understood. Told me that they need more women like me.' She gave a tiny giggle. 'Common as muck, she meant.'

Harper hugged her. Whatever the real reason, she'd tell him in her own good time.

Twenty-Eight

The crowd was large enough to spill out on to Roundhay Road, a pair of bobbies strolling around and keeping genial order. The tram stood on the tracks, fresh paintwork shining on a dull day.

It was a curious looking thing, Harper thought. Smaller than other trams, and the poles that stretched up to the electric wires made it seem a huge insect. If he hadn't seen it arrive he'd have doubted that it could work.

'Look,' Annabelle said, 'there's Billy.'

And it was definitely him, sitting erect at the front of the steam fire engine as it paraded around. He wore his dress uniform, helmet gleaming, proud. The day after they'd found Gordon Carr and Sugden he'd gone back to the fire brigade to work on the engine while he trained to be a fire investigator.

Maybe it was for the best, Harper had decided

306

at the time. Maybe Billy Reed was more comfortable with the certainties of a fire. No grey areas there. And it meant a promotion for Ash. After an hour of talking and wearing him down, the inspector had managed to persuade Kendall that it was the right thing. Detective Sergeant Ash it was now, and he'd grinned wide as a child at Christmas when he heard the news.

The mayor had given his speech, splendid in his ermine and gold chain, talking about opening up Roundhay Park to everyone and the start of a new era for Leeds. The usual rubbish, but people loved it. Reporters from the newspapers took down every word. A brass band struck up *God Save The Queen* when he finished and children waved paper Union Jacks.

Then the ceremony was over and it was time for the main act. Council men and their wives were packed on to the tram. Plenty of the grandees of industry. And finally Annabelle Harper and her husband. Her eyes sparkled as she climbed the steps from the pavement. She'd bought a new gown for the occasion, soft purple with a small bustle, high-necked and trimmed with darker purple velvet.

Everyone was in their Sunday best. He wore the beautiful grey suit she'd had made for him the Christmas before. He always felt rich when he put it on: the only time he knew what it was like to have money.

The bell sounded and the crowd cheered. With a judder the tram started, bunting waving in the breeze. The engine was quiet, no more than a hum. None of the familiar clop of hooves.

307

But it moved as slowly as any horse-drawn tram as it passed by the streets of grimy back-to-back houses before opening out into the light and the grander villas around Harehills.

Annabelle leaned towards him. 'What do you think, Tom? Isn't it wonderful?'

He had to agree. It was something special. Something modern. The world was changing and it was time Leeds changed with it. For most of those on board, this would probably be the only time they ever rode a tram. Not that it mattered. Next summer the working families could clamber on and enjoy the park.

At the terminus the vehicle turned slowly, the green of the fields stretching away to the horizon. Then it was slowly back down Roundhay Road.

The crowds had all vanished by the time they returned to the Victoria. The band had packed up and gone. Inside the pub, the dignitaries fell on the food and drink as if they hadn't eaten in days. Scavengers, the lot of them, Harper thought, shaking his head.

Annabelle was the perfect hostess, moving from group to group, a word here and there. Harper stood alone in the corner, cradling a glass of beer and watching.

An hour later they were done. The plates and the barrel had all been emptied before the last of them left in their carriages. She surveyed all the debris, arms folded under her bust.

'It can wait until tomorrow,' she said, and held out her hand. 'Come on, I'm exhausted.'

Her face was flushed with the excitement and pleasure of the day. She led him up the stairs.

As he closed the door to their rooms she came into his arms with a sigh, her head resting against his chest.

'I enjoyed that.'

'So did I.' In a curious way it was fun to watch the rich at play, greedier than any poor man he'd ever known.

They stayed silent for a minute. He rubbed her back gently, enjoying the warmth of her against him.

'Did you wonder why I turned down that place on the suffrage committee?' she asked eventually.

'Yes,' he nodded. Finally he was going to have his explanation.

'I didn't want to say anything until I was certain.' She pulled away a little and looked up into his eyes. 'But I'm going to have a baby.'

Afterword

In Edwardian times, a case came before the Leeds coroner's court regarding a dead baby, posted in a parcel to a non-existent address and later discovered. Terrible and sad, I have used it, but with one difference: in reality, the police were never able to trace the parcel's sender.

A fire did indeed occur at New Station in Leeds, although it was in January 1892. I've changed the date by a few months. Three platforms were destroyed and one fireman, James Schofield, was killed. The fire began in 'Soapy' Joe Watson's warehouse in the Dark Arches. Rebuilding work began immediately and the other three platforms remained open, as did neighbouring Wellington Station. At that time the fire brigade was part of the police force.

The Leeds Women's Suffrage Society flourished in the early 1890s, as did those in some other Northern towns. Isabella Ford was a leading figure, as was her sister Emily (who was also a fine artist), and Isabella would go on to be instrumental in the formation of the Independent Labour Party in 1893.

Patrick's Martin's description of the people of Quarry Hill is taken from the notebook of the man who was the superintendent of the area for Leeds Town Mission.

Temple Mill was built in the late 1830s. The front design was based on the Temple of Horis at Edfu and the Typhonium at Dendera. When it opened as a flax mill it was the largest room in the world. There was natural light from the conical skylights in the roof – which was originally covered in grass, to retain the humidity flax needs. Sheep were taken to and from the roof in a hydraulic lift to crop the grass. These days it's an arts hub, Temple Works, and a Grade 1 Listed Building.

The first electric tram in Leeds had its inaugural run between Sheepscar and Roundhay Park on October 29th, 1891. The service opened to the public on November 10th.

I'm grateful to all the people at Severn House for their belief in my writing and the way they push my books. To Lynne Patrick, the best editor (and friend) a writer could want. To many who've shown friendship – Candace Robb, Joanne Harris, Thom Atkinson, so many more besides. To Penny, always. To the people who come out to my events, who buy my books or borrow them from libraries. Thank you all.